張愛玲

少帥

The Young Marshal
by Eileen Chang

目　錄

前言

◎宋以朗

　　一九九七年，我的母親鄺文美為了方便學者研究張愛玲，將一批張愛玲遺稿的複印本捐給南加州大學的東方圖書館。這批遺稿成為了南加州大學「張愛玲資料特藏」的重要部分，當中包括未刊英文小說《少帥》的打字稿複印本。我現在家中還有大量張愛玲的書信和作品手稿，正考慮該如何處置。很多人認為應該捐給大學作學術用途，原則上我沒有理由反對，但事實上宋家早在十七年前已經把大批手稿捐到學術機構了，可惜效果未如理想。以《少帥》為例，十多年就這樣過去了，我依然沒有見到任何學者的研究，將來很可能還是會無人問津，所以我決定把它出版。

　　《少帥》是張愛玲當年銳意打入美國市場之作，結果因為各種理由而沒有完成。今天張愛玲的讀者始終是看中文的居多，所以我按照《雷峯塔》和《易經》的先例，找人把《少帥》翻譯為中文。本書的中譯者是鄭遠濤。

　　二〇〇九年出版《小團圓》，我為免眾說紛紜，特地寫了一篇前言交代張愛玲的創作前因後果。但出版前我沒有想過，原來很多人是看不懂《小團圓》的寫作手法的。他們看不出「穿插藏閃」的結構，竟以為是雜亂無章的草稿，令我非常詫異。汲取了那次經驗，我找馮睎乾為《少帥》寫了一篇考證和評析的文章，作為本書附錄。那不是什麼官方解讀，只是我覺得尚算達標的研究，有興趣的讀者不妨參考一下。由於馮文會透露小說情節，讀者切忌跳過小說翻閱這個附錄。

張愛玲——著

鄭遠濤——譯

府裏設宴，女孩子全都走出洋台看街景。街上有個男人把一隻紙摺的同心方勝兒擲了上來。她們拾起來拆開讀道：

「小姐，明日此時等我。」

一群人蜂擁着跑回屋裏。她們是最早的不纏足的一代，儘管穿着緞鞋，新式的「大腳」還是令她們看起來粗野嘈鬧。

「肯定是給你的。」她們把紙條傳來傳去。

「瞎說，怕是給你的吧。」

「這麼多人，怎麼偏偏就我了？」

「誰叫你這麼漂亮？」

「我漂亮？是你自己吧。我壓根兒沒看見是怎樣的一個人。」

「誰又看見了？大家跑起來我還不知道是為什麼。」

周四小姐年紀太小，無須替自己分辯，只笑嘻嘻的，前劉海黑鴉鴉遮住上半張臉。她們留下來過夜。次日那鐘點，女孩子們都說：

「去看看那人來了沒有。」

她們躲在一個窗戶後面張望，撅着臀部，圓鼓鼓的彷彿要脹破提花綢袴，粗辮子順着乳溝垂下來。年紀小的打兩根辮子，不過多數人是十八九歲，已經定了親等過門。她們對這事這樣興沖沖的，可見從來沒愛過。那種癡癡守望一個下午的情態，令四小姐有點替她們難為情。那男人始終沒來。

她自己情竇早開。逢年過節或是有人過生日，她都會到帥府去。那裏永遠在辦壽宴，不是老帥的便是某位姨太太的生辰，連着三天吃酒，請最紅的名角兒登台唱堂會，但是從來不會是少爺們的生日，小輩慶生擺這種排場是粗俗的。總是請周家人「正日」赴宴，免得他們撞見軍官一流的放誕之徒。帥府大少爺自己就是軍官，有時穿長衫，有時着西裝，但是四小姐最喜歡他一身軍服。穿長衫被視為頹廢，穿西裝一副公子哥兒模樣，再不然就像洋行買辦。軍服又摩登又愛國。兵士不一樣，他們是荷鎗的乞丐。老百姓怕兵，對軍官卻是敬畏。他們手握實權。要是碰巧還又年青又斯文，看上去就是國家唯一的指望了。大少爺眾人都叫他「少帥」，相貌堂堂，笑的時候有一種嘲諷的神氣，連對小孩子也是這樣。他們圍着他轉。他逗他們開心，對着一隻斷了線的聽筒講個不停。四小姐笑得直不起身。有一回她去看唱戲的上裝。有個演員借了少帥的書房做休息室，不過已經出場了。

「怎麼你不剪頭髮？」少帥問，「留着這些辮子幹嗎？咱們現在是民國了。」

他拿着剪刀滿房間追她，她笑個不停，最後他遞來蓬鬆的黑色的一把東西。「喏，你想留着這個嗎？」

她馬上哭了。回去挨罵不算，還不知道爹會怎樣講。但原來只是一副髯口。

她在親戚家看過許多堂會，自己家裏的也有。不比散發霉味的戲園子，家裏是在天井中搭棚，簇新的蘆席鋪頂，底下一片夏蔭。剛搭的舞台浴在藍白色的汽油燈光線下，四處笑語喧喧，一改平日的家庭氣氛。她感到戲正演到精彩處而她卻不甚明白，忍不住走到台前，努力要看真切些，設法突出自己，任由震耳的鑼鈸劈頭劈腦打下來。她會兩隻手攔在台板上，仰面定定地瞪視。女主角站在她正上方咿咿呀呀唱着，得意洋洋地甩着白色水袖，貼面的黑片子上的珠花閃着藍光。兩塊狹長的胭脂從眼皮一直抹到下巴，烘托出雪白的瓊瑤鼻。武生的彩臉看上去異常闊大，像個妖魔的面具，唱腔也甕聲甕氣，彷彿是從陶面具底下發出聲音。他一個騰空，灰塵飛揚，四小姐能聞到微微的馬糞味。她還是若有所失。扶牆摸壁，繞行那三面的舞台。前排觀眾伸出手，護着擺在腳燈之間沏了茉莉香片的玻璃杯。在戲園裏，她見過中途有些人離開包廂，被引到台上坐在為他們而設的一排椅子上。他們是携家眷姨太太看戲的顯貴。大家批評這是粗俗的擺闊，她倒羨慕這些人能夠上台入戲；儘管從演員背後並不見得能看到更多。

那時候她還小，還是大家口中的「吳蟠湖那會兒」。再之前是段慶萊時代。「現在是馮以祥了。」「南邊是方申荃。」軍閥們的名字連老媽子都說得上來。她們也許不曉得誰是大總統，但是永遠清楚哪個人實權在握，而且直呼其名。在一個名義上的共和國裏，這是民主政治的唯一而奇特的現象。跟本府老爺關係特殊的老帥是唯一的例外。哪個軍閥起了倒了，四小姐印象模糊。審慎與自矜兼有的心理使他們家諱言戰爭，彷彿那不過是城市治安問題，只要看緊門戶，不出去就行了。「外面正打着呢，誰也不許出去。」同時她聽見遠處的隆隆鎗聲。塾師如常授課，只是教女孩子們英文的英國女人暫時不來了。

「菲碧・周，1925年」——英文教師讓她在自己每一本書的扉頁上都寫上這行字。「菲碧」只是為了方便那老師而起的名字，她另一個名字也只有上課才用。照理她父親會用，可是他甚少有喚她的機會。大家只叫她四小姐。

老帥去年入關，賃下一座前清親王府。偌大的地方設宴請客，盛況媲美廟會，涼棚下有雜耍的，說書的，大廳裏唱京戲，內廳給女眷另唱一齣，近半的院落開着一桌麻將，後半夜還放焰火。她四處逛着，辮子上打着大的紅蝴蝶結，身上的長袍是個硬邦邦的梯形，闊袖管是兩個扁平而突兀的三角形，下面晃着兩隻手腕，看着傻相。大家說少帥同朱家姊妹親近，常常帶她們出去跳舞。他喜歡交際舞。朱三小姐是她眼中無人能及的美人兒，如果他娶的是朱三小姐那該多好！他的妻子很平凡，寡言少語，比他大四歲，相貌還要見老。幸好她極少看見他們在一起。當時還沒有這樣的規矩。他們有兩個孩子。她父親是四川的一個軍閥，曾經救過老帥一命，老帥圖報，讓兒子娶了恩人的女兒。在四小姐看來這又是少帥的一個可敬之處，說起來，他是以自己的人生償還父債。

她家裏人每次提起朱家姊妹，都免不了一聲嗤笑。

「野得不像樣，她們的爹也不管管。一旦壞名聲傳出去，連小妹妹都會受連累的。『哈，就是那大名鼎鼎的朱家姊妹啊』，人家會說。」

四小姐不必提醒也會遠着她們。她自覺像個鄉下來的表親。連朱五小姐都正眼看不得她。除了這一回，她問：「你看見少帥沒有？」

「沒有。」

「找找他去。」

「什麼事兒？」

「告訴他有人在找他。」

「誰呀？」

「反正不是我。」

「你自己去不行？」

「我不行。你去不要緊的。」

「你也大不了多少。」

「我看上去大。」

「我怎麼知道上哪兒找去？要告訴他的又是這樣沒頭沒尾的話。」

「小鬼。人家難得托你一回，架子這麼大。」朱五小姐笑着打她。

她還了手，然後跑開。「想去你自己去嘛。」

跑出了人叢，她便逕直去尋找少帥。到了外面男人的世界，她要當心碰見她父親或是異母的哥哥，貼着牆壁行走，快步躲閃到盆栽後，在回廊上遊蕩，裝做不知道自己在哪裏。在燈光下，院子裏果樹上的一大蓬一大蓬蒼白的花影影綽綽。傳菜的僕役從垂着簾幕的門洞進進出出。到處人聲嗡嗡，絲竹盈耳。她是棵樹，一直向着一個亮燈的窗戶長高，終於夠得到窺視窗內。

2

「哦，他在北京？老帥見了他了？」

「我沒有聽說。」

「他活動是通過老傅。」

「據說老傅跟西南那邊搭上了線？」

「原來是這樣。怎的，他犯得着麼？」

「可不是。廣州那幫人不成氣候的。」

「廣州已經赤化了。」

「那些俄國人越來越不像話了。」

「嘿，咱們今晚只談風月。」

「好啊，話是你說的！你納寵不請我們吃花酒，說說該怎麼罰。」

「哈哈！打哪兒聽說的？小事一樁，哪裏就敢勞動諸位。」

「該罰！該罰！」

「請吃飯！讓貴相好來給咱們斟酒。」

奉上了魚翅羹。

一片「請請！請請！」聲中夾雜「噯，噯——噯，噯——」的低聲央告，單手擋住酒杯，不讓再斟滿。

酒席給外國人另備了十道菜的西餐，但是Ｗ・Ｆ・羅納為防萬一，自己帶了一條長棍麵包來。他名聲夠響亮，可以在這一點上縱容自己與眾不同。他不比同桌的中國人高大，但是身胚壯實，面容普通而和悅，頭髮向後直梳，高鼻梁筆直地指着前方，兩條法令紋沿鼻翼兩側斜伸。他伸手拿自己的水杯。

「有外國酒。」少帥向一個僕人示意。「威士忌？香檳？」

「不用了，謝謝。我不喝酒。」

「羅納先生從來不喝，滴酒不沾，呵呵呵！」教育部總長笑着解釋。

「美國禁酒，」海軍部次長說。他上過英國的海軍學校。

「也禁豬肉嗎？」另一個說道。

「其實來一點波特酒沒關係，很溫和的，」又一個說。

「你不會是禁酒主義者吧？」英國作家貴甫森－甘故作詫異。

「不是。」

「那麼你一定屬於你們某個神秘的教派。」

「不習慣中國菜，」另一個評道。

「也不習慣中國女人，呵呵呵！羅納先生實在是個好人，什麼樣的嗜好都沒有，」教育部總長說。

「不喜歡中國女人，就是不喜歡女人。」 貴甫森－甘說時略一欠身。

「八大胡同代表不了中國女人，」少帥道。

「這話在理！」海軍部次長說。

「可惜外國人能交往的中國女人就只有她們，」貴甫森－甘說。

「正在談什麼？」羅納猜到話題與他有關。

「正替你的男子氣概申辯，」班克羅福特說。他生於山東，父母是傳教師。三個外國人席位相連，讓他們有伴。

「幸好我不懂中文，」羅納道。

「非禮勿聽，非禮勿言，」少帥道。

「待了這些年，完全不懂嗎？」班克羅福特道。

「一句也不懂。我不想學中文，學了反而困惑。」

「也許會抵觸你本身對中國的想法，」貴甫森－甘說。這英國人略有醉意。深色眼睛長得離黑色的一字眉很近，下半張臉闊大，看上去顯胖。初到中國他就趕上了拳民之亂，親歷其境，第一本書便寫這題材，因此出了名。他自然受不了這個來自美國的新聞販子居然也做了中國人的顧問，和他平起平坐。

「別人告訴你的許多話聽不懂其實也好，」羅納說，「有時他們只是客氣，或是想博取好感。」

「他是學不了語言，只好裝犬儒，」 班克羅福特說。

「聽說個性強的人難學會另一門語言，」少帥說。

「你呢？你覺得自己個性弱嗎？」貴甫森－甘說。

「別扯上我。」

「咱們少帥的個性當然是強了。」海軍部次長說，「樣樣都是先鋒，不推牌九，打撲克牌；不叫條子，捧電影明星和交際花。」

「又來侮辱咱們的女同胞了。話說回來，咱們啥時候打撲克牌？」他用中文高聲問全桌。

教育部總長一面搖頭，擺擺手。「撲克牌我不敢奉陪。教育部是清水衙門。」

「是您太謙虛。」

「欸，少帥，上海有份新聞報評出了民國四公子，您是其中一位。」

他哼了一聲。「民國四公子。聽着真損。」

「還有哪些人？」

「有袁弘莊——」

眾人略過不談另外兩個。軍閥之子而已，跟他們相提並論不足恭維。

「弘莊工詩善字，但是哪比得上少帥既懂軍事，又有全才。」

「如今他在上海賣條幅呢。徹底的名士派。」

「他是半個高麗人吧？他母親是原籍高麗的兩位皇貴妃之一。」

「復辟的時候你在這裏麼？」班克羅福特問羅納。

「哪一次？」

「首任大總統當皇帝那一次。」

「其實整場風波是從我開始的。就是在一個這樣的晚宴上，我當時說，究竟是君主制還是共和制於中國最適宜，仍然可以辯論。那些中國人全都馬上說開了，從來沒見過他們那樣興奮。不出幾個禮拜，全國各地便紛紛成立所謂『籌安會』，鼓吹復辟了。」

他對抗了這場他引爆的運動。他幫助一個遭軟禁的反對派將軍藏身洗衣籃，潛逃出北京。將軍鼓動其他省份起事，反對新皇帝。羅納張羅局面讓他退了位，繼續做大總統。但是叛軍堅持要他辭職。羅納只好撫平他對於家人與祖墳安全的憂懼，爭取他下台。如同一個孤獨的冠軍，羅納自己與自己對陣。

「對了，你家鄉是在德克薩斯州嗎？」貴甫森－甘問道。

他微微一笑。「不，奧克拉荷馬州。」

聽着傳譯的中國人無不殷切地定時領首，頭部在空氣中劃出一個個圓圈。現代史沒有變成史籍，一團亂麻，是個危險的題材，決不會在他們的時代筆之於書。真實有一千種面相。

「有人說是一個妓女把他偷運出北京城的。」

海軍部次長用外交辭令向羅納補白：「大家知道肯定有人幫了忙。如果是一個跟他交好的妓女，故事會更加動人。」

「所以我成了妓女了。」

「嘖嘖，你怎麼成？」貴甫森－甘說道。

「徐昭亭在外國做什麼？」羅納問教育部總長。

「借錢呀。」

「為了通常的目的？建軍。」

教育部總長呵呵笑了幾聲，聽上去有點尷尬。徐是段執政的人。執政沒有軍隊，但是有老帥與基督將軍兩座靠山，本來並不需要武備。

羅納重新埋首於他的冷牛排。講完某個長故事便冷不防拋出一個問題，是他的慣伎。聽者一旦沉浸到安全感之中，爭取注意的天性往往會浮現，答案因而更可能接近事實。

中國人似乎依然在談論那次復辟。還有一個關於晚宴東道主和復辟的掌故，羅納當然不會在這裏講。當時老帥已經是統兵滿洲的軍官，北京特意任命了一個與他相得的總督。此人是呈遞秘密請願書，呼籲恢復帝制的十四省代表之一。論功行賞，他獲封一等公爵，老帥則是二等子爵，感到不滿。他召集一大群軍官同行去了總督的官邸，說道：「大人擁立皇上有功，想必要出席登基大典。特來請大人的示，定哪一天起程，我們準備相送。」

總督自知地位不保。「我明晚進京。」

老帥奉陪到底，召集軍官幕僚餞行。滿洲自此再無總督。新皇帝無暇他顧。

「早在遠征高麗的時候他就想做皇帝了，」海軍部次長翻譯道。「他在營帳裏小睡，有個勤務兵進來，見到床上一隻碩大無朋的蛤蟆，驚慌間打碎了一個花瓶。他沒有責罵，只叫那人不要說出去。要是讓滿人知道他們的一個將軍將來是要做皇帝的，那還了得。」

「蛤蟆是皇族的徽號嗎？」貴甫森－甘問道。

「不，只要是大動物。睡夢裏變成大動物據說是個徵兆。實際上，肯定是那勤務兵摔碎了花瓶怕受懲罰，才編造出那樣一個藉口。」

「大蛤蟆，」一屋子喃喃低語。無人敢讚賞勤務兵的急才。首任大總統的面容說穿了確實神似。

不過是會吸引外國人的那一類花哨的迷信而已，羅納想。他對於這些據說令中國人不同的東西不耐煩，因為他知道他們沒什麼兩樣。

「我是從他秘書處的劉子乾那裏聽說這個的。他還真想過娶個高麗公主，將來做高麗國王。」

「因為他是河南人嘛。中原是最早的龍興之地，那裏的人滿腦子帝王將相。他要是生在江南，決不會那麼大膽。」說話的是江南人氏。

「他是個十九世紀中國人，」羅納說，「很有才幹，但是早衰。五十幾歲就老態龍鍾，頭髮和鬍髭全白了。他以為我是親近國民黨的，每次打招呼都說『老民黨，廣州有什麼新聞啊？』」

「羅納先生一肚子軼聞。」教育部總長說完又用英文複述。

「不然還有什麼？」羅納說，「二十年來只有亂紛紛的登場人物，正是軼聞裏的那種腳色。」

「其實你多大年紀了？」少帥說。

「噢，我前兩天看到你，」羅納說。

「在哪兒？」

「在長城上打高爾夫球。」

他大笑。「那兒的球場非常好。」

長城內側的綠草坡上，穿着他寬鬆的白色法蘭絨袴子，令人一見難忘。據說他喜歡一切摩登現代的東西，在奉天學英文時一度與基督教青年會的人接近。他健談而不甚善聽，一旦感到對方在說教便一走了之。父親矮小衰弱，杏核兒眼，鬍髭下露出勉強的笑容。羅納熟悉這種人。奧克拉荷馬州當地有些大亨便出身牛仔，跟老帥一樣。不，確切地說，他本是馬醫。滿洲從前與老西部似乎很相像。馬匹犁田，也用於遠途騎行。他的父親被一個賭徒殺死，為了報仇，他夜闖仇人家，誤將一個女傭射死後，潛逃入伍。多年後他重返故地，很快被捕而越獄成功，給一個村莊做保險隊謀生。保險隊與土匪的界線並不分明，因此傳說他做過胡匪，又稱紅鬍子，也許得名於黑龍江上從事劫掠的白種人部落，但是更可能源自京劇中強盜的標準臉譜。他帶着十餘手足安頓下來，又派人叫來他的妻。他兒子——如今的少帥——生於一個村莊。曾經有個大幫派向他挑釁，他提議與首領決鬥，那人剛一答應，老帥便拔出手鎗將他擊斃。就是那次的快鎗替他打贏了平生第一個大仗，麾下又吸納了百餘人。

　　如今牛仔老了，抽鴉片，許多姨太太。他行事有他自己的一套。羅納在這邊永遠不愁失業。教育部總長是前面幾個政府沿用下來的舊人，老相識了，好兩次要給他聘書。其實，只要是搭上了個中國官員的外國人，就能獲得顧問的頭銜，外加每月兩百元的津貼，讓他默不出聲。自滿清已是如此。當然像貴甫森－甘那樣的顧問不會在乎那兩百塊錢。他新出了一本《孤獨的反共者：他在遠東的奮鬥》，老帥付給他的潤筆想必豐厚。這書由上海一家英國人的書店印行，與他別的著作不同。反共者是指老帥，他在中國獨力抵擋共產主義的潮流。書中籲請西方列強不要干涉他從俄國人手裏收回滿洲的中東鐵路。日本在東北的利益鮮有提及。是日本人委託他寫的嗎？總之以老帥的性格，不見得會那樣相信文字的力量。羅納腦子裏打了個問號，留待日後解疑。

　　他看見少帥起身出了房間，頓覺一陣空虛。方才他侃侃而談，是不是想叫少帥刮目相看？一來也是因為今晚的宴席處處使他想起復辟前夕那一次，同樣的大圓桌，人語營營，蒂芙尼電燈下一片通明，房間是個紅木籠子，雕花隔扇中開月洞門，低垂着杏黃絲綢的帷幔。已經是十來年前的事了，那時候他還是最年青的中國通。偶爾他也納罕自己為什麼留下來。他在這裏做的無非是報導烏煙瘴氣的政局，在酒席上講講故事，寫長信給遠在奧克拉荷馬州庫恩溪的姊妹們大談中國政治。他在這邊永遠不愁生計。中國人念舊，過來人受到尊敬。眼前的權力與財勢總帶着幾分兇險，特別是現在。但是過去，即使只是十年前，也已經醇和得令人緬懷，對首任大總統就是這樣。他是軍閥始祖，一手造成了現狀，不單如此，作為滿族人的最後一個重臣，他是合乎法統的繼位者。是他促成了清朝覆滅又何妨，那是時勢使然，滿清無可救藥也是公認的。他死後，得意門生繼承事業，輪番當上大總統、總理。他們構成了唯一的合法世系。段執政是他創辦的軍事學校的最後一個高材士官，如今卻敗於出身行伍甚或草莽的新軍閥手上。但是所有這些新貴都會扶持某個追隨首任大總統的人，以承國脈。老帥請了段氏出山做他政府的首腦；誰都覺得，這對於老段是淒慘的降格。

「嘿，老民黨！」飯桌上有人喊過來，是首任大總統對他的稱呼。其餘他聽不懂。

「他說老民黨，你的特工同事怎樣了？」

「誰？」

「國姨呀。」

「國姨又是誰？」

「廣州那邊不是稱孫文為國父嗎？這樣，他夫人成了國母，夫人的姐妹就是國姨囉。」

「哪一個姐妹？」

「小妹妹，在這邊使美人計的那個。我們少帥看來也有意思要借聯姻做國舅嘍。」

「別這麼大聲，」有人提醒。

「走了。到北京飯店跳舞去了。」

「說來這一場南北聯盟快要入港了，」另一個說道。

「她將來的嫁妝可不止兩艘軍艦。」

海軍部次長當初帶了兩艘軍艦從廣州叛逃過來，換得官職。

「老帥的意思如何？」

「我們老帥最看重一個忠字。以他對親家的感情，離婚絕對沒戲。」

「這話最好跟那位小姐講講。」

有人讓海軍部次長給羅納翻譯。

「從她還是小女孩那時起，我就很少見到她了。」

「你是他們家的老朋友，有責任告訴他們當心小姐名節受損，叫孫博士身後蒙羞啊。」

少帥在院子裏跟四小姐說話。

「誰找我？」

「不知道。」

「別跑。是誰叫你來的嘛？」

「沒有誰，我高興來就來，高興走就走。」

「那你這麼着急是要去哪兒？」

「去看戲。」

「哪一齣？我跟你一塊兒去。」

「人家在等你呢。」

「誰？」

「問你自己。」

「小鬼，既然你不說，我就不去了。」

「不去就不去，誰稀罕？」

「你不想讓我去。」

「不識好人心。下回看看誰還肯給你帶話。」

「帶什麼話？」

她捶他，兩人在芭蕉樹下扭打起來。

「回來回來，你這是去哪兒？」

「去告訴大嫂。」

　　誰都知道他不怕妻子。這樣說嚇不倒他。但是那夜遲些時候她沒見到他和朱三小姐在一起，想必他並沒有來。幽會地點就是他們倆談話的院子，裏頭一屋子圍在大紅桌布前的豬肝色的臉，有些人面無笑容，站着狂吼，或勸酒或推辭，或邀人划拳，這種屬於男性的儀式於她一向既怪誕，又完全無法理解，圍成一圈的紅母牛被領進了某種比孔子還要古老的祭典之中。那些外國人極力保持微笑，高高的白衣領托出灰暗的深棕色頭部，像照片一樣。難怪他與外國人為伍，不和她父親那樣的人應酬往來。

　　她對自己的針鋒相對久久不能釋懷。在家裏她向來很安靜。「別生事」是洪姨娘的口頭禪。她生母已故，由另一側室帶大。家裏別的孩子都有人撐腰，惟獨洪姨娘早已失寵。他也是幼年喪母，由五老姨太撫養成人。

「他們家那些少爺，父親一背轉身就無法無天了，」洪姨娘說過。

「不像咱們這兒呀，」女傭也附和。

「他們是不好這些。」洪姨娘半眨了眨眼。

她們閒話從前，彼此安撫着。四小姐發現是她父親提攜了老帥。他在東北總督任上特赦了那個匪首，並任命他為統領。革命那年，總督傾向於為滿人保存滿洲。但是革命黨在軍中安插了間諜。一次軍務會議上，有個軍官提議效法他省宣佈「同情革命」，推舉總督做都督。老帥不等輪到自己便起立發言：

「我陳祖望不同情革命。」然後把鎗擱在桌上。

會商無果，總督召來陳祖望，說道：

「革命黨想必是決心起事了，不然也不會暴露身分。我預備隨時以身殉國。」

「大人不要憂慮。我陳祖望有的正是忠心。大人的安全由我來擔保。」

他調來自己的人馬護衛周總督，又借他的號令部署軍隊。革命黨人逃離了東北。然而周總督要把滿洲移交肅親王的計畫被日本人挫敗——可能老帥也暗中作梗。周終於放棄，在北京找了份差事。幾個政府浮沉替換，他也退了休。如今人稱「東北王」的老帥進兵關內。他一手造就的魔王尾隨他跨入北京，雖然是一個心存感激的魔王。

四小姐聽見一個異母兄說「咱們每年給肅親王三萬塊錢」，詫異到極點。他們就像是那種靠豐厚的撫恤金生活的人家，舊例的開銷足以維持，但抗拒任何新的支出。那一回的風波鬧得沸沸揚揚，就是因為洪姨娘在院內裝了一部電話，方便自己安排外出的牌局，而不必用家裏公用的那部。她用的是私蓄。反對的理由是這樣靡費或會招來閒話，彷彿洪姨娘也會有個相好。四小姐無法想像她從前竟是堂子中人。關於她，只知道她進堂子以前家裏姓洪。四小姐記憶所及，從來就沒見過她父親踏進她們的院子。洪姨娘老得快，得以保存顏面，戴金邊眼鏡，穿一件黑大褂，底下棉褲的皺褶在腰間墳起。

「聽說二小姐定了人家了，」一個老媽子悄聲道。洪姨娘也喊喊促促回應：

「哪一家呀？」

「段家。」

「哪一房呀？」

「不知道。說是死了太太的。有肺病。」

「這些都是天註定的。男人身體好，還不是說病就病了。」

「也是啊。」

「有孩子沒有？」

這些話四小姐聽着愕然，但是從來沒想到自己身上。她這個異母的姐姐早已成年了。盲婚如同博彩，獲勝的機會儘管渺茫，究竟是每一個人都有希望，尤其在婚姻尚且遙遠的時候。

她在私塾裏念了首詩：

> 娉娉嫋嫋十三餘，
> 豆蔻梢頭二月初。
> 春風十里揚州路，
> 捲上珠簾總不如。

「是寫給一個青樓女子的，」塾師說。

從前揚州的一個妓女，壓倒群芳的美人與她竟然同齡，簡直不能想像。十三歲，照現代的算法不計生年那一歲的虛齡，其實只有十二。她覺得自己隔着一千年時間的深淵，遙望着彼端另一個十三歲的人。

3

　　她磨了一個表姐過來給她做頭髮，單純為了好玩，前劉海用火鉗燙作卷髮，堆砌成雲籠霧罩的一大蓬。辮子沒動，只拿粉色絲帶緊緊繞了兩寸長短。毛糙的巨型波浪烘托出臉龐與兩根烏油油的辮子。她不知道第二天會不會去帥府，有個姨太太生日。聽說老帥父子倆正在奉天，今年也許不擺酒了。她一夜伏着桌子睡覺，臉埋在肘彎裏，頭髮微微燒焦的氣味使她興奮。

　　他在家。但是在陳家的這些熱鬧中常常會有這麼一刻，盛大的日子在她身邊蕩蕩流過，平滑中略有起伏，彷彿一條太陽曬暖的大河，無論做什麼事都會辜負這樣的時光。那些戲她全都看過了，最好的男旦壓軸才上場。那丑角揮着黑扇子念出一段快板獻壽，誰也不去聽他。她跟着另外幾個女孩子瞎逛。洛陽牡丹盆栽——據說是用牛奶澆灌的——疊成的一座假山，披掛着一串串五彩電燈泡，中間擺得下一張飯桌。今天變魔術的是個日本女人，才在上海表演過的，想必精彩。她們在少帥書房裏議論戲碼單，他好奇地瞥了她兩眼，然後幾乎再不看她。是頭髮的緣故。她頂着那個熱騰騰的雲海，沁出汗珠來。幾個月不見，她現在大了，他不再逗她了。朱家姊妹不在，其他女孩子也都沒什麼話說。他把別人從杭州捎給他的小玩意分贈她們。

　　「咱們走吧，魔術師該上場了，」一個女孩子說。

　　她正要跟着出去，他說：「這柄扇子是給你的。」

　　她展開那把檀香扇，端詳着。

　　「現在是大姑娘了，不再搭理人了。」

「啊？」

「而且這麼時髦。要定親了。」

「哪兒來的這些昏話？」她不禁紅了臉。他以前從來不和她開這種玩笑，老太太們才喜歡這樣說。

「你不肯說。喜酒也不請我吃囉？」

「別胡說。」聽上去不像是戲言了。臨頭災禍陡然舉起她，放到成年人中間。

「唔？那我等着吃喜酒了。」

「呸！」她作勢一啐，轉身要走。「你今天怎麼了？」

「好好，對不起，是我多管閒事。」

「這些話都是打哪兒來的？」

「你真沒聽說？」她第一次看見他眼睛裏有焦急的神色，一閃而過。

「沒有的事兒。」

「唐家人正在給你說媒。」

「沒這事兒。反正我不會答應的。」

他笑了。「你不答應有什麼用？」

「殺了我也不答應。」機會來了，為他而死並表明心跡。

「不如告訴他們說五老姨太認了你做女兒，你的終身有她來安排。」

「我永遠不結婚。」

「為什麼？」

「不想。」

「那你一輩子做老姑娘是要幹什麼呢？上大學？出洋？做我的

秘書陪我一道出洋，好不好？你在看什麼？」 他湊近看看折扇上究竟有什麼東西讓她着迷。

「我在數數兒。」

「數什麼？」

「美人兒。」

他逐一點算花園中亭子裏的彩繪人物。「十。」

「十一。」

「應該是十二。通常有十二個。」

「窗子裏的這個我數漏了。正好是十二。」

「這個我數過。這兒，樹後面還有一個。」

「一、二、三、四……」她數出十個。

靠得這樣近，兩人都有些恍惚，每次得到的數目都不同。他終於一把捉住她，輕輕窘笑了一聲。「這兒還有另一個。」

「讓我數完。」

「這兒的一個呢？一丁點兒大，剛才都沒看見。」

他不放開她的手腕，牽起來細看。「怎麼這麼瘦？你從前不是這樣的。」

她立即羞愧自己始終沒長到別人期望的那麼美，只好咕噥一句：「只不過是最近。」

「最近不舒服嗎？」

「不，只是沒胃口。」

「為什麼？」

她不答。

「為什麼？」

她越是低着頭，越是覺得沉重得無法抬起頭來。

「不是因為我吧？」

他撩起她的前劉海，看她臉上被掩映的部分。她一動不動，迎風光裸着。他的手臂虛虛地籠着她，彷彿一層粉膜。她惘然抵抗着。他一定也知道是徒然。由於他們年歲的差別，他很早以前就娶了親，猶如兩人生在不同朝代。她可以自由愛戀他，彷彿他是書裏的人。不然她怎會這樣不害臊？她忽然苦惱：如果他不懂，她不知道如何才說得明白。他又怎能猜到？跑開只會顯得是假裝羞澀。她跑了，聽見那扇子在腳下嘎吱一響。

出了那房間，她很快便放慢腳步，免得被人瞧見。他沒有追隨她。她既如釋重負又異常快樂。他愛她。隨他們說媒去，發生什麼她都無所謂了。他愛她，永遠不會改變。居然還是下午，真叫人驚異。舞台上的鑼聲隱隱傳來。她寂寞得很，只能去觸摸遊廊上的每一根柱子每一道欄杆。又拐了個彎，確信他不會看見之後，她的步子跳躍起來，只為了感受兩根辮子熟悉的拍打落在肩膀上，不知為何，卻像那鳴鑼一樣渺茫了。

4

「帥府五老姨太派了部汽車來接四小姐，」她父親的院子差人來傳話。

一個男僕領着她去少帥的書房。她停在門口微笑。

「進來，進來。你來了真好。今兒有空，帶你看看網球場，剛蓋好的。會打網球嗎？」

「不會。」

「乒乓球一定會的。」

「不會。」

那男人還會端茶回來。他們默默坐着等待，他低着頭，臉上一絲微笑，像捧着一杯水，小心不潑出來。

那人終於送來了茶，退了出去。

「我有個消息跟你說。」

「上回準是你的把戲。」

「過來這邊坐，你不想人家聽見的。」

「誰要聽這些昏話？」

「嘖，人家替你擔心哪。你聽見什麼沒有？」她搖了搖頭。「那就好。」

「全是你編出來的。」

「不要沒良心。你知道為什麼從此不提了？我叫人向那邊透了點口風，所以他們才會作罷。」

「你跟他們說什麼了？」

「說你已經許給另一家了，不然呢？」

她拿拳頭捶他。「老實說，你是怎麼講的？」

「不過是說五老姨太已經替你想好了一門親事，只是你還太小，還得等幾年。」

「爹要是聽說了怎麼辦？」

「有什麼關係？那也並不過分。」

「也許他們就不許我上這兒來了。」

「如果你不來，我帶鎗上你家去。」

她希望自己被囚禁，那麼他就會為了她而來。「你不過是說笑。」

「不。」

他把她拉到膝上。她低頭坐着，感到他的雙眼在自己的臉旁邊發亮，像個耳墜子一樣。 他順着氣息將她吸進去。即使他們只能有這樣的剎那又如何，她想，已經彷彿一整天了。時間緩慢下來，成了永恆。

「你的眉是這樣走的。」她一隻手指追蹤着，拂過隨觸隨合的眼皮，再小心翼翼沿鼻梁而下，檢點每一件東西，看自己買了什麼。他看起來煥然一新。一擁有就不同了，正如畫片有別於書裏的插圖。

「你沒去過北戴河？青島還要好。咱們要去那裏。你學游泳。能這樣抱着你睡一晚就好。」

她的微笑僵了一點。

「光是抱着。我小時候有一回出去打獵，捉到一隻鹿，想帶回家養，抱着它在地上滾來滾去，就是不鬆手。最後我睏得睡着了，醒過來它已經跑了。」

她緊摟着他，要擠掉他胳臂間的空虛。

「它挺大的，比我那時候大多了。」

「你那時候有鎗嗎？」

「沒有，還不讓我帶鎗。只有弓箭和一把小刀。」

「那是在東北。」

「嗯，是很好的獵場。」

「天氣非常冷嗎？」 她父親做東北總督時，母親就在當地的堂子裏。她自幼只有父親，從未覺得自己是半個東北人。其實她長得相當像他，同樣是長而直的眼睛，鵝蛋臉五官分明。他退開一點，微笑看着她。

「真想吃了你，可是吃了就沒有了。」

「有人來了。」她聽見院子裏有聲。

「這兒沒有人來。」

「那天我們大家都在這裏。」

「我單獨在這兒的時候不會放人進來的。」

單獨與某人相對？比如朱三小姐嗎？已經不重要了。在一個亂糟糟的世界，他們是僅有的兩個人，她要小心不踩到散落一地的棋子與小擺設。她感覺自己突然間長得很高，笨拙狼犺。

「少帥，上頭有請，」一把聲音從走廊盡頭喊來。

他父親要他應酬訪客。他去了差不多一個鐘點才回來，又把她放在膝頭，撫摸她的腳踝。傍晚他再一次給叫了去。不一會僕人過來說，汽車會載她回家。

下趟五老姨太請她過去，汽車駛進一條僻靜的街，拐進長胡同，停在一幢她從未見過的宅子前面。汽車夫打開車門。她略一躊躇，便用頭巾掩面，像乘坐黃包車的女人要擋住塵沙。她帶着這張輕紗般的鴨綠色的臉走進去，經過一群穿制服的衛兵，他們在前院外一間亮着燈的房裏打麻將。他在下一進院子裏等着她。

「這是誰的房子？」

「我的。總得有個去處才行，家裏沒一刻清靜。」

「我不知道你有自己的房子。」

「沒機會常來，所以是這個樣子。帶你走走吧。」

「這裏沒有別人？」

「沒有。」

好像在一幢荒廢的房子裏扮家家酒。每個半空的房間要怎樣處置，他們倆都很有想法。臥室倒是家具齊全。窗簾低垂，梳妝枱上的瓶瓶罐罐在半黑中閃爍着。

「誰住這裏？」

他很快地關了門。「這間是客房，有時我會叫一幫朋友過來通宵打撲克牌。旁邊這個房間有一張炕，我打算拆了鋪上地板，以後咱們就可以跳舞了。」

他們走了一圈。

「朱三小姐常來？」

「唔，來過一兩回。」

之後她不大說話。回到客廳，他說：「你不一樣。我們會永遠在一起的。」

「不能。」

「為什麼？」

「你太太。」

「那只是為了老帥。我一向沒虧待她，畢竟當初也不是她的主意。我同她會達成某種安排的，不過由我和老帥談就行了。」他向來稱「老帥」，彷彿他只是他父親的一個部將。孝順是舊派的美德，使他有點難為情，他喜歡歸之於軍紀。

「現在馬上說什麼是沒用的，你年紀太小。只會害你被囚禁。」

「你說過你會帶鎗來救我。」

「對老丈人最好還是不要用鎗。」

她笑着扭身脫開。不知為什麼，這新的前景並沒有使她驚異。他們的無望於她本來就不是什麼藉口，如今更拋諸腦後。他也愛她；

有了這個神奇的巧合，什麼事都有可能。

「我不想要這裏，可是很難找到另一處既近帥府，又不喧鬧。還要有地方安置衛隊。」

「他們要是去帥府接我怎麼辦？」

「會給我打電話的。到時再過去也不晚。」

「癢。」她捺住順着她的法蘭絨袖管摸索的手。

「你怎麼穿了這許多衣服？今天太晚了，改天我開汽車帶你去西山。」

「你會開汽車？」

「很容易的。」

「我們可以在西山騎毛驢兒。」

「我們租來騎。我挺想在西山住的。那外國新聞記者羅納在西山有個別墅，蓋在過去禁苑裏的一座廟上頭。最近他才說起來。第一次直奉戰爭的時候，他在西山前線四處走動，看見地上有一根彎彎曲曲的電線，撿了起來，邊走邊繞線團。我們有幾個人走過去衝他呼喝。他只是豎起大拇指說：『老帥很好。』然後搖頭：『吳蟠湖不好。』他們笑着放他走。這一來戰地電話被切斷，東北軍後撤，局勢翻轉了。所以照他說，是他害我們打了敗仗。」

「他不怕講出來？」

「他邀我作客，看他電鈴上纏着我們的電線。這些洋人自以為多麼勇敢。他們一走進鎗林彈雨馬上就停火了，怕殺掉一個洋人。除了在中國，哪裏有這種絕對安全的歷險呢？」

「他們說你喜歡洋人。」

「跟他們一起很高興。比較坦率。我最討厭拍馬屁的。」他探

身揮了揮煙灰，別過頭來吻她，一隻鹿在潭邊漫不經心啜了口水。額前垂着一絡子頭髮，頭向她俯過來，像烏雲蔽天，又像山間直罩下來的夜色。她暈眩地墜入黑暗中。

仍舊是有太陽的下午天，四面圍着些空院子，一片死寂。她正因為不慣有這種不受干涉的自由，反覺得家裏人在監視。不是她儼然不可犯的父親，在這種環境根本不能想像；是其他人，總在伺機說人壞話的家中女眷，還有負責照顧她的洪姨娘與老媽子。她們化作樸拙的、未上漆的木雕鳥，在椽子與門框上歇着。她沒有抬頭，但是也大約知道是圓目勾喙的雌雉，一尺來高，有的大些，有的小些。她自己也在上面，透過雙圈的木眼睛俯視。他的手拉扯着她的袴管與絲綢長襯袴，心不在焉地滑到長筒襪上。坐在他身上使她感到極其怪異，彷彿有一個蒙着布的活塞，或是一條揮打着的返祖般的尾巴，在輕輕椎擊她。小時候老媽子們給她講過脊柱下端尾骨的笑話，也讓她摸過自己的尾骨。「這是割掉尾巴以後剩下來的。人從前有尾巴。」儘管暗地裏彷彿還沒有完，她依然疑心不是真的。她不想問他，大概總與性有關。也許只有置之不理才不失閨秀風度。

從黃昏開始，鼓樓每隔半個鐘點擂八下鼓。鐘樓隨即響應，宣告夜晚與道德宵禁的來臨。

「我以前居然沒注意到，」她說。「聽上去像古時候。」

「鐘鼓樓是明朝建的。」

「從那時候起每天晚上都這樣嗎？」

「嗯，滿人也照舊。」

「我們為什麼還要這樣？現在有時鐘了。」

「可不是嗎？民國建立十五年了，還是什麼都沒變。」

他拉鈴繩，腳步聲近了便喊「擺飯」。在隔壁房間晚膳，左右無人。他捧着飯碗向她微笑。只他們兩人同枱吃飯，終於真的當家了。她窘得百般糾結，只得放下飯碗。

「怎麼了？」

「沒什麼。你吃。」

一塊灑了古龍水的新毛巾架在邊桌的熱水盆上保溫。他吃完飯，她便浸了浸毛巾，絞乾給他，才遞過一半已經轉身要走，覺得自己在服侍丈夫似的，不由得難為情。她側身避開回頭微笑，倏然串成一個動作。他着迷地捉住她的手，但她抽回去了。

「出來吧，」他喚道。

他們在遊廊上望月。他摟着她，腰間暖意像風中火焰一樣拂拭她的背脊，使她詫笑。大紅柱子映出藍色的月光。

「想想真是，我差點兒回不來了。」

她抓緊他。「什麼時候？上回你在奉天時？」

「唔，出了事，我們有個軍官倒戈，基督將軍也在裏頭。」

「我好像聽說關外打仗了。」

「是差點兒打起來了。我們的主力部隊開赴奉天，離城只有幾里。老帥的專列上東西堆得滿坑滿谷，預備隨時開走。」

「去哪兒？」

「大連。」

「大連……那是你本來要去的地方。」

「是要去。那時候我跟奉天斷了聯繫。甚至有謠言說我也是叛黨。」

「怎麼會這樣？」她小聲說。

「就因為姓顧的和我看法相近，關係也不錯。」

「他們怎麼能說這種話？你自己的父親。老帥不信吧？」

「老帥非常生氣。」

「可是……現在好了？」

「現在不提了。當然我也有錯，應該更留神的。」

因此他更有理由不對他父親提出她的事或是任何要求，至少在目前。但是這又算得了什麼，根本比不上他們倆幾乎失之交臂的恐怖，想想已經覺得心寒，彷彿他整個人就在她眼前瓦解，在指縫間溜走。但是這張藍光勾畫的臉就在這裏，向她俯視微笑，嘴唇冷冰冰壓上來。他就在北京城這裏，鐘鼓延續着夜更，外頭聲音更大，黑夜的奇異與危機更覺迫切。古城後千迴百轉的時光兔窟和宮殿都在剎那間打通，重門一道一道訇然中開，連成一個洞穴或隧道。

「你該走了，」他說。「我們不要坐一輛汽車。」

「五老姨太這樣喜歡你，怎不認你做女兒？」洪姨娘說。

「我不想。」

「傻孩子。有個富有的乾媽多好。她會給你找到一門好親家的。」

「洪姨娘從來沒一句正經話。」她向前一倒，下頷抵在桌子上，玩弄手邊的小物件。

「倒真是。指望你爹唄，就拿你做人情送出去了。當然這是我跟你講體己話。」

「你儘管扯，誰要聽。」

「我知道你不會說的。」

是否一語雙關？不會的，她很快把這想法排斥到意識外。

「你洪姨娘沒說什麼？」他問。

「沒。」

「要是他們知道你到這兒來，孤男寡女，一定會認為你給占便宜了。有嗎？」他笑着把臉湊上去看她，她一再躲避。「有嗎？」

她蜷曲身子緊挨沙發邊。

「要是他們真問你了你怎麼說？」

「照實說。」

「那麼再把你嫁出去也還不晚。」

「那我就說謊，」她隔了一會說。

「沒有用的。呵，真是沒辦法了我就把你劫走。」

「老帥會氣得不得了。」

「一定的。他特別敬重你父親。」

「咱們該怎麼辦？」

「沒關係，反正我跟老帥已經很僵了。」

她不喜歡與他並躺在沙發上，但是這樣可以久久凝視彼此的臉。只恨每人多生了一條胳臂。幾次三番藏掖不了，他說：「砍掉它。」下午的陽光往牆上的鏡子投下一道小彩虹。她彷彿一輩子也沒有感受過這樣的平靜安穩。沙發靠背是地平線上遙遙起伏的山巒，在金色沙漠般的沉靜中，思想紋絲不動。房間裏開始暗下來了。她的微笑隨暮色轉深，可怕的景象令他瞇縫着眼。他把臉埋進她披拂的、因結辮而捲曲的頭髮裏。

「不知為什麼，你剛才像一個鬼。」

「哪一種鬼？」

「尋常的那種。有男人迷了路，來到荒郊野外的一幢大宅前，給請進去跟漂亮的女主人吃晚飯。共度一宵後，他走出宅外回頭一看，房子沒有了，原先的地方只有一座墳山。」

可見他跟她一樣害怕這道門內的一切都是假的。

「有一種無日無夜的感覺，只有一個昏暗的黃褐色太陽，好像在陰間。」

「那是因為我們成天關在這兒。」

「我一輩子沒有跟誰這麼長時間待着。」他窘笑。「人家問我這些天都忙什麼去了，怎麼總不見影兒。」

「不知道他們在你背後怎麼說。」

「我恨不得告訴他們。」

「要是他們說我是你的丫頭，我也不管。」

丫頭比姨太太容易說出口。但即使她一面說一面連自己也感動，意識深處還是有一絲懷疑。也許她隨時能夠叫一聲「騙你的！」然後笑着衝出去。她隨時可以停止。她會坐到他懷裏，紐扣解開的襖子前襟掩人耳目地留在原位，鬆開的袴頭與沒有打結的袴帶一層層堆在腰際。他沿着暖熱的皺褶一路摸索下去，她躲在壁櫥裏等待被發現，有一陣莫名的恐懼。每一下撫摸就像悸動的心跳，血液轟隆隆地流遍她，渾身有一陣傾聽的靜默。彼此的臉咫尺天涯，都雙目低垂，是一座小廟的兩尊神像，巍巍然凸出半身在外，正凝望一個在黑暗中窺探肚臍上紅寶石洞眼的竊賊。

他的頭毛氄氄的摩擦着她裸露的乳房，使她有點害怕和噁心。她哪裏來的這樣一個吮奶的成年兒子？她見他首先空洞地瞥一眼起了雞皮疙瘩的粉色乳頭，然後才含進嘴裏。那癢絲絲的吸吮又在不斷磨擦她，針刺她，彷彿隔着一層金屬篩網在擠壓。他轉向另一邊時，

她低頭看看那個緩緩平伏的蒼白小三角形，不無憂慮。他終於惘然地抬頭，眼睛紅光迷離，重新揀起香煙。她拉直衣服，走到鏡子前整理劉海。在那片回復原狀的黑色大方塊的遮蔽下，她對他微笑，又向下伸展手臂，十指相扣像忍住一個呵欠似的，以掩飾輕微的狼狽。這動作使她的衣袖像亭子的簷角一樣挑起來，褲管下也露出白色L形的腳，繡鞋、襪子全是白的。他伸一伸手，也沒抬高，她立即又回到他旁邊。

　　兩性間的基本法則她一竅不通，連赤條條躺在他的身軀下，也覺得隨時可以起來走開。在她的重負中間有一隻袋，軟篤篤輕柔柔，形成一個令她不安的真空。他的手來回摸索他窄窄的背脊，但是他一衝動起來她便沉着臉，僵着身體。應當等到「洞房花燭」──追溯到穴居時代的新婚夜。如果她不為那晚保留什麼，連他也會責怪她。而且如果哪天──雖然她儘量不讓自己這樣想──她一踏出這道門，這房子就變作墳山呢？這裏發生的只存在於他們兩人之間，一旦回到外面各自生活，便會融化得無影無蹤了。

　　他想起有一個推不掉的約會。汽車會回來接她。她後來意識到他有點生氣，感到忽忽若失。

　　「只有這辦法。過後誰也奈何不了我們了，」他說。

　　她一張臉別開枕在沙發靠墊上，微微點頭。他們一直沒有走近臥室。

　　「嗳，辦不到的，」她帶笑說道，彷彿是要她吞下一隻瓶，甚至於一個有圈形凸紋的陶罐。

　　「疼。」

　　「馬上就不疼了。」他停下好幾次。

「不行，還是疼。」

「我們今天要辦完它。」

還在機械地錘着打着，像先前一樣難受，現在是把她綁在刑具上要硬扯成兩半。突然一口氣衝上她的胸口。就在她左一下右一下地晃着頭時，只見他對她的臉看得出神。

「我覺得要吐出來了。」

他又再不停吻她，趕緊回到正事，古來所謂的魚水之歡和鴛鴦交頸舞。不如說是一條狗在自顧自的撞向樹樁。她忍不住大笑，終於連淚水也笑出來了。他苦笑，泄了氣。他又再撐起四肢蹲伏，最後一輪細察了地面，才伸直身子來輕吻她，摟她入懷。

「也算是做完了，」他彷彿借此下台似的說。

回復平靜後，他們難得又可以假裝能一覺睡到天明。她詫異他睡着了。落地燈黃黯的光線下，這個陳設西洋家具的中式房間起了奇異的變化。熟悉的几案櫥櫃全都矮了遠了，貼牆而立，不加入戰鬥。他蜷身側臥，忽然看上去很平凡，很陌生，是新造的第一個男子，可以是任何人，根本不值得費那麼多工夫來製作。

然而每一次重見都如隔數年，她又一而再的變了。他們向對方咧嘴一笑，心照不宣。因此也不會一塊兒坐，也儘說些閒話。他拉她站起來的時候，她說不要，會疼的。

「我們一定要搞好它。」

他拉着她的手往沙發走去。彷彿是長程，兩人的胳臂拉成一直線，讓她落後了幾步。她發現自己走在一列裹着頭的女性隊伍裹。他妻子以及別的人？但是她們對於她沒有身分。她加入那行列裏，好像她們就是人類。

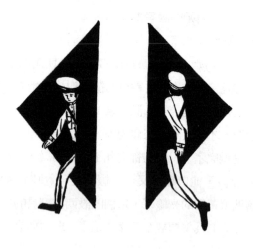

5

「這兩天風聲不好，」洪姨娘與老媽子們竊竊議論。

她以為東北打完仗了？傳說北京城外發生了刺殺。誰也不出門，正門上了閂，還用大水缸頂住。如果少帥的汽車來過接她，也沒有人跟她說。

她已經就寢了，照顧她的老媽子走進來，神色鄭重地悄聲說：

「少帥來了。」

他在門外。她連忙穿衣服。

「吃驚吧？」

她只說了聲「這麼晚！」彷彿除此以外在臥室會見男客也沒什麼不妥。老媽子走了，得體地虛掩房門。

「你怎麼進來的？」

「闖進來的。告訴過你如果你不來，我會闖來嘛。」

「瞎說。」

但是他一身軍服，手鎗插在鎗套裏。

「前院知道嗎？」

「我從離你最近的那個後門進來的，他們不會知道。一個僕人開的門，他認得我是誰。」

見到他仗着權勢施展穿牆過壁的魔法，她禁不住興奮。在這個房間見到他，有一種異樣的感覺——這裏於她早已經太小了，近乎破落，只有童年的頹垣敗瓦散滿一地。但是她慶幸可以打破咒語，不再受困於他們的鬼屋。他們出來了，這裏是日常世界。在這房間裏她曾經對他百般思念，難道他看不出？常有時候她夜裏從帥府的壽宴回來，難得看到他一眼，然而感受卻那麼深刻，那麼跟她的舊房間格格不入，以致她只能怔怔望着窗子，彷彿在聽音樂。微弱的燈光映在黑漆塗金木框內空空的黑色窗格上，泛棕褐色。她不走到窗邊，只正對窗前站着，任一陣濕風像圍巾般拂拭她的臉，這時候現實的空氣吹着面頰，濃烈的感覺瀰漫全身，隨又鬆開，無數薄囂囂的圖案散去，歡樂的歌聲逐漸消散。相比那樣喧騰的感覺之河，他來到這裏的真身只像是鬼魂罷了。

「是不是要打仗了？」

「現在傳言很多。」

那老媽子會不會端茶過來，把會客的幌子維持下去？難說。也許這會兒正在生爐子。

「大家都鎖起門來待在家裏？」

「怕遇上搶劫。」

「他們是怕誰？基督將軍已經跑了。」

「馮還有部隊在這裏。在西城門。」

勢力較弱的基督將軍怎麼會是老帥的長期盟友，她一直不大明白，他們決裂後的情形更加使她困惑。

「被刺殺的是誰？」

「徐昭亭，」他望着別處咕噥道。又是一個不需要她記住的人名。「馮幹的。」

「在火車上。」

「嗯，我差點坐了同一趟車，」他帶笑說。

「啊？」他的另一個世界，那個由無數難記的人名和沉悶的政治飯局匯聚而成的大海，突然波濤洶湧地掩沒了房間。

「給徐昭亭送行的飯局我也在座，他叫我跟他一塊兒坐火車，反正我本來也要去趟天津的。他們原定在鐵軌上埋伏炸藥，不過運兵車太多，沒法下手。最後他們把他拽下了火車。這一來都知道是誰幹的了。」

「你沒去真是萬幸。」

「所以我想，不管了，既然想見你我就要過來。」

她報以微微一笑。那老媽子還回不回來？

「老帥生氣嗎？」

「當然氣。首都附近出了這種事。」

「會不會打起來？」

「現在人心惶惶。段執政辭職了。徐是他的人，剛從國外考察回來。」

他起身關上房門。

「別，你還是走吧。」

「現在走，和之後走一樣壞。」

她看着他把皮帶掛到床闌干上，手鎗的皮套與金環暗啞的球根狀鐵枝對襯，恍若夢境。

「洪姨娘肯定會聽到的。」

「她大約已經知道了。」

「她不知道。」

「大家都睡下了。」

「她能看見我這邊還亮着燈。」

「關掉。」

「別關。我想看見你，不然不知道是什麼人。」

他面露不悅。除了他還可能有其他人？但是她要看見他的臉，像一朵從大海冒出的蓮花般降臨，不然就無法知道發生什麼事，只會在黑暗中覺得痛。蚊帳半掖着，以便在緊急關頭他可以抓起手鎗。要是讓人知道了洪姨娘會怎樣？老媽子呢？她在害人，叫她們以後沒法在這家裏有口飯吃。這是罪過，卻又奇異地安全，彷彿鑽進閣樓裏藏身。難得這次他們有一整夜的時間，就像對於院落的鳴蟲來說，這已經是一生一世。她喜歡那第一下接觸，彷彿終於擁有着他，一根軟而滑的肉餌在無牙的噬嗑間滑出，涼颼颼的，挑逗得她膝蓋一陣酥麻。但是立即轉為疼痛。

「給我說個好聽的就可以馬上完了。說你是陳叔覃的人。」

不知怎麼她就是說不出口。

「說你喜歡我。」

「我喜歡你。我喜歡你。」

他立即發了瘋似的快馬加鞭，背部中了一箭，哼哧哼哧喘着氣還是馳騁不休，末了俯身向前，仍舊不鬆開，一股熱的洪流從他體內湧出。

「有蚊子。」

「咬到了？在哪兒？」他用指尖蘸了唾沫，揉搓那塊地方。

她微笑。一定是他小時候在鄉下學的。他們還是安全地身在半夜。他是一件她可以帶上床的玩具，枕邊把玩的一塊玉。關了燈，她只依稀能辨認他仰臥的側影。

「你沒有我那麼快樂。」她覺得他面帶愁容。

「因為我年紀比較大。像個孩子哭了半天要蘋果，蘋果拿到手裏還在抽噎。」

「你一直要什麼有什麼。」

「不是的。」

可惜她不能走進他沒有她的那些年：一個個荒涼的庭院，被古老的太陽曬成了黃色。她要一路跑進去，大聲喊着「我在這兒！我在這兒呀！」

他從床邊探下身去，在蚊香盤上點燃香煙。

「今晚飯桌上談的都是徐昭亭。」

「究竟為什麼要殺他？」

「他在拉攏各路人馬結盟對付基督將軍。他回來的時候東南那邊接駕似的歡迎他。不過哪裏都很把他當一回事兒。他在英國應邀出席閱兵典禮，觀禮台上只有給英皇和皇后坐的兩把椅子，他看了臉色很不高興。於是喬治五世起身讓他和瑪麗皇后並坐，自己跟軍官們站在一起。」

「他是軍人嗎？」

「外國人叫他徐將軍。他們把誰都稱作將軍。其實他是個政客。小胖子。白金漢宮有一次開園遊會，他的高級秘書帶太太出席，那女人年過五十了，裏小腳，穿中國衣裳，但是她丈夫要她戴一頂很大的簪花草帽。有個年青的秘書不贊成，可是那高級秘書是前清的舉人，天下事無所不曉，說『哪有外國婦女白天出門不戴帽子的？』離御帳大約有六百碼的路，那女人小腳走不快，風還把她的帽子吹跑了。那年青秘書追趕帽子，可帽子在風裏忽左忽右，忽上忽下，好一會兒才抓住。喬治五世捧着肚子哈哈大笑。」

她竭力壓低笑聲不讓外面聽見。他拉過她的手，覆住那沉睡的鳥，它出奇地馴服和細小，帶着皺紋，還有點濕。

　　「過後徐昭亭跟那年青人說：『你大概沒有考慮吧，這對英皇是大不敬。』那秘書說：『那麼那美國首席大法官呢？他拍着英皇的背，一邊跺腳一邊大笑。』徐沒再說什麼。第二天倫敦泰晤士報講了追帽子的新聞，沒加評論，但是批評了休斯大法官，儘管他是英皇的老朋友。」

　　「他們還去了哪些地方？」

　　「美國。哪裏都去到了。徐在蘇聯跟他們外長齊翟林舌戰了一場。那邊是以接待國家元首的禮數歡迎他。」

　　「為什麼？」

　　「中國人除非是軍人，否則誰也不把你當真。徐是北洋集團的耆老。」

　　「我想去看看巴黎和義大利。」

　　「咱們會去的。過兩年吧。」

　　又在擂鼓撞鐘了，每半個鐘點一次的報時。鐘鼓樓依然在中國深處，警報着黑夜的危險，直通千百年前，一分鐘比一分鐘深入和古老。

　　「老段拍電報到上海叫他不要回來。老段替他擔心。但是他想，堂堂專使不敢回京覆命，勢成國際笑話。再說東北在打仗，他也想趁機撈一把，那老狐狸。他覺得這是老段的機會。於是他向天津英國領事館借了一輛汽車，車頭揚着英國國旗開到北京。這次不知怎麼他沒有提防。命中註定的。」

　　「坐上火車就去了。」

「嗯，叫是叫專列，不過是普通火車上拖一節車廂。每停一站都有軍樂隊歡迎他，還要等很長時間給引擎加水。車站燈火通明，被兵士層層圍住，就像莫斯科歡迎他的儀式那麼隆重。有個軍官上了火車，說要找徐先生。他秘書說專使身體不舒服，讓來客坐上座，但是他坐了下首。」

「火車也分上座下座？」

「也不是臥鋪。我們中國人嘛，總是先禮後兵。所以他們便聊了起來，軍官說他是張督辦派來的，問徐先生在哪裏。秘書咬定他身體不適。徐喝多了，在另一節車廂睡覺，被說話聲吵醒了，揉着眼睛走了出來。秘書說：『怎麼樣，我說專使身體不舒服吧？』」

他把她的手拉回來。

「那軍官站了起來。徐終於讓他們都重新坐下，然後說：『我身體抱恙，一路上只好謝絕招待。』『張督辦已經等了一晚上，還請徐先生賞光。』『沒有工夫。』『火車多停一會無妨。』『我得了重感冒，改天再拜訪督辦吧。』『司令部特為準備了茶話會歡迎徐先生。』『半夜三更開什麼茶話會？』『有急事洽商。』『什麼事那麼急？我已經派人到蒙古和馮先生洽商一切了。』那秘書插話說：『馮先生徐先生都是一家人，無事不好商量。』但是那軍官揚一揚手巾示意，立即有十幾個兵士湧上車廂，扶着徐下了火車。」

「怎麼他們在附近還有司令部？」

「他們是沿着鐵路來擺平各樣事情的。」

她永遠沒法明白兩個軍閥怎麼可以各據一條鐵路分治北京，而且剛打完一仗，一方竟會容許另一方這樣悠然撤退。

「他們在司令部鎗斃了他？」

「不不，在田地裏，趁黑幹的。已經夠駭人聽聞的了。基督將軍氣得直跺腳，他們把他的計畫搞砸了。」

這些人變了小小的殉葬俑，青綠釉的襖子底下穿着黃袴子，打着敝舊的陶土補丁，他們倆可以把頭靠在同一張枕席上仔細觀看。

「老段自己惹的禍。他向來利用老馮對我們玩弄手腕，事變嚇得他膽戰心驚，看見老馮坐困蒙古，幾十萬部隊軍心離散，不知道他下一步要怎樣。結果老馮做了這件事。他聽說老段幾天沒去辦公，可把他逼急了，便幹掉老頭子最得力的副手。老段失了臂膀，怕他怕得要死，連自己家裏都不敢大聲說話。」

「他在蒙古也會聽到？」

「他到處安插了特務，對誰都跟蹤。我今晚在這裏他也會知道。」

她觸了一下電，想到基督將軍是替他們保密的心腹好友，幾乎暖在心頭。

「你出去的時候沒有危險嗎？」

「沒有。」

「不會打仗吧？」

「估計還要有一場決戰。」

「因為刺殺的事？」

「反正是徐一死，他搞的反共同盟看起來就要實現了。大家都想倒馮。」

「他又信基督教，又是共產黨。」

「他是偽裝的。蘇聯每個月給他六萬，還不計他拿到的軍械。」

「那麼他並不真的是共產黨，只是假扮出來的？」

「也不見得好多少。大家說起赤禍，都說是洪水猛獸。照我看來一個大家挨窮的國家裏有別的東西更可怕。大概對於年紀大的人來說，共產就是什麼準則都不要了。比方說老帥，他就恨共產黨。」

「這些人不很多？」

「我們抓到的就不少。也有些是大學生，真可惜他們被蘇聯利用了。」

「他們被抓到就只有死了。」

「嗯。」

她見過犯人的首級，偶爾吊掛在城門旁電線杆上。「不要看，」坐黃包車或是汽車路過的時候老媽子會這樣說。她只有一個印象，彷彿是髮根把五官全都拉扯得翹了起來，如同箍着網巾的京劇腳色，腮頰與額頭上一道道紅痕也像是舞台化妝。她害怕，好在沒人知道是誰……洗衣的老媽子李婆有一回講起她村裏有人被捕。當夜大家都在院子裏乘涼，老媽子們坐小板凳，四小姐躺在竹榻上，平滑的床板如墓碑般冰冷。黑沉沉一大片的星空朝她壓下來，是一個正在塌陷的穹頂，碩大無朋，看得她眼花撩亂。她很想找到古詩所謂的「北斗闌干」。那個夏夜儘管就在外頭的同一個院子裏，可是已經好像過了一千年。

「他們抓他的時候他正在賣糖人兒，直接逮到司令部去了。到處抓人呐。」

「如今就是這樣，」另一個老媽子感歎。談起時事，每個人都啞着嗓子小聲說話。

「聽他們講這事兒都嚇死了。問斬那天，判官坐在公案後面，前邊站兩行扛着來福鎗的兵。那四個人犯跪成一排。斬條貼在竹簽上，放在公案上。判官查對了姓名，拿起毛筆在一張斬條的名字上勒一道朱紅，像投槍似的投到地下，這時候兵士們就大吼一聲。有個兵撿了斬條插到人犯的衣領後面，四個人都這樣對上了號。突然間判官踢翻了桌子，一轉身跑了。要把煞嚇走。」

「煞是什麼？」四小姐說。其他人都訕訕地笑。

「沒聽說過歸煞？」洪姨娘道，「人死了，三天之後回來。」

「煞是鬼？」

「或許是地府的凶神吧。我也不大清楚。問李婆。」

「他們說呀是一隻大鳥。歸煞那天大家躲起來避邪。但是有些好事的人在地上灑了灰，過後就有鳥的爪子印。」

「據說呀但凡有殺人，甚至只是有殺人的念頭，煞都會在附近。」洪姨娘道，「所以那個判官要保護他自己。」

她已經坐直了身子，慶幸自己在黑暗中被熟人包圍着。

「人犯上身剝光了在騾車上遊街，前邊一隊兵，後邊一隊兵，兩邊又各有兩行兵。監斬官騎馬跟在最後，肩膀上一條大紅綢子掛下來，新郎倌兒一樣。兩個吹喇叭的開道，吹的是外國兵衝鋒的調子，『噠噠啲噠噠啲』。兵士們齊聲喊『殺啊！』看熱鬧的也跟着喊『殺啊！』」

「嘖！這些人，」一個老媽子說。

另一個短促地笑了一聲。「門房裏老是有人說『看砍頭去』。」

「這些男人呵！而且成天沒事閒着，哪像我們。」

「講下去呀，李婆。後來呢？」四小姐說。這話她們聽了也笑。

「後來？後來那四個人在城門外跪成一排。劊子手走到第一個跟前，先用力拍了拍他脖子後面估摸尺寸，大刀一落，頭踢到一邊。

輪到第四個，就是那和我同村的，他看了前面那些，昏過去了。醒來就躺在牢房地上。他是陪斬的。」

「陪斬的？」洪姨娘疑惑地咀嚼這幾個字。「唔，有人做貴賓，有人只是請來陪他的。」

「過了幾天就把他放了。到底也不大肯定他是奸細。」

「那怎麼不繼續關在牢裏？」四小姐說。

「讓他長年累月白吃白喝呀？他們就是想嚇唬嚇唬他。不過他回了家沒幾個月就死了。」

「嚇破了膽，難怪的，」洪姨娘道。

「嗐呀，現在這時世還是深宅大院裏好，」李婆道，「聽不見外邊的事兒。」

雖然這故事早於他的時代，她不知怎麼並不願意告訴他。那一定是吳蟠湖的時候。現在做法肯定不一樣了吧？可是一說起其實什麼都不會改變，他就難免惱火。

他把煙灰彈到地板上的蚊香盤裏。「小聲說了半天，喉嚨都說疼了。」

「我們別說話了。」

「那樣會睡着的。」

「也許你最好現在走，趁着天沒亮。」

他忖了一忖。「沒關係。五點不到我就會睡醒。」

「你怎麼知道你會？」

「行軍習慣了。」

「如果打起來，你就要走了。」她本來不想說這話。

「我會找個人照應你的。」

「你睡覺時把手放在這兒嗎？」

「小時候會。放在那裏似乎最安全，不知為什麼。」

「我也一樣，但老媽子總是拉開我的手，就不再放了。」

但是他的手夾在她腿間，似乎像插進口袋裏那麼自然。他一個吻弄醒了她。周圍灰茫茫一片。

「不不，你不是要走了麼？」她叫喊，他已經一條腿壓向她，身子滑上來。

有一會並不痛。海上的波濤在輕柔地搖晃她，依然是半夢半醒。他們的船已經出海，盡是詭異的一大片灰濛濛。然而他們渾濁的臉發出一股有安全感的氣味，令他們想起床上的一夜眠。

他穿衣的時候她坐了起來，摸一摸他的肩膀、背脊與肘彎。

「別起床，那僕人可以領我出去。」

「不要穿鞋。」

他略一躊躇，顯然是愛面子。「不要緊的。」

她聽見他走在過道石板地的腳步聲，一路清晰刺耳。她心裏發冷，很清楚事到如今洪姨娘一定是知道了。但還是照樣理好床鋪，燒蚊香的錫碟裏的煙蒂也一個個揀了出來，洗臉時趁機把那條藏着的毛巾也洗了。毛巾浸在熱水盆裏，隱隱聞見一股米湯的氣味，這粥水也被視為生命的源泉。

6

「現在外邊亂得很，」洪姨娘私下裏透露。「你爹去發起了一個地方保安會，跟清朝倒掉的時候一樣。但是現在不比當年了，那時候老帥只是他手下一員部將。這回老帥一定點過頭，你爹斷不會自作主張的。」

四小姐知道她話鋒所向。

「他們家的老大算是好的了，沒被寵壞。他媳婦是配不上他，但朱三小姐的事都傳成那樣子，他到底沒讓她進門。那就有些意思了。」

提起朱三，四小姐仍舊不動聲色，繼續撥弄手裏的九連環。

「其實像他們這樣的人家，娶兩個媳婦平起平坐的又有什麼？老帥也許不肯讓年青人娶兩房，但也許是顧到朱家的名譽。除非是另一種姑娘，出身不一樣的人家。姑娘家最要緊的是名譽。外邊的人，抓住一點點話柄就講得滿城風雨。就拿你爹說，尤其是他現在又出山了，儘管大家都知道他跟陳家是老交情，他至少也不想顯得自己聽命於人。要是人家說他為了討好姓陳的什麼都肯呢？你知道你爹的脾氣。就連老帥也不會插手——說到底是當爹的處罰兒女。還不要說我，我自己也會落下罪名。也不用我叨念，你自己心裏頭都有數。」

她自己為此而死也願意，但是洪姨娘和老媽子怎麼辦？她們是她的地獄。只是她對地獄沒有執念。眼前她不必言語，低着頭就是了。洪姨娘的反應已是極度溫和。儘管如此，他與她的事旁人只要一提就是褻瀆，令她不由得繃緊了臉退縮。旁人看上一眼便已是誤解。

洪姨娘沒有再說什麼。當務之急是阻止他又一次登門。他沒再來。

事關自尊，四小姐不去問他將來。他不提，不表示他忘了。如果他試過跟父親談而因此受辱，他也不會願意告訴她。東北的叛變之後，他長跪了一日乞求父親的寬宥，這就從來沒有告訴她。她是在一個親戚家裏聽說的。

她一見到他便不擔心了，什麼事都像對鏡微笑一樣明晰。只是每次他去打仗，兩人一別數月的時候，她才開始憂慮自己的處境。她想去他家裏看看五老姨太以及他的孩子們，甚至於他的妻。他們是她唯一的親人，她在自己家裏只與陌生人同住。五老姨太常說起他的童年：

「他喜歡守在院子裏一個池塘邊上，等穿着新衣裳的人洋洋得意走過來，就扔一塊大石頭到水裏，濺別人一身的水，自己拍着手笑。人家多窘呀，只好說：『少帥怕人是吧？』嘻嘞，那頑皮勁兒。他長大一些的時候我成天提心吊膽的，怕在他父親跟前沒法交代。」她耷拉着膨鬆的眼皮，語氣驕傲。

五老姨太全靠他才有如今的地位。她從前是小縣城的一個妓女。如果他戰死了，四小姐能想像自己如何投奔五老姨太，抱着她的膝蓋跪地哭泣，懇求收留，說着這種場合的套語：「我生是他家的人，死是他家的鬼。」少女去給情人送葬，一身素服：

「白綢衫兒，白綢裙兒，
黑頭髮紮了白綢手巾兒。」

這叫做望門寡：未婚夫死了而少女希望為他守節。在那關係鬆散的大家庭裏，有他待如生母的老姨太，有他待如妻子的半老婦人，如果多加上一個她呢？她們不會拒絕？她太年青了，還不知道自己的心志，最終會改嫁，敗壞他們家聲。平常不過的說辭。自會有人押送她回到自己家，她父親羞怒之下會殺了她。

陰曆年之前他打來電話。「是我。我回來了。」

一聽見他的聲音她就彷彿霎時往後靠在實心牆壁上，其實她還手握話筒，動也沒動。汽車開過來接她。

「回來了？」洪姨娘說。

「嗯。」

現在能用電話約定幽期，才不枉洪姨娘當初為了裝私房電話而引起的麻煩與猜疑。洪姨娘的沉默使她一陣愧疚。那老媽子如今則是終日潛行，彷彿懷着鬼胎，隨時要生出一個什麼妖怪來。

長久圍攻以後，他打贏了南口之戰。他在前線一度患上痢疾，聽人建議拿鴉片作為特效藥，有了癮。

「休養好了就請個大夫來幫我戒了。」

他不願意讓她看見他躺下抽大煙，雙唇環扣粗厚的煙嘴，像個微突的鳥喙。鴉片就如堂子裏的女人，是他父輩的惡習，兩者都有老人的口涎味。

「想我了麼？」他一隻胳臂摟住她，探身過來看她別過一旁的臉。問題彷彿有性的意味。「想我了麼？」

她終於僵着脖子不大由衷地點了點頭。

「我嘴上有沒有那個味兒？」

「沒有。」不過是一種讓人聯想起老人的隱約的氣味。在她心目中，鴉片是長者的一種殘疾。然而戰爭沒有給他別的還算僥倖。

「朱三小姐要嫁人了。」

「哦？嫁誰？」

他咕噥了一個人名。

「是做什麼的？」

「政客。她可以嫁得再好些。」

他們談到別處去了。忽然她向着他咧嘴一笑，脫口道：「我真高興。」

「我早就知道你憋不住要說了。」他半笑半嗔，而且似乎厭恨她環抱着的撫慰的手臂。

次日晚上八點後他打來電話。「是我。我今年想再見你一次。」

她也立即想到不然就是隔了一年才見面。「今天太晚了。」

「明天是除夕。」

「算了，不行的。」

「說是看戲好了。車子馬上來。」

「好吧。」

「我跟他們看戲去，」她向洪姨娘咕嚕一句。

「噴！馬上就過年了，各有各忙，哪有這時候還周圍逛的。你爹一定要說了。」她聲音很輕卻語帶威嚴，簡直是他在說。

默然片刻，洪姨娘轉身向老媽子，快速地喃喃吩咐：「到前頭去說一聲，帥府來接四小姐看戲去。」

老媽子走了。

「好了，還不趕緊收拾收拾——前頭沒說什麼才好，但你也不能這個樣子出門。」

他們真的去看了一場電影。從此他常帶她出去看戲，在有舞會的飯店吃飯。要麼他是逐漸豁出去了，要麼就是非要逼出個結果來。他的醫生每次都跟着來給他打戒煙針。她把頭髮盤起，以顯得好像剪短了，身上的新旗袍與高跟鞋平時存放在他們幽會的房子裏。人人都議論他們，但是她絲毫不在乎，不像在洪姨娘面前。人言只是群眾的私語，燈光與音樂的一部分。她沒機會聽見老帥的話：

「他討小找誰不行，偏偏是我老朋友的女兒。我成什麼人了？就算他沒有娶親也絕對不能結婚。我們陳家沒有先上床後進門的媳婦。」

她父親走了他的第一步棋。

他把她喚到跟前，說道：「我和北京大學的校長談過了，他答應讓你入學做旁聽生。看看一兩年內能不能把功課趕上去吧。」

沒說為什麼兄弟姊妹裏獨獨讓她進學堂。就當是時代在變，女大學生的婚姻前途有時候比較看好。實際上，上學給了她自由，一整天都可以自己安排。如果她墮落了，那是現代教育有問題，現成的替罪羊。不加管束任她撒野，總也強於由人非議她父親把她給了陳家做小。兩家之間未曾言明的緊張關係至此緩和。倘若事情吹了也許還是可以嫁掉她。朱三小姐不是嫁了？

洪姨娘贏得奇異的勝利，四小姐平生第一次見她精神振奮。忍受了這些年的忽略與輕視，她終於都報了仇。那男人怕了。她的孩子有靠山，他認了下風。四小姐前所未有地成了她的親女兒。她盡情吐出心中的憂慮：

「現在時世還不太平，你最好自己做好打算，不要一味拖延。老帥因為他對唐家人的感情，肯定是為難的。可你也不去爭那個虛名嘛。看在你爹份上，他總也不會虧待你。關鍵是少帥要找到合適的人跟他父親談，一個說得上話的人。全靠你自己拿定主意了。男人向來是不急的。」她微笑輕聲說着，對於提起她青樓時代的閱人經驗感到遲疑，也當心不要暗示他或許和別人一樣沒長性。「我不過是旁觀者提醒你一句，看得出你也不是個沒主見的人。人家會怪我為什麼早先不說你。說了又有什麼用。母女一場，徒然傷感情。」

四小姐仍舊默然。到了這時候，從前什麼都不告訴她是無禮又傷人。但是怎麼對她說他們倆從來不談這些？

「朱三小姐嫁了人，還給丈夫謀了個官職呢。你們摩登的人也無非是這樣。」

她對朱三小姐的婚事一聲不吭，洪姨娘似乎特別佩服。現在是因為覺得她冷漠才愛她，這讓她有點不安。

北京照常慶祝中秋節，儘管正跟北伐的廣州政權——途中已分裂為南京和漢口兩個政府——交戰。他早早已經去了河南前線，但是這天依舊是她一生最快樂的中秋節。她請了一個孤身留在北京的女同學過來，其後陪她走回宿舍。家裏的人力車落後幾步跟着，累了可以隨時上車。灰牆灰瓦的矮房子使馬路更顯寬闊。遠處劈嚦啪啦放着鞭炮，附近也偶爾嘭的一聲空洞地炸響，嚇人一跳。商店都上了排門，人人回家吃團圓飯去了。長街一直伸向那灰藍的天空，天上掛着一個冰輪似的月亮。一說話風就把面紗往她嘴裏吹。她披着每個女大學生都有的那種深紅色絨線圍巾，一路晃着給朋友帶回去的那盒月餅。兩人走在電車鐵軌上，直到一輛電車衝她們直壓過來，整座房子一樣大，噹噹響着鈴，聽上去彷彿是「我找到的人最好，最好，最好，最好。」 恰恰是她小時候一直想要的：站在舞台正前方，兩隻手攀着台板無論如何也靠得不夠近。如今鐃鈸在她頭頂頂上鏘鏘敲着。

次日他打電話來。原來前一天已經回來了。

「跟他太太過的中秋節。」洪姨娘哂笑一聲，憤憤不平。

她只微笑。她自己也是要跟家裏人吃團圓飯。

「梁大夫呢？」他讓她在身邊坐下的時候，她環顧了房間。

「那忘八羔子。被我攆走了。」

「怎麼回事？」她從來沒見他這樣生氣。

「他給我打的戒煙針是一種嗎啡。」

「用嗎啡戒鴉片？」

「他是故意的，好讓我積重難返。」

「他到底是什麼人？」

「我發現他是楊一鵬的人。」

她搜索腦中面目模糊的人名冊。老帥最信任的那位副手？

「為什麼？」

「他恨我。出了顧興齡的事情以後，明擺着憎恨我。」

東北那場叛變。難道他是說他確曾參預？

「那次主要是要整掉他。」

矛頭並不完全指向他父親？罪行之大立即使她眩暈。造反的皇太子是什麼下場？關押，賜死──面朝紫宮叩首謝恩，喝下毒酒自盡。無論他做了什麼，那也表明他是男子漢，不僅是某人的兒子。也許她還有點悲哀，因為他做了不會為她而做的事。

「可他們說你──」她剎住了口。

「說我嫖妓賭錢昏了頭，自己兵營裏發生什麼都不知道？」

「不過是說你大意了。」

「我還沒那麼傻。不錯，我常跟姓顧的在兵營俱樂部打撲克牌。我們比較好的年青士官裏他算一個。我們倆都想革新，但只要楊一鵬還在就沒有機會。最後沒有別的辦法。倘若不是日本人插手就已經成功了。」

「他們為什麼支持老帥？」

「他們不想俄國人在東北坐大。顧興齡和基督將軍結了盟，而他跟俄國人是一夥兒。」

她無法想像他站在基督將軍那邊反對他父親。其後他在南口擊敗了馮以祥。今年兩方又在河南對壘，這次馮屬於南方陣營。

她的沉默使他多說了幾句替他父親辯護：「有些人說老帥親日。東北緊挨着高麗，他當然不能不敷衍日本人。但他總是這個態度：小事可以談，大事一定拖。現在他連小事也拖，大事絕對免談。甚至於為滅掉顧興齡而定下的協議，他也從未執行。」

「顧後來怎樣？」

「鎗斃了。」

一時間兩人都不做聲。他能撿回一條命，是因為他是親生兒子。

「你不能告訴老帥被騙的事？那些戒煙針。」

他略一搖頭又半眨眼睛，表示決無可能。但是同時會有別人向老帥告狀，說他年紀輕輕成了癮君子。

「前幾天出了件好笑的事，可見我們周圍這些人是個什麼德性。有報告說南方軍襲潰了首任大總統的墳，於是有人提議我們也要回敬，去污毀孫文的屍骸。」

「孫中山葬在這兒？」

「在西山。幸虧那天有個老國民黨葉洛孚在場。他勸老帥說現在不興幹這種事了，而且首先要查清楚。查出來不是國民黨，是基督將軍的駐軍幹的。砍了樹，房子也洗劫了，但是沒有擾動墓裏。葉就跟老帥說，既然孫文遺體正好在北京，我們應該加以保護，表示我們有器量。於是老帥派了一支小分隊到碧雲寺去。果然沒兩天廟裏就來了幾個帶着鋤頭鑱子的人，見這兒有兵駐守，徘徊了一陣子又跑了。」

「他們是誰？」

「齊永福的人。」

她猜度是首任大總統的舊部。

「我們也不算落後。國民黨自己，兩年前他們的右派鬥不過左派，失勢了，不惜大老遠從廣州跑到這邊敵界來，在總理靈前開了個會，後來被人稱作西山會議派。孫夫人自己──對遺體施行防腐永久保存，就是她的主意。」

「他還是生前的樣子？」她叫道。

「嗯，她跟列寧學的，她親共。當然她推在丈夫的頭上，說他說過最好能保存遺體。孫的追隨者很錯愕。首先花費就非常大。最後蘇聯送了他們一副玻璃棺材。」

「她美不美？」

「眼睛很大。」

「是她還是她妹妹更美？」

「妹妹更活潑。孫夫人也活潑，只是他們剛來她丈夫就病倒了。他們在天津下船的時候，我代表老帥去迎接。我們到達北京那天下雪，從火車站坐汽車出來，除了歡迎團體還有大批的群眾。大雪紛飛，屋頂上、樹頂上全是人。」他近乎氣憤地直衝着她說。「在天津群眾也是一樣多，只不過警察局長為了討好段執政把他們趕散了。」

「孫中山真是那麼偉大的人？」

「關鍵是他代表了共和的理想。辛亥革命時大多數人都不知道在發生什麼事。可是到民國十三年，他們真的想要共和了。好比女人剛結婚的時候並不懂得怎麼回事，後來才喜歡。你會嗎？」

「不知道。我又沒結婚。」話一出口她便懊悔，彷彿在提醒他。

「哦，『沒結婚』。翅膀長硬了，呃？說說你是誰的人。」

「少來。」

「你是誰的人？說說。」

「少來。那一回孫夫人的妹妹也跟着他們？」

「沒有，只是夫婦倆。他是應邀過來組織政府的。他的追隨者滿懷希望，覺得他會當選大總統。他一到便去拜訪老帥，我也在場。寒暄過後，老帥馬上站起來說：『我陳祖望是個粗人，坦白說一句，我是捧人的。今天我能捧姓段的，就可以捧姓孫的。我惟獨反對共產。假如我們要搞共產，我陳祖望是寧可流血也不要赤化。』這幾句話吹到老段耳朵裏，他更是疑神疑鬼了。其實那一回才談了半個鐘點。孫文當然不承認親共。可是有老段在，已經坐着那把交椅了。孫回到飯店，跟幕僚開會直到深夜，當晚就生病了。」

「他是這樣死的！」

「病了幾個月才去世的。老段一直沒有去探望，葬禮也不出席，托詞腳腫穿不上鞋。堂堂一國元首會沒有鞋子穿！」

「至少他脫身了。」

「如今他正在看我們的笑話。他一下野政府就真空了。代理內閣有我們全部盟友的代表，當然維持不下去。內閣辭職以後，誰也不願意就任。老帥很生氣，說『隨便找些人就行』。政府雇的人已經停薪半年了。遜帝溥儀仍舊每個月拿到三萬塊，是我們私人的錢。皇權統治遺留下來的，就只有這份對所有上等人的尊敬。本來老百姓也不過是指望『豫人治豫』、『魯人治魯』而已。政府再不好，本省人總比外人強些。我們儘量由得各地自治。任何當地人只要有武裝力量，足以把本土管起來，就能從我們這裏得到一官半職。」

聽上去形勢很壞。「戰爭會不會打到這裏？」

「戰爭的事難講。論實力，我們沒什麼好怕。去年馮的部隊在南口把戰壕挖得很好，不過我們的加農炮火力也夠猛，集中開火幾天以後，地皮都掀翻了。廣州原本是土鎗土炮的革命黨，現在有了蘇聯的軍械和顧問，我們的盟友自然敵不過。像吳蟠湖，他接到自己前線快要潰散的報告，就派出大刀隊砍殺逃兵。他的兵早已聽說大刀隊要來，向着火車窗裏掃射他們。結果大刀隊都不敢下火車。」

「這些盟友有什麼用呢？」

「可不是，個個都只顧自己。吳挨打的時候，東南那邊方申荃按兵不動，儘管他本來可以輕易切斷南方軍的補給線。輪到他吃了敗仗，就賄賂長腿給了他去奉天的安全路條，親自過來乞援，路上隱姓埋名穿便服，因為他一個敗兵之將不配穿軍裝。老帥見他這樣忍辱負重，就派長腿出兵幫他奪回了東南五省。」她聽說過他們的長腿將軍。「老帥就是那樣。對敵人也識英雄重英雄，向來慷慨，給人留點面子。他最不能容忍的是以下犯上。所以長腿摽着老方奉承老帥，說服他自己出面做政府首腦。下屬不算數，但同儕的支持⋯⋯」

「他當上了大總統？」她囁嚅道。

「沒有，不是總統總理，只稱大元帥。這是老帥謙抑的行事做派，一輩子只喜歡從旁輔佐。這樣已經是破例了。」

他突然頓住了。她也聽說過那句俗語「變古亂常，不死則亡」。年紀大的人改變習慣是個壞兆頭。

「南邊也亂糟糟的，」她說。

「他們有自己一套搞法。」

「他們是共產黨？」

「不再是了。南京跟英美搭上線，甩掉蘇聯了。現在蘇聯希望我們來遏制南方。老帥不賣帳，下令搜查了蘇聯大使館，把他們搞顛覆的密件都公佈了出來。這方面他們不遺餘力，有一段時間似乎他們就要在中國實現赤化了。」

「在南邊？」

「在南方軍所到之處。集會鬥爭地主，分田，把男裝裁短——長衫是上等階級的標誌。而且攻擊教堂和教團，彷彿是義和拳的重演。洋人確實招人厭恨，因為政府待他們總是一副奴才嘴臉，替他們說話，跟從前沒分別。傳教師在農村勢力很大。排外一直盛行，共產主義便打着這個旗號滲透。老百姓心裏有不平，給他們隨便一個出口都會發洩的。不過共產黨正在遭到清洗，他們不比義和拳長久。」

「孫夫人的妹妹現在結婚了嗎？」

他微微一笑。「不知道，沒聽說。」

「她多大了？」

「跟我差不多大。」

「她不會已經二十七了吧？」

「我不知道，她自己沒講過。洋化的女人不提自己年齡的。」

「她總不能永遠不結婚吧？」

「這些基督教徒說不準。」

「不是因為你？」

「不，不會。」

「她一定喜歡過你。」

「她正一心找個中國的領袖，恰好我有機會繼承這個位子。」

「你說得她那樣無情。」

「她自然是以她姐姐為榜樣。」

「她非常美？」

「不是。」

「不，說老實話。」

「出洋念書的人別有一種清新可喜的氣質，況且她也沒有沾上一身男子氣回來，叫人討厭。」

「幸好老帥不會讓你離婚。」

「哪裏就到那一步了。」

「你不想娶她嗎？」

「即使想過，我也是在大處着眼。男人也有希望跟某一家結親的，好比一個亮燈的門廊，人人路過都看兩眼，因為正好是你沒有的東西。自從那一回群眾在大雪裏等候孫文，可以跟那樣一個人發生的任何關係我都願意發生。」

「但是你總要喜歡那姑娘。」

「那當然。我以前常想這些，不像現在，沒有雜念了。」

「老帥知不知道？」

「他當成笑話兒──他兒子娶一個『吹鼓手』的女兒做媳婦！那是她父親的外號兒，他從前在上海附近傳教，彈簧風琴。」

這位社交新星，如今在她自己的往事中是一個親切的人物。「不知道她為什麼不結婚。」

「可能她也難。以她的年齡，即便是早幾年，她遇見的男人應該都結了婚了。」

他拉了鈴繩，從另一個院子叫來新雇的醫生給他注射，與前任

醫生用的藥劑一樣。

他仍舊鬱鬱不舒。「咱們去趟西山吧。」

「這麼晚，城門都要關了。」

「會給我們打開的。」

他們帶着醫生鑽進汽車的時候，天已垂暮。從遠處城門傳來敲鑼聲，漸成悠長狂亂的嗆──嗆──嗆──嗆──嗆──嗆，警報着敵軍來襲、火災或洪水，世界的末日。汽車繞開了剛好趕上擠進城來的一輛輛騾車。一個警衛跳下汽車的踏腳板，喊叫着往前跑去。城門再次開啟，鐵灰色城牆矗立在黑色塵土上，汽車從當中的隧洞穿過。

長途行車，彷彿真把他們帶到了他鄉。抵達西山飯店後，他們卻沒有走進餐廳，免得碰見認識的人。只在金魚池邊徘徊，李醫生進去代點汽水。她戴着墨鏡，蒙着一層面紗。

「你像是個軍閥的姨太太，到這兒來跟小旦幽會，」他說。

倒也沒那麼浪漫。他們在樓上套房與醫生吃晚飯，談到上午回去前要遊覽哪些地方，顯然是要過夜。她可以說是同學家留宿，但是也懷疑自己太過分了。

野外寂靜得不自然，這西式旅館也一片死寂。北京城與它那守夜的鐘鼓、市井的私語，都彷彿很遠了。徹夜不歸，又是在飯店裏，她毫無羈束，以至於不再受法律的保護。她可笑地覺得自己是被搶來的新娘，落在一個陌生的村子裏，終於受他支配。奇怪的是他看上去也忸怩，脫衣的時候不朝她看，帶一絲微笑，眼睛很明亮。她想擺脫那異樣之感，很快上床鑽進被窩，他一上來就溜到他臂彎裏。他卻掀開被子，在燈光下慢慢檢視她。

「你幹什麼？」

一隻獸在吃她。她從自己豎起的大腿間看見他低俯的頭，比例放大了，他的頭髮摩擦着她，使她毛骨悚然。他一輪急吻像花瓣似的向她內裏的蓓蕾及其周邊收攏，很難受。俘獵物的無奈與某種模糊的慾望在她內心輪流交替：要設法離開，不然就輪到她去吞噬他，拿他填滿自己。她好幾次試着起來。終究又還是他在上頭向她微笑，臉泛微紅。她讓他來，近乎解脫般喘氣，不斷呷着甲板上搖晃的半杯酒。他一次次深扎進去，漸漸塞滿她，忽然像魚擺尾一樣晃到一邊，含笑望着她的臉。他停下來又看又摸。

「大了，呃？這個可不是長大了麼？」

但是他們整夜都沒怎麼說話，不似往常。

7

父親把她喚到書房去，用談公事的口吻壓低了聲音說：

「現在時局緊張，老帥要把全家遷回奉天，今晚就啟程。他叫你也一塊兒去。也許最好是這種時候了——兩家都省心。看在我們交誼的份上，他一定把你當親生女兒看待的。不過，從今以後你也要學會做人了。現在全靠你自己了。讓洪姨娘給你收拾行李，東西和傭人倒不必多帶。想要什麼晚些可以再送過去。就是要穿暖和點，關外冷。等時局平靖些你可以回來，你洪姨娘也可以去看你。」

她經歷了一趟奇妙的旅程。專列上的陳家人把她當做來長住的外甥女那樣招待。少帥夫人責不旁貸，親自打點她的起居。她以後不再喊她大嫂了，改口叫大姊。關外是中國的北極，從前無數哀怨的公主與嬪妃出塞和親，嫁給匈奴王。起伏不休的褐色山巒，橫披着長城這條由成對的烽火台扣起的灰色帶子，看得她驚喜不已。窗子裏的景致永遠一個樣子，同一幅畫屏不停地折疊開展，克喇嗵踢——克喇克！克喇嗵踢——克喇克！沒完沒了。

翌晨火車第一次停站，她望着停在旁邊鐵道上的一車兵。兵士們都站着，彷彿半身露出車外。一個農家子弟，雙頰凍得紅撲撲的，吃着大餅油條早餐。他瘦削的臉與脖子從棉制服裏伸出來，就像揣在芝麻大餅裏的油條末梢。他們在幾尺之外說說笑笑，卻聽不見一點聲音。她瞪大了眼睛，心口周圍有種愉快的震顫；後來她覺得那便是預感。她到奉天的次日，老帥經同一路線返回時被人用炸藥暗殺了。少帥的歸途也有危險，但是他打扮成普通兵士乘坐運兵車，不坐車的路段則急行軍，終於也安然到達。

正當局勢一片混亂，眾人又在籌備喪事的時候，他的出現彷彿是從天而降。聽說他父親最後一句話是「小六子回來了沒有」，他哭了。他在族裏排行第六。

他知道她在這裏。留守北京，預備情勢緊急便帶她去東北的副官拍了電報到前線給他。

「爹在那樣千頭萬緒的時候也想到了我們，」他對她說。

「他們說是日本人幹的，」她說。

「十有八九。」他的眼睛在軍帽的陰影下奇異地閃爍着——晚上他依然戴帽，遮掩因喬裝剃光的頭。

他歷劫歸來，這對於她是他們倆故事的一個恰當結局，從此兩人幸福快樂地生活在一起。童話往往是少年得志的故事，因此這種結局自有幾分道理。在那最敏感的年齡得到的，始終與你同在。只有這段時間，才可以讓任何人經營出超凡的事物，而它們也將以其獨有的方式跟生命一樣持久。十七歲她便實現了不可能的事，她曾經想要的全都有了。除了據說是東方女性特有的嫻靜之外，如果所有的少妻都有某種自滿的話，她則更甚，因為她比她知道的任何人都更年青，更幸福。一種不可動搖的篤定感注入了她的靈魂，如同第二條脊梁。她生命中再也不會有大事發生了。

「先前我們聽說老帥已經動身回奉天，都覺得看情形是要撤退了。」他告訴她，「我們在那裏扶乩玩兒，更深人靜的，心想不如問問戰事吧。乩仙在沙盤上批了『大帥歸矣』，我笑了起來：『我們太神機妙算了，誰不知道大帥在回家路上？』當晚就接到了電報。」

火車是在皇姑屯的鐵路橋上被炸毀的。

顯然他在那故事中找到安慰。如果真有任何形式的鬼神，則他父親可能仍在左近。他被各方敵友派來的弔客包圍着：基督將軍、國民黨、日本人、山西王，在葬禮上全都各有說客，敦促他訂約，結盟，承認政權。他對長腿將軍關上了東北的門戶，任他被人掃蕩。他對東北的日本顧問停發津貼，又邀請Ｗ・Ｆ・羅納前來。此人有臨危仗義的名聲。

「他們說這裏鎗斃了兩個人。」她的老媽子悄聲對她說。

「在哪兒？」

「辦公樓那邊。」

她稍後聽說其中一個是楊一鵬，害他染上嗎啡癮的那個。晚上他進來更衣。

「哦，替我拿褲兜裏的銀元來。」

他喜歡把玩那枚錢幣，還拿去鍍了金。此時握在手中掂量着，面帶微笑。

「昨晚楊何的事我拿不定主意，就擲了銀元。」

「不！」她心中一沉。

「一直有人跟我說他們靠不住。」「叛亂」、「政變」這些嚇人的詞極少直說。「可是也說不準。人總會妒忌，我和楊一鵬合不來又是盡人皆知的。現在不是記仇的時候。我最後告訴自己，正面逮捕，背面處決。三次作準。」

「全是背面？」

「三次都是。我懷疑這銀元一面輕些，又試了三次，正面處決。而三次都是正面。」

遞來的錢幣上是首任大總統蓄鬍髭的渾圓頭像，她縮了縮。她不迷信，但是她信他。他很快把它放進口袋裏，見不着了。

「我很難過，因為老帥的緣故。」

「現在他會明白的，」她說。

「他只跟楊見了一面就讓他去開辦兵工廠，那時楊剛從日本留學回來。老帥用人一向這樣，不管是親戚還是陌生人。」他提高聲音，聽起來因嗓門拉開而變尖，她不由得看了看他。他父親識人有方，卻從來不指望他，可見他不成器。起先她沒悟到這一層，只是混混沌沌想起他父親其他讓他不以為然的親信，比如長腿將軍。

「那一回在南邊打仗我和長腿住一個房間，只隔着一道簾子，」他曾經說，「他叫了三個女人，還不停問我，要一個吧？我只好拿毯子蒙頭，假裝睡着了。」

但是到了上海，他包下一個飯店房間，與長腿還有別的軍官推牌九，無日無夜，一個多星期裏倌人進進出出穿梭領賞。他們玩樂的那一套，他更在行，而他偏好的是他們碰不了的女人。

「有一回長腿為了個清倌人大鬧了一場。臨上前線，他從上海堂子裏叫了個清倌人。用處女開苞交好運，跟用犧牲祭旗是一個道理。結果他沒有『見紅』，就要老鴇『見血』。其實誰敢耍他？肯定是那姑娘已經跟人有染，不敢告訴老鴇罷了。」

　　然而長腿究竟是老帥那樣的風雲人物；他自己不過是兒子，雖然打了許多仗，卻依然未經風浪。一向都有人確保他不會失敗，或至少不會丟臉。

　　「我問楊何關於兵工廠和鐵路的事。他們要先去核查。這一回我把他們叫到這兒來，他們還是含糊其辭。我走出房間。一分鐘後，門打開，幾個軍官進來射倒了他們。」他小聲說着，驚恐地微笑。「羅納才聽說了這事兒。他一定覺得他闖到賊窩來了。」

　　「你有沒告訴他原因？」

　　「我把正面背面的事也說了。」

　　「那怎麼行，人家會怎麼想？」

　　「他見我比起在北京的時候變化那麼大，想必早已大吃一驚了。」他看着鏡中的自己。

　　「你瘦了。還沒有從回來的那趟路緩過勁兒來。」

　　她像家裏其他人一樣，樂意將他的毒癮看成是麻煩的小病——儘管偶有竊議，也不過視為阿基里斯之踵而已。只要父喪的危機一過，他就會有時間去醫治了。目前壓力還太大。

　　「像那些唱京戲的，」他說，「有點名氣的角兒都抽大煙，不然應付不了緊張的生活。」

　　「也為了安撫他們的女戲迷嘛，」他有個朋友俏皮地說。

　　他笑了起來。「他們確實有這個問題。」

從前常有一幫年青人跟他一道騎馬，都是些軍官或大地主的兒子。如今他在清朝皇帝的北陵建了新別墅，邀他們過來開狩獵派對。四小姐喜歡北陵那些巨大的建築，經滿族人淡化的撒馬爾罕風格相當簡樸，被高大的松樹林環抱着。別墅不過是一組紅磚小房子。她聽說這些聚會上有姑娘。他說那是他的壞名聲招來的謠傳。另一次則是打獵後賭錢，有幾個人的太太也過來參加。某人的太太「盯得好緊」。兩人都覺得非常可笑。

　　府裏人仍舊叫她四小姐，但是外面現在都知道他有兩個太太。大姊慶幸自己絕處逢生。假如四小姐不是已經來了，他父親身故後他大概會想要離婚的。依現在的情形與時世，離婚肯定是不提了。三年守孝期也把婚慶排除在外──原本是個棘手難題。從簡的擺酒請客又太像是納妾。「過些時候再看看老帥的意思吧，」五老姨太曾經說。現在問題全解決了，只消在家裏安安靜靜磕幾個頭。她地位平等，但於法律不合。

　　他們三人住在一個院子裏。大姊說這樣方便，他可以隨時拿到衣服與物品，不必傳送。仍想操持家事的妻子歷來有這種安排的權利。她基本遂願。另外兩人太滿足，沒什麼好挑剔。這府第是微縮版的北京故宮。穿過一道牆和假山花園，就是三層的辦公樓，木雕花飾門楣，掛着老帥手書的一塊橫匾「天理人心」。花園門頭上刻着另一句題銘「慎行」。周圍是一溜僕役警衛住的房子，有手鎗護衛隊與汽車隊。

　　「新房子蓋好了咱們叫羅納來一塊兒住，」他說，「目前他還是待在飯店裏舒適些。」

　　「他成家沒有？」她說。

「結過一次婚。」

「在美國？」

「不是，這些年他從來沒回去過。他們是在中國認識的，兩人來自同一個州。他當時一定想家了。她嫌他太迷戀中國，走掉了。」

她笑起來。「只有外國女人才介意這樣的事。」

「至少傳說是那樣的。他倒是出了名的正人君子。宋秘書把他比作周遊列國的孔夫子，想找到一個君主運用他的教誨來治國。去年為了阻攔他南下，老趙專門成立了統計局，好讓他痛痛快快地收集數目字。美國人相信數目字。他一個月有一千元經費。老趙說：『那羅納真迂，一千塊錢是給他的，沒想到他當真雇人發薪水。』這還不算，北京陷落後他自掏腰包發工資。南京答應他會保留統計局，但是最終也沒有把錢還他。」

她喜歡聽他們談話，給了她一種前所未有的感覺，彷彿坐在一個高高的亭子裏，敞風向陽，眼光越過曠邈平原一直望到黃河。一切都在她面前，即使由於陌生的人名地名而模糊不清，更因羅納不準確的發音愈加混亂。他也說到一些不可思議的事，包括他自己付錢給反對二十一條要求的抗議者。她在大學那年聽說，那場示威遊行是學生運動與民族覺醒的里程碑。但是她相信他，儘管她同時也有一絲懷疑與不忿，在他口中彷彿人人都是蠢材，比如他描述的孫中山：

「有個新聞記者問：『孫博士，您是社會主義者嗎？』他轉向我問：『我是嗎？』我說：『你是國民黨人所應是的一切。』」

「大博士現在終於隆重遷葬了，和明朝皇帝做鄰居，」少帥道。

「葬在一個最浮誇的大糖糕裏。有一萬多人請願，抗議為了開路運棺材上山而拆除他們的房子。」

「怎麼遺體又不供瞻仰了？費了那麼大的勁兒來保存。」

「他們跟共產黨決裂了，不想仿傚列寧。」

「你怎麼看那個剛剛跟他成了連襟的繼位人？現在他雙手捧着神主牌了。」

她豎起耳朵。就是那個人娶了他的舊愛。

「我其實不怎麼認識他，只是經他的連襟們介紹過。」

「他們是連襟政制。」

「法律上他真的離婚了嗎？」難得一次開口，她謙謹地對着少帥問。他們依東方人待女性之道，這類交談沒有她的份。

「是的，」羅納答道。

「鄉下老婆好辦，」少帥說。

「這椿事可不是把老婆攔在鄉下那麼簡單。況且他不止於此，還改信了基督教。」

「他兒子聲討他是怎麼回事？」

「那是他在他的親俄時期送去蘇聯的兒子。俄國人總是叫兒子去聲討父親。那小夥子是青年團的。中國共產黨一份地下刊物登了他寫給母親的公開信，譴責他父親背叛了革命。」

「還有，把勸他不要逛堂子的母親踢下了樓梯，」少帥嘿嘿笑着說。

「那是他在上海經商時的事。」

「是他離掉的那個太太嗎？」她問。她見過素瑚小姐與他訂婚的照片，褶紋的雪紡紗裏着圓圓的肩膀，波浪燙髮底下一張略大而柔和的臉，眉目含笑；他穿軍裝站在她身後，高瘦俐落。她愛不愛他？她得到了她一直尋覓的——中國的領袖。而她是他自己挑選的，不是他依父母之命娶的那個女人。這就有極大的分別。

「他在證券交易所賺到一百萬是真有其事？」

「崩盤的時候賠回去了。」

「那是足以刺激一個人參加革命的。」

「他早參加了，在陸軍學校裏。不過國民黨在上海失敗以後，許多人轉入地下，有的就在交易所做事，在堂子裏會面。他在那圈子似乎混得不錯，待了十年。」

「他擅長一百八十度的倒轉。」

「他把握住危機，乘勢登上了極頂。問題在於一切都沒有改變。舊勢力集結起來，內戰打不完。至今南京也做不出一件革新的事。我留下的時間不長，但也看清楚了他們在混日子。現在我不叫他們Nationalists（國民黨），改叫Nationa-lusts（國賊黨）。」

「嗯，一樣的老中國。要是我們能殺掉幾百萬人就好了。也許那樣我們就可以有作為。」

「那是布爾什維克的方法。」

「奏效就行。」

「那我不敢肯定。『大實驗』已經進行了快十年，他們還是鬧饑荒。軍事上蘇聯誰也不怕它。」

「在這邊它至少幫我們收回了漢口的外國租界。」

「租界其實最不必操心。只要全國其他地方夠和平有序，也能吸引一樣多的外國資金。你們各省連貨幣都沒有統一。」

「要是我們可以把國家交給某個可靠的強國，託管個二十五年多好。」

「不幸無法辦到。」

「我的大多數同胞會責怪我這樣說，但他們沒有試着立一番事業，或者說從來沒有機會去試試。」

「我明白你為什麼會有激進的名聲了。」

「只不過是因為我父親的地位，我講話更自由而已。」

「我很高興你不隨大流，把一切歸罪於外國人和不平等條約。其實中國需要更多的外國資本、更多的監督局，而非較少。雖然我作為區區一個新聞記者跟外國銀行團鬥過兩次，我還是這樣認為。」他隨即講起自己的故事，怎樣施計讓他們放棄了列為貸款擔保的土地稅。

「羅納話很多，但是不該講的事他絕對不講。」一年多以後他告訴她，「他知道楊何的事情。他們曾經派人去上海見他，提出付兩千英鎊讓他到倫敦洽談，借款一千五百萬英鎊來開發東北。他說那是辦不到的。他剛來這裏的時候向那兩人提起這事，他們很快岔開不談了。他覺得奇怪，疑心他們是想用那筆錢搞政變。我處決了他們以後，如果他馬上告訴我這件事，我一定受用極了，但是他什麼都沒說。他這人有擔當。無論誰找他參謀他都保守秘密。」

「那你是怎麼知道的？」

「他才說起來的，現在我們很熟了。」

羅納說服他戒毒，又親自打點他的膳食，推薦了幾樣他自己最喜歡的保健食品。他可以幾個鐘頭滔滔不絕，論證瓊脂和麥麩哪一種更有益處。他讓他減少派對，一同打高爾夫球、游泳、釣魚，帶他去遠足，讓他耗盡體力。有人擔心山徑上會有刺客埋伏。自從他承認南京是中央政府，日本關東軍的將官們便揚言要「教訓陳叔覃，他背叛了我們。」

她喜歡看見他們倆像男童軍一樣出行。但是他的健康惡化了，醫生建議他閉關靜養至少一個月。

「外面一定會傳說我死了，」他立即說，「會發生叛亂，讓日本人有機可乘。」

他再度依賴嗎啡。「等我們有了合適的醫院，我第一個去治療。」

斥資興建了一所大學、一個現代港口之後，醫院的計畫便無以為繼了。移民從戰亂頻仍的北方與中原湧來。最近一場戰爭規模空前，雙方各有五十萬人上戰場，犧牲三十萬人。無論是南京政府、基督將軍還是和他結盟的山西王，都敦促少帥加入他們的陣營。他申明反對內戰的立場，但是他們鍥而不捨。

午餐時她聽見羅納說：「至今沒有人去碰。惟獨這件事體現出中國國民的一致性。」竟是焦慮的聲口。

「中國人只是把它看成不平等條約的一部分，」他說。

「如果他們托詞於海關自主權而奪走海關，為什麼安置一個英國人做稅務司？把一個英國人換成另一個，這我不能理解。」

「老殷在山西孵豆芽太久了，辦外交沒有經驗。」

「還偏偏選中貴甫森－甘這麼一個人。」

「他夠沒良心嘛。又是名作家。」

「所以他不怕來到這幫演鬧劇的軍閥中間做隨便什麼事。饒有趣味，寫寫又是一本書了。」

他們打高爾夫球去了。她隨後便聽說：「我們要參戰了。」

她以為早有共識，他要盡可能長久地保持中立。

「條件必須是國民黨清理門戶，開放政府。」羅納先前說過，「空頭支票不算數。」

她不希望他去打仗，所以熟知反對的各種理由：留下半空的東北，日本人會趁虛而入。東三省比中國其他地區都更工業化。國民政府的代表乘車參觀兵工廠，三個鐘點才走畢全程，振奮不已。東北地大物博，開發它，就比插手內戰更有利可圖。算起總帳來，老帥那些戰爭是得不償失的。

　　「所以你這裏也有孤立主義者，」羅納曾經說。

　　「羅納為什麼那樣討厭那英國人？」她問。

　　「哦，貴甫森－甘。待在中國的外國人裏面他是一種典型，一心想着多撈好處。羅納自己對錢向來很有原則。」

　　「他們認識很久了？」也許做妻子的往往疑心丈夫的至交在利用他。她感到愧疚不安。

　　「對，在北京。貴甫森－甘寫了許多關於中國的書，據說很精彩。羅納也寫東西。」

　　「『文人相輕，自古而然，』」她笑着引用古語。

　　「這是幾時的話？」

　　「不知道。也許是魏晉時候的吧。」

　　即將降臨的考驗沉重地籠罩着他們。他要投身於新聞報上所謂的中原大戰、問鼎之爭。日本人支持另一方。她從不希望讓他經受任何考驗，因為這些都不公正。老話是不以成敗論英雄。

　　他入了關。在北京找到公館後，立刻如約讓她和大姊一道過去。他不住大帥府，防止別人將他與舊政權混為一談。東北人這次是以和平之師前來。他的大軍一壓境，仗便打完了。

　　關於這次行軍，他津津樂道的是貴甫森－甘的故事。

　　「他寫信到司令部給我，答應送來兩百萬現款，此後每個月一百萬，條件是我讓海關保持獨立。我叫他過來面談。

「羅納問：『你為什麼這樣做？』

「『我想看一個英國人丟臉。』

「『小心點。大家會認為你們只是談不攏。』

「『你在場做證人好了。』

「『我不知道。他會認為你感興趣的。萬一你們談得成什麼，你會多了一個朋友而又少了另一個。因為我只好離開你了。』」

羅納先前也一度這樣威脅。他在奉天遇見一個老相識，是英國的從男爵，曾經在印度的公職機構做事，後來在公使館任職。

「你在這邊做什麼？」羅納問。

「少帥請我來做他的顧問。」

在家晚飯時少帥宣佈：「羅納丟下了烏紗帽。妒忌得跟女人似的。」

「什麼妒忌得跟女人似的，」大姊說，「你捫着胸口問問自己的良心。」

「於是貴甫森－甘到司令部來了。他說：『你一定得讓我官復原職。』

「我問為什麼？

「『因為我們合作可以賺大錢。』

「『你是指從海關搶錢。』

「『倘若你不幫我，我不知道該怎麼辦。』

「『問殷錫三去。』

「『他跑了。』

「『那你也跑唄。』

「『給我一個禮拜行不行？』」

「『為什麼？』」

「『我要照顧好我雇用的人。』」

「『給你一個禮拜榨乾海關！我限你一天之內把它還給接收機構。』」

「他匆匆忙忙走了。兩天以後他的一個雇員因為分贓糾紛鎗殺了他。天曉得一個外國人要在中國橫死有多難。他大概是義和拳以來第一個死於非命的外國平民。英國終於不派軍艦干涉了。」

在難以置信的勝利之後，最初的日子如在雲霧，就只有這故事令她覺得那是真的。貴甫森－甘可謂那場戰爭唯一的犧牲者。三十萬無名死者是他參戰前的事。山西的殷氏到大連暫避，後來仍舊回去做一省之王。基督將軍下了野，帶着老婆和精兵躲到山東一座風光旖旎的山上。南京並不追究到底；全國通緝他們已是足夠的懲罰。要不是那英國人死了，一切都會惘惘如夢，彷彿一場枕頭大戰，線頭裂開，拍打出毛茸茸的雲霧。她感到司令部的那場會談是他人生的第一個高峰。他終於證明了自己，還是在羅納面前，而羅納就是全世界。

「有一件怪事，」羅納道，「從他第一本書上，能看出拳民之亂給他最深印象的是搶掠。想不到他三十年後為此喪命。」

「《北京實錄》，」她說。

「嗯，很好的第一手記述，垂涎的模樣躍然紙上。」

「他還寫過一個短篇小說叫〈搶掠〉。」

「哦？講什麼的？」

「同樣的故事。」

「英國人、印度人和哥薩克人搶掠皇宮？」

「嗯，他八年後把它重新寫成一個短篇。」

「活見鬼了。」

「原來你也看他的書，」少帥得意地說。

「我也好奇嘛。那時候你們都在講他。」

他喜歡在羅納面前炫示她，但她通常不說話。羅納待她也謹慎規矩，較少注意她，不比對待帥府裏的未婚女孩子。他平素喜歡跟少女打趣，尤其是會說英文的。然而一個男人有兩個太太，不管他們看上去多麼摩登，還是視為守舊派更安全。

「他始終在給他們找藉口，」羅納道，「他們是德瑞克的海盜團夥，從劫掠者手裏劫財。滿族自己則是從明朝皇帝那裏劫來的。至於外國人掌管的海關，他們的財富是帝國主義掠奪的果實，雖然這話對於他也許太布爾什維克了些。」

「這麼說他只是按照自己一貫的信念做的了，」少帥道。

「作家是不該這樣的。吠犬不噬嘛。」

他受任全國陸海空軍副總司令，與羅納一起坐飛機到南京出席國民會議。風傳他回不來了。南京會留着他，再不然他父親的老部下也會接管東北。他兩個月後返回。他已結束了軍閥時代。下一次南行，太太們也與他同坐一架私家飛機。終於是二十世紀了，遲到三十年而他還帶着兩個太太，但是他進來了。中國進來了。

THE YOUNG MARSHAL

英文原稿

Eileen Chang

1

At the house party all the girls came out on the veranda to look at the street. A man down below tossed up a sheet of paper folded into a twin-hearts knot. They picked it up, untwisted it and read:

"Young lady, wait for me this time tomorrow."

They rushed indoors in a body. They were the first generation with unbound feet. Even in satin slippers the new "big feet" made them seem like a boisterous crowd.

"This must be for you." They passed the slip of paper around.

"Says who? More likely for you."

"Why me of all people?"

"Who told you to be so pretty?"

"Me pretty! That's you yourself. I never even saw what sort of a person it was."

"And who did? I had no idea what happened when everybody started running."

The fourth Miss Chou was too young to have to protest. She just grinned from under the bangs that blacked out the top half of her face. They stayed overnight. The next day at the same hour the girls said:

"See if the man is here again."

They hid behind a window and peered out, hippy with their posteriors thrust out in the figured satin trousers and their thick pigtail hanging down the cleavage. The young ones had two pigtails. But most were eighteen, nineteen and engaged to be married. They were so excited over this it was plain that they had never been in love. Fourth Miss was a little ashamed of the way they kept watch all afternoon. The man never came.

She herself had been in love a long time. She went to the Marshal's House on all birthdays and festivals. There it was always somebody's birthday, either the Old Marshal's or one of the concubines', not the sons' as it was bad taste to celebrate a youngster's birthday with three days' feasting and command performance by all the best-known actors. The Chous were invited on the "central" day so there was no danger of their running into more rowdy elements like the army officers. The eldest son of the house was an officer himself. Sometimes he appeared in a long gown, sometimes a western suit but she liked him best in uniform. Men's gowns were considered decadent and western clothes foppish, or like a compradore. A military uniform was both modern and patriotic. Soldiers were different, they were strong-armed beggars. The officers were feared in a different way. They had all the real power. When they happened to be young and mannerly they seemed to be the country's only hope. The Young Marshal as everybody called him was very handsome. When he laughed he had a sarcastic look, even with children. They followed him around. He carried on a conversation on a dead telephone for their benefit. She could not stand up for laughing. Once she went to watch the singers make up for their roles. An actor was using his study as a retiring room but the actor was on.

"Why don't you cut your hair?" he asked. "Why these pigtails? We're a republic now."

He chased her around the room with a pair of scissors. She was laughing until he held out a bushy black bunch to her.

"Here, you want to keep this?"

She burst out crying. At home they would scold and what would Father say? But it was only a false beard.

She had seen many private performances at relatives', in her own house too. Unlike the musty theaters these were in a courtyard under a roof of fresh matting casting a summery shade. The new stage lit by blue-white gas lights and the hubbub of a holiday crowd totally transformed home life. The feeling that something wonderful was going on that she did not quite catch drove her to go in front, see better, somehow protrude herself, get hit on the head by the shattering gongs and cymbals. She would put her hands on the stage boards and stare upward. The heroine stood right above her piping her song, plucking her own sleeve showing off the flowing white cuff. Her headdress of black-ringed brilliants flashed blue. Two long slabs of rouge from eyelid to jaw marked off a narrow white nose. The warrior's painted face loomed large as a devil's mask. His singing also came out in a bottled boom as if from behind a clay mask. A kick and leap flung up dust that Fourth Miss could smell, stinking slightly of horse dung. There was still something she was missing. She circled the three sides of the stage hand over hand. Those sitting in the front row reached out to protect their glasses of jasmine tea placed between the footlights. At the theaters she had seen people ushered onstage out of the wings in the middle of a performance and chairs set out for them in a row. They were important people with their family and concubines. It was said to be vulgar showing off but she envied them up there in the midst of things although it was doubtful they could see more from behind the actors.

That was when she was little. In the days of Wu Pan-hu as they say. Before that was Tuan Ching-lai's time. "Now it's Fung Yih-shiang." "In the south it's Fang Shen-chuen." Even the amahs knew the war lords by name. They may not know who the president was but they always knew who was actually in charge, and called him by his name, the one curious instance of democracy in a nominal republic. The Old Marshal was the only exception in this house because of his special connection with the master. Fourth Miss was hazy about their reigns and change-overs. A combination of snobbery and caution kept the wars out of polite conversation and reduced them to the level of city crime talks, a matter of staying in and watching the doors. "There's fighting outside. Nobody goes out," She would hear along with the boom of distant guns. The resident tutor taught as usual but the Englishwoman would not come for the girls' English lessons.

"Phoebe Chou, 1925," the teacher had dictated the line on the flyleaves of all her books. The name Phoebe was just for the teacher's convenience. Her other given name was also not known outside the schoolroom. Her father was supposed to use it but he seldom had occasion to address her. She was just called Fourth Miss.

The Old Marshal coming inside the Pass last year had rented the former palace of a Manchu prince. The parties on its huge grounds were as big as a fair, acrobats and minstrels under the mat awning, Peking opera in the big parlor, another performance for the ladies in the second parlor, mahjong in every other courtyard, fireworks after midnight. She drifted around with big red bows on her pigtails, her long gown a stiff trapezoid. Wide sleeves jutted out flat and triangular above the wrists that dangled foolishly by her sides. People said the Young Marshal was sweet on the Chu sisters and often took them out dancing, of which he was very fond. She wished he was married to the Third Miss Chu, the most beautiful girl she had ever seen. His wife was homely and silent, four years older than him and seeming much older still. Fortunately she seldom saw them together. The rules of the day did not call for it. They had two children. She was the daughter of a war lord in

Szechuan who had saved the Old Marshal's life once. In gratitude he married his son to his benefactor's daughter. To Fourth Miss it was one more thing to admire in the Young Marshal, to have paid his father's debt with his own life, so to speak.

She never heard the Chu sisters mentioned at home without a snicker.

"Running wild and their father lets them. Once the bad name is out even the youngest will suffer by it. 'Ha, the famous Chu sisters' people will say."

The Fourth Miss Chou did not have to be warned off them. She felt like a country cousin. Even the Fifth Chu ignored her except this one time when she asked, "Have you seen the Young Marshal?"

"No."

"Go look for him."

"What for?"

"Tell him somebody is looking for him."

"Who?"

"Not me anyway."

"Can't you go yourself?"

"I can't. It's all right for you."

"You're not much older."

"I look older."

"How should I know where to look? And just to tell him

something without head or tail."

"Little devil. People seldom ask you anything and you put on airs." The Fifth Chu hit her laughing.

She hit back and ran. "You want to go, go yourself."

Rushing out of the crowd she went straight to look for the Young Marshal. Once out among the men she had to watch out for her father and half brothers, keep close to the wall, run for cover behind potted flowers, wander around the corridor walks pretending she did not quite know where she was. Fruit blossoms appeared in pale masses where the lights touched them in the courtyards. Servants bearing dishes went in and out the curtained doorways. A hubbub everywhere and music instruments being tuned. She was a tree growing toward a lighted window all her life, at last tall enough to peer in.

2

"Oh, is he in Peking? The Old Marshal seen him?"

"I haven't heard."

"He works through Old Fu."

"Is there talk that Old Fu has hitched a thread on the southwest?"

"Is that so. Hardly worth his while, what?"

"That's it. Canton will never amount to anything."

"Canton has gone Red."

"The Russians are getting out of hand."

"Hey, tonight we speak only of the wind and moon."

"All right, you there! You took in a pet without feasting us, now say how you should be punished."

"Ha ha! How did you get to hear? I didn't dare disturb you all for such a trifling matter."

"Punish! Punish!"

"Stand dinner! Make your honorable pet fill our cups."

Sharkfins were served.

"Chin chin! Chin chin!" And "Ai, ai—ai, ai—" little cries of warning with a hand covering the wine cup to stop it from being refilled.

There was an alternative ten-course western dinner for foreigners but W. F. Ronald brought a loaf of bread just in case. He was well-known enough to indulge in this one small eccentricity. He was no bigger than the Chinese but well-built, with an ordinary pleasant face, hair combed straight back, a high nose pointing straight out with two wry lines at the base. He reached for his glass of water.

"There is foreign wine." The Young Marshal signalled a servant. "Whiskey? Champagne?"

"No, thanks. I don't drink."

"Mr. Ron never drinks, not a drop, heh heh heh!" the Minister of Education explained laughing.

"America prohibits wine," said the Under Secretary of Navy who had studied in the naval academy in England.

"Is pork also taboo?" another said.

"Actually a little port won't hurt. Very mild," said the another.

"You're not a Prohibitionist are you?" The English author Gravesend-Kemp pretended alarm.

"No."

"Then you must belong to one of your fascinating sects."

"Not used to Chinese food," observed another.

"Or Chinese women, heh heh heh! Mr. Ron is really a good man, no hobbies of any kind," said the Minister.

"Anyone who doesn't like Chinese women doesn't like women," Gravesend-Kemp said with a little bow.

"Eight Big Alleys don't represent Chinese women," the Young Marshal said.

"Hear, hear!" said the Under Secretary.

"Unfortunately they're the only ones a foreigner can get to know," Gravesend-Kemp said.

"What is this about?" Ronald gathered that it had to do with himself.

"Your manhood is being defended," said Bancroft, born in Shantung of missionary parents. The three foreigners were placed side by side to keep each other company.

"A good thing I don't speak the language," Ronald said.

"Hear no evil, speak no evil," the Young Marshal said.

"Not at all? After all these years?" said Bancroft.

"Not a word. I don't want to. It's just confusing."

"It may contradict your own ideas about China," Gravesend-Kemp said. The Englishman was a little high. His dark eyes were set close to the level black eyebrows. The lower part of his face was big, making him look fat. He was famous for his first book about the Boxers' Rebellion, which he had been here in time to see. Naturally he could not stand the American newspaper hack turned advisor to the Chinese like himself.

"It's just as well not to understand a lot of what you're being told," Ronald said, "when people are just being polite or trying to give a good impression."

"He's just a poor linguist masquerading as a cynic," Bancroft said.

"It is said that people of strong character have difficulty learning another language," the Young Marshal said.

"What about you? Would you call yourself a weak character?" said Gravesend-Kemp.

"Leave me out of this."

"Certainly a strong character, our Young Marshal," said the Under Secretary, "pioneer in everything, poker instead of dominoes, movie actresses and society girls instead of singsong girls."

"Insulting our women again. That reminds me, when are we

going to play poker?" he called across the table in Chinese.

The Minister shook his head and waved a hand. "In poker I dare not keep you company. The Ministry of Education is a poor organization."

"You're too modest."

"Hey, Young Marshal, a Shanghai newspaper elected the Four Princes of the Republic. You're one."

He sniffed. "Princes of the Republic. That's a good swear word."

"Who are the others?"

"There's Yuan Hun-chuang—"

All comments passed over the other two, mere war lords' sons, less flattering comparisons.

"Hun-chuang is a poet and calligrapher but no match for the Young Marshal in military matters and all round brilliance."

"He's selling calligraphy in Shanghai. A real bohemian."

"Half Korean, isn't he? His mother was one of the two imperial concubines from Korea."

"Were you here during the restoration?" Bancroft asked Ronald.

"Which one?"

"The first president turning emperor."

"As a matter of fact I started the whole business. It was at just such a dinner as this. I was saying it's still debatable whether China is best suited to a monarchy or republic. And that set all the Chinese talking at once. Never saw them so excited. Within weeks the so called 'Security Planning Society' sprang up all over the country boosting restoration."

He had fought the movement he touched off. He helped a dissident general under house arrest, smuggling him out of Peking in a laundry basket. The general stirred up other provinces against the new emperor. Ronald arranged for him to abdicate and continue as president. But the rebels insisted on retirement. Ronald had to quiet his fears for the safety of his family and ancestral graves before he would resign. Like a lonely champion Ronald had played both sides of the game.

"I say, are you from Texas?" Gravesend-Kemp said.

He smiled. "No, Oklahoma."

The Chinese listening to the translation nodded so steadily and heartily their heads made circles in the air. Contemporary history was unwritten and unsorted, a dangerous subject never to be committed to writing in their time. Truth has a thousand faces.

"Some has it that a singsong girl smuggled him out of Peking."

The Under Secretary added diplomatically to Ronald, "People knew somebody must have. It makes a better story if it was the girl he was going with."

"So I became a singsong girl."

"Tch, tch, how could you?" Gravesend-Kemp said.

"What's Hsu Chow-ting doing abroad?" Ronald asked the

Minister.

"Borrowing money."

"For the usual purpose? Build up the army."

"Heh heh heh heh!" the Minister sounded slightly embarrassed. Hsu was the Premier's man. The Premier had no army and ought not to need any with two protectors, the Old Marshal and the Christian General.

Ronald returned to his cold steak. He had this trick of suddenly shooting out a question after one of his long stories. When a listener was lulled into a sense of security the natural desire to compete for attention was apt to surface and the answer was more likely to be truthful.

The Chinese seemed to be still talking about the restoration. There was that story about mine host and the restoration, of course Ronald would not tell it here. The Old Marshal was already the ranking officer in Manchuria at the time. Peking saw to it that he got a governor he got along with. This was one of the fourteen governors who had sent in secret petitions for restoration. As a result he was created duke, first class. The Old Marshal was viscount, second class. The Old Marshal was not pleased. He got up a large group of officers to go with him to the governor's house saying, "Your Excellency being kingmaker will want to attend the coronation. We're here to beg for instructions as to the date of starting, so we can prepare the send-off."

The governor could see that he had to go. "I leave for the capital tomorrow evening."

The Old Marshal played it out to the end, gathered all the staff for the farewell feast. Manchuria never had another governor. The new emperor had his hands full.

"He wanted to be emperor as far back as the Korean expedition," the Under Secretary translated. "He was taking a nap in his tent. An orderly came in and saw a huge frog in the bed, was so scared he broke a vase. He did not scold, just told the man not to talk. Dangerous if the Manchus knew one of their generals was going to be emperor one day."

"Is frog a royal emblem?" Gravesend-Kemp asked.

"No, any big animal. Turning into one when you are asleep is said to be a sign. What really happened must be the orderly was afraid to be punished for breaking a vase and so invented the excuse."

"A big frog," the murmur ran around the room. No one dared praise the orderly for a quick imagination. The first president had rather looked like one.

Just the sort of colorful superstition that would interest foreigners, Ronald thought. He had no patience for these things that supposedly make the Chinese different, because he knew they are not.

"I had this from Liu Tze-chien who was in his secretariat. He actually considered marrying a Korean princess to become king of Korea."

"He's from Honan, that's why. The seat of the earliest dynasties. The mind is influenced by the royal traditions. He'd never have dared if he was born south of the Yangtze," said a man from south of the Yangtze.

"He's a nineteenth century Chinese," Ronald said. "Very capable, but he aged early. Quite worn out in his fifties, hair and moustache all white. He got the idea that I'm for the Nationalists. Greeted me every time with '*Lao ming-dang*, old Nationalist, what's new in Canton?' "

"Mr. Ron has a bellyful of anecdotes," the Minister said and repeated it in English.

"What else is there?" Ronald said. "The last twenty years was just a jumble of personalities, the kind that figure in anecdotes."

"How old are you anyway?" the Young Marshal said.

"Oh, I saw you the other day," Ronald said.

"Where?"

"Playing golf on the Great Wall."

He laughed. "Very good golf links."

Quite a memorable figure in his wide white flannel trousers on the green grass of the inner slope. He was said to be fond of all things modern, had been close to the Y. M. C. A. people in Mukden while learning English. Talked better than he listened, got away the minute he sensed advices and lectures. The father was a sloe-eyed frail little man with a forced smile under the moustache. Ronald knew his type. In Oklahoma they had local big shots who had started life as cowboys like the Old Marshal. No, he was a horse doctor, to be exact. Manchuria seemed to have been very much like the Old West. Horses ploughed the land and were ridden across great distances. To avenge his father who was killed by a gambler he got into the enemy's house at night and shot a maid servant by mistake. He ran away to join the army. Years later he came back, was promptly arrested but escaped from prison. He hired himself out as protector to a village. It was difficult to tell between protectors and bandits, hence the legend that he had been a *hu fei*, bearded bandit, also called red beard, possibly originating from marauding white tribes on the Amur but more likely a reference to the standard make-up for robbers in Peking Opera. With a dozen men under him he settled down and sent for his wife. His son the present Young Marshal was born in a village. On being challenged by a large gang he proposed a duel with the leader who had no sooner said yes when the Old Marshal whipped out a pistol and shot him dead. So by a quick draw he won his first important battle and absorbed a hundred new men into his following.

The cowboy had grown old, smoked opium and kept many concubines. He had his own way of doing things. Ronald could always get a job here. The Minister of Education was an old acquaintance, a carry-over from former governments, and had made him offers. The fact was practically any foreigner who accosted a Chinese official would be given the title of advisor and 200 Yuan a month just to keep him quiet. It had been so since Manchu times. Of course advisors like Gravesend-Kemp were not after the 200 Yuan. The Old Marshal must have paid him a tidy sum for his latest book, "The Lonely Anti-Communist: His Struggles in Far Asia". Unlike his other works this one was published by a British bookstore in Shanghai. The Anti-Communist was the Old Marshal, the only bulwark against Communism in China. The western powers were urged to give him a free hand to take back from the Russians the Chinese-Eastern Railway in Manchuria. Japanese interest in Manchuria was scarcely mentioned. Did the Japanese commission the book? It was not like the Old Marshal anyway to place such trust in the powers of writing. Ronald made a mental note to find out.

He noticed the Young Marshal get up and leave the room, and suddenly felt empty. Had he talked to impress the Young Marshal? Partly it was because the dinner tonight so reminded him of the other on the eve of the restoration, the same big round table and buzz of talk, Tiffany lamps and an overall white glare, the room a rosewood cage, curlicue partitions with moon gates cut out of them, hung with apricot silk. That was already a dozen years ago when he was the youngest old China-hand. Sometimes he wondered why he stayed. What is he doing here, reporting on the murky political scene, telling stories at dinnertables, writing long letters on Chinese politics to his sisters in Coon Creek, Oklahoma. There is always a living for him here. The Chinese don't forget people easily. Has-beens are respectable here. There is something sinister about present power and wealth, especially now. The past even as recent as a decade ago has mellowed enough for nostalgia, as with the first president. Aside from being the granddaddy of war lords, the maker of things as is, he inherited the mantle of authority from the Manchus as their last chief official. Nevermind that he helped bring them down. That's the trend of the times and it is generally agreed that the Manchus are impossible. After he died his favorite pupils took turns succeeding him as president or premier. They constitute the only legitimate descent. Premier Tuan, the last of the star cadets of the military school he had founded, lost out to the new war lords risen from the ranks or worse. However all these upstarts have tried to maintain continuity by supporting one of the first president's men. The Old Marshal has got Tuan out of retirement to head his government, a sorry come-down for Tuan, everybody thinks.

"Hey, *lao ming-dang* !" what the first president had called him, being shouted across the table. The rest he did not understand.

"He said Old Nationalist, how is your fellow spy?"

"Who?"

"The Aunt of the Country."

"And who is that?"

"In Canton aren't they calling Sun Yatsun the Father of the Country? That makes his wife the Mother of the Country, and her sister will be the Aunt of the Country."

"Which sister?"

"The little one who is here as beauty bait. It looks like our Young Marshal has a mind to be the country's uncle by marriage."

"Not so loud," somebody cautioned.

"Gone. Off to the dance at Peking Hotel."

"So a north-south alliance is in the offing," another said.

"She will bring in more dowry than two battleships."

The Under Secretary of Navy had got the post by defecting from Canton with two ships.

"What does the Old Marshal think?"

"Our Old Marshal is great on loyalty. With his feeling for his in-laws, divorce is out of the question."

"Better tell that to the lady."

The Under Secretary was told to translate to Ronald.

"I've scarcely seen her since she was a little girl."

"As old friend of the family it's your duty to tell them she may lose her virtue here and lose face for the late Dr. Sun."

The Young Marshal was in the courtyard talking to Fourth Miss.

"Who's looking for me?"

"Don't know."

"Don't run. Who made you come anyway?"

"Nobody made me. I come and go as I please."

"So where're you going now in such a hurry?"

"To the show."

"Which show? I'll go with you."

"People are waiting for you."

"Who?"

"Ask yourself."

"Little devil, so you won't tell, then I won't go."

"Then don't go, who cares?"

"You don't want me to."

"That's the thanks I get. Next time see who will take a message
for you."

"What message?"

She struck him and they wrestled under the banana palm.

"Come-back-come-back, where're you off to?"

"To tell Big Sister-in-law."

Everybody knew he was not afraid of his wife. That wouldn't
scare him. But she did not see him together with the Third Miss
Chu later that evening and thought he did not come. Theirs was
the rendezvous, in the courtyard just outside the roomful of liver-
ish faces around the scarlet tablecloth, some standing up bellowing

unsmiling, urging wine or declining it or challenging another to finger game, in the kind of male ceremoniousness that had always struck her as grotesque and completely incomprehensible, a circle of red cows being led through some temple ritual older than Confucius. The foreigners smiled fixedly, faded sepia heads resting on tall white collars like photographs. How like him to be with the foreigners instead of people like her father.

She could not get over how she had answered back. At home she was very quiet. "Don't start anything" was Aunt Hung's constant admonition. Her mother was dead, she was brought up by another concubine. All the other children had backing while Aunt Hung had long been out of favor. He had also lost his mother early and had been reared by the Fifth Old Concubine.

"Those young masters of theirs, no law, no heaven, the minute their father's back is turned," Aunt Hung had said.

"Not like us here," the amah agreed.

"They don't go in for these things," Aunt Hung half winked.

They chatted about the old days, putting each other right. Fourth Miss discovered that her father had given the Old Marshal his start. As viceroy of Manchuria he had granted amnesty to the bandit leader and made him a captain. Came revolution, the viceroy's inclination was to save Manchuria for the Manchus. But there were revolutionist plants in the army. At a military conference an officer suggested that they follow the example of other provinces and declare themselves "sympathetic to the revolution" but retain the viceroy as military governor. The Old Marshal stood up and spoke out of turn:

"I Chan Tzu-wong don't sympathize with the revolution," and slapped his gun on the table.

After the conference which got nowhere the viceroy summoned Chan saying:

"The revolutionaries must be all set to act or they wouldn't have revealed themselves. I am ready to die for the emperor."

"Your Excellency need not worry. I Chan Tzu-wong happen to have a thing for loyalty. I'll be responsible for Your Excellency's safety."

He moved his own men in to guard Chou and ordered troops about in his name. The revolutionaries fled Manchuria. But Chou's plan to turn it over to Prince Su was foiled by the Japanese, possibly by the Old Marshal too. Chou finally gave up and took a job in Peking. As the governments rose and fell he retired. Now known as "king of the northeast" the Old Marshal pushed inside the Pass. The monster he had made had followed him to Peking although it was a grateful monster.

Fourth Miss was so surprised when she heard a half brother say, "We give Prince Su thirty thousand a year." Theirs was like a family of well-off pensioners, with enough to keep up the old rules but discountenanced by any new expenses. There was the great fuss when Aunt Hung put in a telephone in her courtyard so she could arrange to go out and play mahjong without using the family phone. She was paying for it herself, she had money of her own stowed away. The objection was that such extravagance might give rise to gossip. As if Aunt Hung could have a lover. Fourth Miss could not see her as a singsong girl. All that was known about her was that her last name was Hung before she entered the singsong house. Fourth Miss did not remember ever seeing her father in their courtyard. Aunt Hung had grown old quickly to save face, put on gold-rimmed spectacles and a black gown bulging in the middle from the fold of padded trousers.

"There's talk that Second Miss is engaged," an amah whispered and Aunt Hung whispered back:

"Which family?"

"The Tuans."

"Which branch?"

"Don't know. A widower they say. With lung trouble."

"These things are all in the stars. A healthy husband can also sicken."

"That's true."

"Any children?"

Fourth Miss heard them with consternation but never thought of it in terms of herself. Her half sister had always been a grown-up. The lottery of blind marriage gave everybody hope no matter what the odds were, especially when it was far in the future.

She learned this in the schoolroom:

> "Slenderly swaying, just over thirteen,
> A nutmeg on the bough in early March.
> On three breezy miles of Yangchow road,
> At all the windows with pearl blinds up
> There's none as fair."

"Written for a courtesan," the tutor said.

It was inconceivable how the most beautiful courtesan of old Yangchow had been the same age as herself. Thirteen was actually twelve by modern reckoning which did not count you as a year old at birth. She felt the gulf of a thousand years looking across at the other thirteen-year-old.

3

She pestered a cousin to do her hair for her just for fun, curl the fringe with hot tongs and top it with a smoky rise. The pigtails were left untouched, tied for two inches with tightly wound pink silk thread. The mass of coarsened waves somehow set off the face and the lacquered plaits. She did not know whether she would be going to the Marshal's House the next day, one of the concubines' birthday. They may not celebrate this year. Both father and son were said to be in Mukden. She sat up all night sleeping face down in her arms on a table. The hair's slightly burnt smell excited her.

He was home. But as often happened at those circuses at the Chans' there came a point when the great day streamed by passing over her, smoothly bumpy, a big sun-warmed body of water, and there was nothing to do worthy of a day like this. She had seen all the operas. The best female impersonators did not come on till late. Nobody listened to the comedian waving his black fan with a patter of tributes to the birthday lady. She milled around with several other girls. A mound of potted peonies from Loyang, said to be watered with milk, was wired with colored electric bulbs leaving enough space inside for a table set for dinner. Today's magician was supposed to be good, a Japanese woman who had just played Shanghai. They talked about the programme in the Young Marshal's study. He had glanced at her curiously, then scarcely looked at her again. It was the hair-do. She steamed under the hot cloud of crimpy hair. She had not seen him for months. He no longer wanted to tease her now that she was older. The other girls, no Chus among them, did not have much to say either. He gave them knick-knacks some people brought him from Hangchow.

"Let's go. Time the magician is on," a girl said.

She was going with them when he said, "Here's a fan for you."

She opened the sandalwood fan and looked at it.

"A big young lady now. Won't speak to people any more."

"What?"

"So stylish too. Getting engaged."

"What nonsense is this?" She colored automatically. This was one thing he had never teased her about. Old ladies liked to do it.

"You won't tell. Won't invite me to the wedding either?"

"Stop that nonsense." It no longer sounded like a joke. The disaster suddenly lifted her up and put her among the adults.

"So? I'll be waiting for the feast."

"Pei!" she pretended to spit and turned to go. "What's the matter with you today?"

"All right. Sorry for being a busybody."

"Where did this talk come from?"

"Haven't you heard really?" For the first time she saw a gleam of anxiety in his eyes.

"There's no such thing."

"The Tangs are making a match for you."

"No such thing. I'll say no anyway."

He laughed. "What's the use of your saying no?"

"Kill me and I'll still say no." Here it came, the opportunity to die for him and to let him know.

"How about telling them the Fifth Old Concubine has adopted you, so she will see to your marriage."

"I'm never going to marry."

"Why?"

"Don't want to."

"What do you want to do if you're going to be an old young lady all your life? Go to college? Go abroad? Go as my secretary, all right? What are you looking at?" He crowded close to see what she found so engrossing in the fan.

"I'm counting."

"Counting what?"

"The beauties."

He pointed to each painted figure in the garden and pavilions as he counted them. "Ten."

"Eleven."

"Ought to be twelve. It's usually twelve."

"I missed this one in the window. That's twelve."

"I got her. And here's one behind the tree."

"One, two, three, four…" She got ten.

Their nearness so confused them it came out different every time. Finally with an embarrassed little laugh he pounced on her, "Still another one here."

"Let me finish."

"What about this one here? So small we didn't see."

He did not let go of her wrist and held it up for examination. "Why so thin? You weren't like this before."

Immediately ashamed of not having turned out as pretty as she had promised to be, she mumbled, "It's only lately."

"Aren't you well?"

"Yes. I just can't eat."

"Why?"

She did not answer.

"Why?"

The more she kept her head down, the heavier it weighed, impossible to lift.

"Not because of me?"

He pushed up her bangs to see the hidden half of her face. She held still, nude and windblown. His arms were so loose around her it felt like a coat of powder. She struggled foggily. He must know too that it was no use. The difference in their age had him married long ago. They might as well have lived in different dynasties. She was free to love him as if she found him in a book. Otherwise how would she have been so shameless? Suddenly mortified, she did not know how to explain if he did not know. And how would he guess? Run and it would just seem like acting shy. She ran and heard the fan crunch underfoot.

Once out of the room she soon stopped running for fear of being seen. He was not following her. She was immensely relieved and happy. He loved her. Let them make their matches, it no longer matter what happened to her. He loved her, he always would. Surprisingly it was still afternoon. The clang of gongs came over faintly from the stage. She was so lonely she had to touch every pillar and post on the corridor walk. After taking another turn, definitely out of his sight, she skipped just to feel the familiar patter of pigtails on her shoulders, somehow as dim and far away as the sound of the gongs.

4

"Fifth Old Concubine of the Marshal's House has sent a car for Fourth Miss," the message came to her courtyard from her father's.

A man servant showed her to the Young Marshal's study. She stopped at the door smiling.

"Come in, come in. A good thing you came. Nothing to do today. Show you the tennis court. Just been put in. Do you play?"

"No."

"Ping pong surely."

"No."

The man would be back with tea. They sat waiting in silence, he with bent head and a slight smile as if he was holding a cup of water he was afraid to spill.

The man finally came and was gone.

"I have news for you."

"I guess it was your trick."

"Sit over here. You don't want people to hear."

"Who wants to hear such nonsense?"

"Tch, people are worried for you. Did you hear anything?" She shook her head. "Good."

"You made it all up."

"Don't be without conscience. Do you know why nothing more was said? I had people drop a hint to the other side so they wouldn't go any further."

"What did you tell them?"

"That you're spoken for, what else?"

She beat him with fists. "Honest, what did you say?"

"Just that Fifth Old Concubine has a match in mind for you, only you're too young, it has to wait a few years."

"What if Father hears?"

"What of it? Nothing wrong with that."

"Maybe they won't let me come here any more."

"If you don't come I'll come to your house with a gun."

She wished she was locked up so he would come for her. "You're just fooling."

"No."

He pulled her to his lap where she sat with bowed head feeling his eyes glow beside her face like a jewel on her ear. He breathed her in. What if they could only have moments like this, she thought, it already seemed like a whole day. Time slowed down to eternity.

"Your eyebrows go like this," she traced them with a finger, then along the eyelids that fluttered down at her touch, and carefully down the center of the nose, checking each item to see what she had bought. He looked all new. Ownership made a difference, the way a picture card differed from a picture in a book.

"You haven't been to Peitaiho? Tsingtao is still better. We'll go. You learn to swim. If only I can have one night's sleep holding you like this."

Her smile stiffened slightly.

"Just hold you. Once when I was little I went out hunting and caught a deer. I wanted to take it home and keep it. We rolled over and over on the ground, I just will not let go. In the end I was so tired I just fell asleep. When I woke up it was gone."

She hugged him tight to squash the emptiness in his arms.

"It was quite big. Much bigger than I at the time."

"Did you have a gun?"

"No, I wasn't allowed to. Just bow and arrow and a knife."

"That was in Manchuria."

"Yes, it's good hunting country."

"Is it very cold?" Her mother had been a singsong girl there when her father was viceroy. Having been raised as her father's daughter only she never thought of herself as half Manchurian. Actually she looked rather like him with the same chiseled oval face and straight eyes. He drew away to look at her smiling.

"I'd eat you, but then there'd be no more."

"Somebody's coming." She heard a sound in the courtyard.

"Nobody comes here."

"All of us were here the other day."

"Nobody's let in when I'm here alone."

Alone with someone? Like the Third Miss Chu? It no longer mattered. They were the only two people in a cluttered world where she had to be careful not to step on all the chess figures and bric-a-brac scattered on the ground. She felt herself lumbering in sudden tallness.

"Young Marshal, topside calls," a voice shouted from down the corridor.

His father had visitors for him. He came back in nearly an hour to sit her on his knees again and stroke her ankle. At dusk he was called away once more. After a while the servant came to announce that the car would take her home.

The next time Fifth Old Concubine sent for her the car took her to a house she had never seen before in a long alley off a quiet street. The chauffeur held the door open. She hesitated and drew the head scarf over her face the way ladies kept out of the dust on ricksha rides. She went in with the filmy turquoise face past uniformed guards playing mahjong in a lighted room off the front court. He was waiting for her in the next courtyard.

"Whose house is this?"

"Mine. I have to have some place to go to. Never any peace in the house."

"I never knew you have your own house."

"I don't get to come here often. That's why it's in such a state. Come take a look around."

"Nobody else here?"

"No one."

It was like playing house in a deserted building. They both had ideas of what to do with all the half empty rooms. The bedroom was fully furnished however, complete with bottles and jars on the dressing table glinting in the half dark with curtains drawn.

"Who lives here?"

He closed the door quickly. "It's a guest room. Sometimes I have friends over to play cards all night. This other room has a brick bed, I was going to have it taken out and put in floor boards so we can dance."

They made the round.

"Does the Third Miss Chu come here often?"

"Yes, she was here once or twice."

She did not talk much afterwards. Back in the parlor he said, "You're different. We'll always be together."

"Can't."

"Why?"

"Your wife."

"That was only on account of the Old Marshal. I've always been fair to her. After all it wasn't her idea. I'll come to some arrangement with her, but it's a matter between me and the Old

Marshal." He always said the Old Marshal as if he was just one of his father's officers. Filial obedience was an old virtue that embarrassed him a little, he liked to put it under military discipline.

"No use saying anything just now, you're too young. It will only get you locked up."

"You said you'd come for me with a gun."

"Still best not to train a gun on a father-in-law."

She twisted away laughing. Somehow the new prospects did not surprise her. Their hopelessness had been no pretext with her, yet was already forgotten. Anything was possible after the miraculous coincidence of his loving her too.

"I wanted to give up this place but it's difficult to find another so near the house but out of the way. And there has to be room for the guards."

"What if they go and fetch me at the Marshal's House?"

"They'll telephone me. Plenty of time to get over there."

"Itchy." She pinned down the hands groping up her funnel sleeves.

"What's all this you've got on? It's too late today, I'll drive you to West Hill some time."

"You can drive?"

"It's easy."

"We can ride donkeys in West Hill."

"We'll rent donkeys. I'd like to live there. The foreign reporter

Ronald has a villa there, did over a temple in the emperor's hunting park. He was telling about it the other day. In the first Chih-Feng war he walked around the front lines in West Hill and saw a wire trailing on the ground, so he picked it up and rolled it up as he went. Some of our men came yelling to him. He just stuck up a thumb and said, "Old Marshal very good," then shook his head: "Wu Pan-hu no good." They laughed and let him go. With the field telephone cut off the Manchurian army fell back and that turned the tide. So according to him he lost us the war."

"He wasn't afraid to tell it?"

"He invited me to come and see his electric bell wired with our piece of wiring. These foreigners think they're so brave. They walk into a rain of bullets and it stops, for fear of killing a foreigner. Where else but in China can you have such adventures without the least danger?"

"They say you like foreigners."

"They're fun to be with. More outspoken. I hate flatterers most of all." He leaned forward to knock off cigarette ashes and turned around to kiss her, a deer taking a lackadaisical sip from a pool. A lock of hair hanging down his brow, the head came down at her like a lowering sky or the quick nightfall in the mountains. She dipped dizzily into darkness.

It was still sunny afternoon and dead quiet with all the empty courtyards around them. Precisely because she was unused to such privacy her family seemed to be watching. Not her father whose remoteness and dignity made it inconceivable under the circumstances, but the others, the women of the house always waiting to put in a bad word, and Aunt Hung and her own amah who were responsible for her. They took the shape of birds carved roughly of unpainted wood perched on the rafters and over the door. She never looked up but she had some idea of them, round-eyed hook-beaked hens over a foot high, some larger, some smaller. She herself was up there looking down out of the wooden eye of double circles. His hand strained at her trouser leg and long silk under-pants and slid absently down the stocking. Sitting in his lap she had the oddest sensation of being flogged gently by some muffled piston or an atavistic thumping tail. The amahs had jokes about the tail bone at the base of the spine and had made her feel her own when she was a child. "It's the stump of the tail that has been cut off. Mankind had tails before." She doubted it happened even while it seemed to be going on underground. She did not want to ask him, it probably had to do with sex. Perhaps the only ladylike thing to do was to ignore it.

Starting from twilight the Drum Tower sounded every half hour with eight drum beats. The Bell Tower immediately tolled its answer, announcing the coming of night and the moral curfew.

"Funny I never noticed it before," she said. "It sounds like ancient times."

"The towers were built in Ming Dynasty."

"It's been like this every night since then?"

"Yes, the Manchus continued it."

"Why do we still do it? There're clocks now."

"Why indeed? We've been fifteen years a republic and nothing is changed."

He pulled a bell cord and shouted "Serve dinner" at the approach of footsteps. The dinner was set out in the next room with no one around. He smiled at her over his rice bowl. Eating at the same table by themselves they were real householders at last. Her embarrassments tied her in such knots she could not finish eating.

"What's the matter?"

"Nothing. You eat."

A new towel sprinkled with cologne was spread over a basin of hot water on the side table to keep it hot. When he had finished she put the towel in and wrung it dry for him, turning to go even before she had handed it over, ashamed of acting so wifely. Leaning away she smiled over her shoulder all in one quick movement. Entranced he caught her hand but she pulled away.

"Come out here," he called.

They looked at the moon on the corridor walk. He held her to him and the warmth of his loins swayed her back like a blown flame so that she laughed in surprise. The moonlight was blue on the scarlet pillars.

"Just think, I almost didn't come back."

She clutched him. "When? The last time you were in Mukden?"

"Yes, there was trouble. One of our officers turned on us. The Christian General was in it too."

"I seemed to have heard there was fighting outside the Pass."

"A near thing. The bulk of our troops marching on Mukden, only a few miles away. The Old Marshal's train all stoked up ready to leave."

"Leave for where?"

"Dairen."

"Dairen…That's where you were going."

"I suppose. I was cut off from Mukden at the time. There was even talk that I was mixed up in the uprising."

"How was that?" she whispered.

"Just because Koo and I belonged to the same company and got along all right."

"How can they say such a thing? Your own father. The Old Marshal didn't believe it?"

"The Old Marshal was very angry."

"But…Not now?"

"It's not mentioned any more. I was at fault of course, should have been more watchful."

That was more reason why he could not speak to his father about her or anything else just now. But all this was nothing compared to the chilling terror of their nearly missing each other, that seemed to dissolve his solidity right in front of her eyes and between her fingers. But here was the blue-limned face smiling down at her and the cool pressure of his lips. Here he was in Peking, the drum and bell continuing the night watch, louder outdoors, with a more pressing sense of the wonders and dangers of the night. For a moment it opened up the palaces and rabbit warrens of time behind the old city, all the double doors looking straight through one another as they swung open, to make a cavern or tunnel.

"You'd better go," he said. "We won't go by the same car."

"Fifth Old Concubine is so fond of you," Aunt Hung said. "Why not adopt you?"

"I don't want it."

"Silly. It's good to have a rich adopted mother. She'll make a good match for you."

"Aunt Hung never says a decent thing." She slumped forward to rest her chin on the table, fiddling with little objects at hand.

"No, really. Leave it to your father and you'd be given away as present. Of course this is just between you and me."

"Talk away, nobody's listening."

"I know you won't tell."

Was there a double meaning? No. She quickly put it out of her mind.

"Your Aunt Hung didn't say anything?" he asked.

"No."

"If they know you come here where we're all by ourselves they'd certainly think you've been taken advantage of. Have you?" Laughing he tried to look into her face which she kept turned away. "Have you?"

She clung to the side of the sofa bending over it.

"If they really ask you what are you going to say?"

"The truth."

"Then it's still not too late for them to marry you off."

"Then I'll lie," she said after a moment.

"That's no use. Well, worst come to the worst I'll kidnap you."

"The Old Marshal will be very angry."

"That goes without saying. He has a special regard for your father."

"What shall we do?"

"Nevermind. I'm in bad standing with the Old Marshal anyway."

She did not like to lie down beside him on the sofa but this way they were able to gaze into each other's face longer than ever. The only annoying thing was that each had one arm too many. After various efforts to tuck it away he said, "Chop it off." The afternoon sunlight made a small rainbow on the wall mirror. She could not remember ever having known such peace and safety. Not a thought stirred in the golden desert-like calm with the mountain ridge of the sofa back looming on the horizon. It began to get dark in the room. Her smile deepened with the twilight. A look of dread pinched his eyes small. He buried his face in her loosened hair, wavy from the braiding.

"I don't know why, just now you were like a ghost."

"What kind of ghost?"

"The usual. A man lost his way and came upon a big house in the wilderness. He was invited in for dinner with the beautiful lady of the house. After spending the night together he walked out and looked back and no house, just a burial mound where the house had stood."

So he was afraid like her that it was all make-believe inside this door.

"There's that feeling of no night or day, just a dim yellow-brown sun like in the city of the dead."

"It's because we're cooped up here all day."

"I've never spent so much time with anybody in all my life," he laughed embarrassedly. "People are asking what I'm so busy at these days, why I'm never around."

"I wonder what they are saying behind your back."

"I'm dying to tell them."

"I won't mind if they say I'm your slave girl."

Slave girl was easier to say than concubine. But even as she was saying it, feeling moved by it herself, there was a faint suspicion at the back of her mind. Perhaps she was capable of shouting any time "*Pieng ni duh*, fooled you!" and run out laughing. She could stop any time. She would sit in his lap, the unbuttoned flap of her jacket hypocritically kept in place, the layers of opened trousers top and untied belts piled around her middle. There was something terrifying about the long reach down those warm folds and her hiding in the cupboard waiting to be discovered. His touch palpitated like a heart pumping thunders of blood through her and a listening silence. Their faces were close, yet remote, both with eyes down, idols towering half out of the little temple they shared, contemplating the thief in the dark prying at the ruby eye in the navel.

His head rubbing furrily against her bare breast frightened and revolted her slightly. Where did she get such a grown son to suckle? She saw him first regarding the goosepimply pink nipple with an expressionless eye before taking it in his mouth. The half itchy drawing on it also grated and needled like pressing it through a wire sieve. She looked down worriedly at the small pale triangle being flattened as he turned to the other one. Finally he raised his head blindly, a red haze over the eyes, and picked up his cigarette. She straightened her clothes and went to the mirror to tidy her bangs. Shaded by the big black square, now in place, she smiled at him and covered the slight awkwardness by stretching her arms downward with fingers interlaced in the attitude of a suppressed yawn. This jerked her sleeves up like the uptilted roof corners of a pavilion, and under the trousers the white L's of feet, stockings and slippers all white. He extended a hand without lifting it and she flew back to his side.

Being ignorant of any kind of basic rule between the sexes, even lying naked under him she felt free to get up and leave any time. A soft weightless bag made a disconcerting vacuum in the middle of her load. She ran her hand up and down his narrow back but when he grew restive she was close-faced and rigid. This had to wait for the "cave room and flowered candles", the wedding night going back to the cave-dweller's time. Even he would blame her if she did not keep something back for that night. And although she would not let herself think it, what if this house was to turn into a burial mound behind her one day the minute she stepped out the door? What happened here was only between the two of them, melting away without a trace when they each went back to their lives outside.

He remembered an appointment he could not get out of. The car would come back for her. She realized afterwards that he was a little angry, which was enough to make her feel lost.

"This is the only way. Then nobody can do anything about us ever," he said.

She nodded slightly with her head turned away on the sofa cushion. They never went near the bedroom.

"No, it's impossible," she said half laughing as if asked to swallow a bottle or rather a grooved ringed earthen jar.

"It hurts."

"It won't in a minute." He stopped several times.

"No, it hurts."

"We have to get this settled today."

The senseless ramming went on, as impossible as ever, now getting to be a racking pull splitting her into two. A sudden rush of air was forced up her chest. Between tossings of her head from side to side she saw him look thoughtfully into her face.

"I feel like throwing up."

He kept kissing her and hurrying back to his business, traditionally called the joy of fish in water and the dance of mandarin ducks with necks crossed. More like a dog butting at a tree stump for some reason of its own. She burst out laughing, finally laughing so hard there were tears in her eyes. He grinned ruefully, deflated. After a final crouch on all fours to examine the ground closely he stretched out to kiss her lightly and hold her to his side.

"It counts as done," he said face-savingly.

Peace returned and with it the luxury of pretending they could fall asleep and stay the night. To her surprise he was asleep. The Chinese room with western furniture had changed curiously in the dark yellow light of the standing lamp. The familiar tables and bureaus were ranged lower all round, farther away, backed against the wall to keep out of the fight. He lay curled up on his side, suddenly common-looking and unknown, the first man newly created that could be anybody, not worth the labors that produced him.

But it always seemed years before they met again and left her quite changed. They grinned at each other with the secret between them. It made them sit apart and talk of other things. When he pulled her to her feet she said no, it would hurt.

"We have to fix this."

He pulled her by the hand toward the sofa. There seemed a long way to go and the length of their arms left her a few steps behind. She found herself walking in a procession of muffled women. His wife and the others? But they had no identity for her. She joined the line as if they were the human race.

5

"The sound of the wind is not good these few days," Aunt Hung and the amahs were whispering.

She thought the fighting was over in Manchuria? Something about an assassination just outside Peking. Nobody went out. The front gate was barred with big water jars pushed against it. If the Young Marshal's car had come for her she was not even told.

She had already gone to bed when her amah came in and whispered straight-faced, "The Young Marshal is here."

He was at the door. She dressed hurriedly.

"Surprised?"

"So late!" she said, as if otherwise there was nothing untoward about receiving men guests in the bedroom. The amah was gone, appropriately leaving the door slightly open.

"How did you get in?"

"I forced my way in. I told you I would if you don't come."

"You didn't."

But he was in uniform complete with pistol in holster.

"Does the front of the house know?"

"No, I came by the backdoor nearest you. A servant let me in. He knows who I am."

She thrilled at the magic of power that enabled him to pass through walls. It felt odd seeing him in this room that was outgrown, almost dingy, filled with the debris of childhood now behind her. But she was glad to break the spell that confined them to their phantom house. Here they were out in the everyday world. She had thought of him so much in this room. Couldn't he tell that? She used to come back at night when she had scarcely seen him at one of those birthday parties but with impressions so strong and so at odds with her old room she had to fix her eyes on the window as if listening to music. The reflection of weak lamplight browned the empty black panes framed in black-and-gilt wood. Without going to the window she was standing right in front of it, open to a damp wind blowing like a scarf on her face as the feeling came over her with the air of reality against her cheeks, then coming unstuck again, the multitude of filmy patterns drawing away, the exultant singing receding. Compared to such clamorous streams of sensations his actual presence here was ghostlike.

"Is there going to be fighting?"

"Lots of rumors around just now."

There was no telling whether the amah would help keep up the pretense by bringing tea. Perhaps she was starting the stove this minute.

"Everybody is staying home with locked doors?"

"Afraid of looting."

"Who are they afraid of? The Christian General has run away."

"There still are Fung's troops here. At the west city gate."

It was never quite clear to her how the Christian General kept on as a lesser partner to the Old Marshal, and still more confusing after their falling out.

"Who was this man that was assassinated?"

"Hsu Chow-ting," he mumbled looking away. Another of those names she was not supposed to remember. "It was Fung's doing."

"On a train."

"Yes. I could have been on that train." He half laughed.

"What?" That other world of his, the sea of unmemorable names and boring political dinners, suddenly reared up and flooded the room.

"I was at the dinner that saw Hsu off and he asked me to come along for the ride. I was thinking of running over to Tientsin anyway. They were going to mine the tracks, but with so many troop trains, the schedule was all upset. In the end they just dragged him off the train. That's how everybody knows who did it."

"How lucky you didn't go."

"That's why I was thinking, I don't care, I wanted to see you so I came."

She smiled back weakly. Was the amah coming back or no?

"Is the Old Marshal angry?"

"Of course. To have this happen so near the capital."

"Is there going to be war?"

"There's a lot of confusion just now. Premier Tuan has resigned. Hsu was his man. Just back from a trip abroad."

He got up and closed the door.

"No, you better go."

"It's just as bad to go now as later."

She watched him hang his belt on the bed rails, the dreamlike juxtaposition of the pistol holster against the bulbous iron railings ringed with faded gold.

"Aunt Hung is sure to hear."

"She probably knows already."

"No she doesn't."

"Everybody has gone to bed."

"She can see my light is still on."

"Turn it off."

"No, don't. I want to see you or I wouldn't know who it is."

He looked displeased at the very idea that there could be anybody else. But she had to see his face hanging over her like a lotus risen out of the sea, otherwise she wouldn't know what was happening to her, just pain in the darkness. The mosquito net was half tucked up so he could grab the pistol in case of emergency. If this got known what was to happen to Aunt Hung? And the amah? She was fouling their lots, making it impossible for them to go on with their meagre lives in this house. It was sinful, yet curiously safe like burrowing into the attic. For once they had the whole night, as lifelong as to the insects cheeping in the courtyard. She liked the first contact when she seemed to be getting him at last, a soft smooth flesh bait coolly slipping out of the toothless bites, a tantalization that melted the knees. But it became painful immediately.

"Say something nice to me so I can finish right away. Say you're Chan Shu-tan's man."

Somehow she just could not say it.

"Say you like me."

"I like you. I like you."

Off he went on his frantic ride and rode on after an arrow shot in the back made him grunt and pant, finally falling forward still hanging on, the hot flood pouring out of him.

"There're mosquitoes."

"Were you bitten? Where?" He licked a fingertip and rubbed the spot.

She smiled. He must have learned that as a small boy in the country. They were still safely in the middle of the night. He was a toy she could take to bed with her, a jade piece to fondle beside the pillow. With the light out she could just make out his profile facing up.

"You're not as happy as I am." She thought he looked sad.

"It's because I'm older. Like a child that cried and cried for an apple, still sniveling when he has got it."

"You've always had everything you wanted."

"No, I didn't."

She was sorry and wished she could go into all the years without her, the deserted courtyards yellowed by an ancient sun. She would rush in shouting "I'm here! I'm here!"

He leaned over the side to light a cigarette from the incense coil on the floor, supposed to keep mosquitoes away.

"All the talk was about Hsu Chow-ting at tonight's dinner."

"Why was he killed anyway?"

"He was getting up a coalition against the Christian General. The southeast gave him a royal welcome on his way back. But he was made much of everywhere. He was asked to review troops in

England. When he found there were only two seats on the platform for the king and queen he looked displeased. So George V got up and let him sit with Queen Mary while he stood with the officers."

"Was he an army man?"

"Foreigners called him General Hsu. They call everybody general. He's a politician really. Little fat man. At a garden party in Buckingham Palace his senior secretary brought his wife, over fifty, with bound feet and dressed in Chinese clothes, but her husband wanted her to wear a big straw hat with flowers. A young secretary was against it. But her husband being a scholar with an imperial degree, second grade, knew everything in the world. 'Is there a foreign woman who'd go out in daytime without a hat?' he said. It was about six hundred yards to the royal tent and her bound feet could not walk fast. The wind blew her hat off. The young officer ran to get it but it rolled left and right and up and down and took a long time to catch. George V laughed with both hands holding his belly."

She tried not to be heard laughing from outside the room. He pulled her hand over and closed it around the sleeping bird, strangely tame and small, wrinkled and a little moist.

"Hsu spoke to the young man afterwards: 'You may not have stopped to consider, it's great disrespect to the English king.' The secretary said, 'Then what about the American chief justice? He was slapping the king's back, jumping up and down laughing.' Hsu said no more. The next day the London Times gave an account of the chase without comment, but criticized Chief Justice Hughes although he's an old friend of the king."

"Where else did they go?"

"America. All over. In Russia Hsu had a debate with their foreign minister Chinchirin. There he was welcomed as a head of state."

"Why?"

"No Chinese is taken seriously unless he's a military man. And he was an old-timer of the Pei-yang clique."

"I'd like to see Paris and Italy."

"We'll go. In a couple of years."

The drum and bell towers sounded the half hour. They were still deep inside China, deeper and older by the minute as the warning against dangers in the dark led far back into the centuries.

"Old Tuan telegraphed him at Shanghai not to come back. Old Tuan was afraid for him. But he thought it would be an international joke if the Special Envoy dared not come back to Peking. Also because of the fighting in Manchuria, he thought to take advantage of the situation, the old fox. He saw a chance for Old Tuan. So he borrowed a car from the British consulate in Tientsin and was driven to Peking flying the British flag on the radiator cap. Somehow he didn't take precautions this time. It's fate."

"He just took a train."

"Yes, supposed to be a special train, just a car hitched to the regular train. Brass bands to welcome him at every stop and a long wait to water the engine. The station was brightly lighted and surrounded with troops, as grand as his reception in Moscow. An officer came aboard and asked for Mr. Hsu. The Envoy is not feeling well, his secretary said and asked the man to sit in the upper seat but he took the lower."

"Even on a train there's an upper and lower seat?"

"Not berths either. With us Chinese it's always ceremony first, war later. So they chatted. The officer said he was sent by Commander Chang and where was Mr. Hsu? The secretary insisted he was not well. Hsu was in another compartment sleeping off his wine. The voices woke him up. He came out rubbing his eyes. 'Didn't I tell you the Envoy is not well?' the secretary said."

He pulled her hand back.

"The officer stood up. When Hsu finally got them all seated again he said, 'I'm not feeling well, had to refuse all invitations along the way.' 'Commander Chang has been waiting all evening. Will Mr. Hsu please alight.' 'There's no time.' 'The train will wait.' 'I have vicious influenza. I'll call on the Commander another time.' 'There's a tea party at headquarters to welcome Mr. Hsu.' 'What tea party, at midnight?' 'Urgent consultation.' 'What's so urgent? I've already sent somebody to Mongolia to talk over everything with Mr. Fung.' And the secretary put in, 'Mr. Fung and Mr. Hsu are

like one family. Nothing between them that cannot be arranged.'
But the officer signalled with a handkerchief and about a dozen soldiers swarmed up and helped Hsu off the train."

"How is it they still have headquarters near here?"

"They're winding up their affairs along the railroad."

She would never understand how two war lords could share
Peking each with a railway to himself, and one allowing the other
to clear out in such a leisurely fashion after a fight.

"They shot him at headquarters?"

"No, no, in the fields, pitch dark. A great scandal as it is. The
Christian General stamping his feet at the way they bungled his
plan."

These people became little funereal dolls in green glaze jackets
and yellow pants with worn earthen patches, that they could examine together with their heads on one pillow mat.

"Old Tuan himself touched it off. He'd always played Fung
off against us, now he was scared at the upset, worried what Fung
was going to do next, cornered in Mongolia, his hundreds of thou-
sands of troops falling apart. So this is what he did next. The news
of Old Tuan not coming to office for several days so unnerved him
he struck down the old man's righthand man. Left to himself Old
Tuan is terrified of him, dared not talk loud even in his own house."

"He'd hear in Mongolia?"

"He has spies everywhere. Everybody is followed. He'd know

I'm here tonight."

She was electrified and almost had a warm feeling for the Christian General, the confidante who would not tell on them.

"Wouldn't it be dangerous when you go out of here?"

"No."

"There's not going to be war?"

"I guess there still has to be a show-down."

"Because of the assassination?"

"Well anyway, with Hsu dead his anti-Communist coalition seems to be coming true. Everybody set on toppling Fung."

"He's a Christian and a Communist too."

"He's a fake. Russia pays him sixty thousand a month not counting all the arms he get."

"Then he's not a real Communist, just pretending?"

"That doesn't make him any better. To hear people talk of the red menace, it's *hung shui mung sheuh*, great flood and predatory animals. It seems to me there are worse things, in a country where everybody's so poor. I suppose to older people it means the end of all standards. Like the Old Marshal, Communists are the one thing he hates."

"There aren't many?"

"We've caught many. Some college students too. A pity they were used by Russia."

"They're killed when they're caught."

"Yes."

She had seen the occasional head strung on the electric pole by the city gate. "Don't look," the amah would say as their car or ricksha passed it. She just got an impression of all the features on the face being pulled up by the roots of the hair like Peking opera actors who wear these tight net kerchieves. A red streak here and there on the cheek and over the brows seemed part of the make-up. She was afraid but as long as nobody knew who it was—The wash amah Li Paw had once said that a man from her village was caught. She told the story when they were all sitting in the courtyard taking the breeze at night, the amahs on low stools, Fourth Miss lying on her back on a cot of sliced bamboo that made a smooth slab as cold as a tombstone. The big black sky pin-pointed with stars bore down on her with all its weight, a tremendous crushing dome that the eye could not endure. She was looking for the Dipper lying down as in an old poem. That summer night itself seemed like a thousand years ago, although it had been right outside here in the same courtyard.

"Selling candy dolls when they caught him and took him to Headquarters. Catching people all over."

"That's the way it is nowadays," said another amah. Everybody spoke in a scratchy whisper when it came to current affairs.

"Scares you to death to hear them tell it. On the day of execution the judge sits behind the aproned table, with two lines of soldiers before him carrying rifles. The four prisoners kneel in a row. Four markers are lying on the table, stuck on bamboo splits. The judge checks the names, picks up his writing brush and runs a red stroke through the name on a marker and tosses it down like a spear. At this all the guards give a big yell. One of them snatches it up and sticks it on the back of a prisoner's collar. One by one all four are marked. Suddenly the judge kicks the table over, turns and runs away. To scare off the *shah*."

"What's that?" said Fourth Miss. The others tittered at her question.

"Never heard of the return of the *shah*?" Aunt Hung said. "The dead coming back three days after death."

"*Shah* is the ghost?"

"Or the demon of death itself. I don't really know. Ask Li Paw."

"They say it's a big bird. People hide on the day the *shah* returns, to keep out of harm's way. But some were curious and sprinkled ashes on the floor. They found bird prints."

"*Shah* is said to be around whenever there is killing or even a thought of killing," Aunt Hung said. "That's why the judge has to protect himself."

She was sitting up by now glad to be surrounded by familiar figures in the dark.

"The prisoners stripped to the waist are paraded on a mule cart, a column of troops in front, a column behind and two rows on either side. The execution supervisor comes at the end riding a horse, with a red sash over his shoulder like a bridegroom. Two trumpeters clear the road blowing the foreign tune for the charge, da da dee da da dee. And all the soldiers yell, '*Sha*-ah! Kill!' And the crowd shouts after them, '*Sha*-ah!' "

"Tch! These people," said another amah.

Another half snickered. "At the gate house they always say 'Go see the beheading.' "

"These men! And with so much time to themselves. Not like us."

"Go on, Li Paw, what happens next?" said Fourth Miss, and this also made them laugh.

"What happens? Outside the city gate the four are lined up kneeling. The executioner comes up to the first man, claps him hard on the back of the neck for size, swings the sword once and kicks the head away. He was getting to number four who saw it all. That was the man from my village. He fainted, and woke up lying on the prison floor. He was the execution companion."

"Execution companion," Aunt Hung bit into the words dubiously. "Yes, there's the guest of honor and there're others invited just to keep him company."

"They let him out in a couple of days. They weren't so sure he was a spy."

"Then why didn't they just keep him in prison?" Fourth Miss said.

"And feed him for years? They just wanted to give him a scare. But he died a few months after he got home."

"Fear split his gall and no wonder," Aunt Hung said.

"Hey ya, in times like these," said Li Paw, "It's a good thing that in a big deep house you don't get to hear things."

Somehow she did not feel like telling him the story although it was before his time. It must have been in Wu Pan-hu's days. Surely they did things differently now? But he was always touchy on the point that nothing really changed.

He flicked cigarette ashes into the incense dish on the floor. "I've got a sore throat from whispering."

"Don't let's talk."

"We'll fall asleep."

"Maybe you'd better go now. Before it's light."

He reflected for a moment. "It's all right. I'll wake up before five."

"How do you know you would?"

"I'm used to it in camp."

"If there is war you'll be going." She had tried not to say this.

"I'll have somebody watch out for you."

"Do you ever sleep with your hand here?"

"When I was little. It seemed the safest place to put it, somehow."

"Me too, but the amah always pulled it away so I stopped

doing it."

But his hand tucked between her legs seemed all right, like hand in pocket. He woke her with a kiss. It was grey all round.

"No. No, aren't you going?" She cried when he threw a leg over her and slid up.

For a while it was not sore. She was still half dreaming cradled on a rough sea. Their boat had gone out in the eerie uniform greyness. But their stale faces smelled safe, reminder of a night's sleep in bed.

She sat up as he dressed, snatching a feel at his shoulders, back and elbows.

"Don't get up. The man will be around to show me out."

"Don't wear your shoes."

He hesitated a moment. It would embarrass him. "No, it's all right."

She heard his footsteps going down the stone-paved corridor, excruciatingly distinct to the end. Her heart went cold. She knew for certain now that Aunt Hung knew. Still she tidied the bed and picked up the cigarette butts in the tin dish of incense coil. When she washed her face she managed to wash the hidden towel. Soaked in the basin of hot water it smelled faintly of thin rice gruel, also thought of as a source of life.

"Things are in great disorder outside," Aunt Hung confided. "Your father went and got up a local security council, same as when the dynasty fell. But what a change of position. The Old Marshal was just one of his officers then. This time he must have given permission or your father wouldn't have gone ahead with it."

Fourth Miss knew what was coming.

"Their eldest is a good boy, considering. He stood pampering well. Although his wife is no match for him, for all the talk about the Third Chu he never did take her into the house. That's something."

Fourth Miss did not flinch at this about the Third Chu. She went on playing with the brass-ring puzzle.

"Actually in a family like theirs, what if there are two wives both just as great? The Old Marshal may not allow it for such a young man, but it may also have to do with the Chus' reputation. If it's a different kind of girl now, from a different sort of family. A girl's reputation is most important. People talk all over town before there is anything to speak of. Take your father, especially now that he's active again. Even if everybody knows of his connection with the Chans he wants at least to seem independent. What if people say he'd do anything to please the Chans? You know your father's temper. Even the Old Marshal won't interfere—after all a man punishing his own children. Not to say me, I'd be held guilty myself. I needn't go into all this, it must have occurred to you."

She herself was ready to die for it but what about Aunt Hung and her amah? They were her hell. Only she was not obsessed with hell. For the moment she was not expected to say anything as long as she bowed her head. Aunt Hung was being extraordinarily mild about it. Even then she could not help hardening and shrinking at the desecration of the thing between him and her merely by mentioning it. Just for other eyes to look on it was to misunderstand.

Aunt Hung said no more. The most important thing at the moment was to stop him from paying them another visit. He did not come again.

It was a point of honor with Fourth Miss not to ask him about the future. Just because he did not mention it did not mean he had forgotten. If he had tried speaking to his father and met with humiliations he would not want to tell her. He had never told her that he knelt for a whole day asking his father's forgiveness after the Manchurian rebellion. She heard this at a relatives' house.

She was never worried the minute she saw him. Everything was as clear as smiling into a mirror. Only when he had gone to war and she had not seen him for months her position began to weigh on her. She wanted to go to his house and see the Fifth Old Concubine and his children, even his wife. They were her only kin. At home she lived among strangers. The Fifth Old Concubine often spoke of him as a child:

"He used to wait by a pond in the courtyard for people in new clothes who seemed well-pleased with themselves. He'd throw a big stone into the water splashing all over them and clap his hands and laugh. People were too embarrassed to say anything except 'Did the Young Marshal get a fright?' Hey-ya, the naughtiness, and when he got older, the worries and jitters I had, from having to account for him before his father," she said proudly with her puffy eyelids down.

She owed her position largely to him. She had been a small town prostitute once. If he got killed in the war Fourth Miss saw herself go up to her and kneel down crying hugging her knees begging to be taken in. "Alive I am a person in his house; dead I shall be a ghost in his house" was the set piece on such occasions. The maiden went to her lover's funeral dressed in mourning:

"White silk blouse, white silk skirt,
White silk kerchief on black hair girt."

It would be a case of *wong mung gua*, widowed by looking at the door, when a girl who had lost her fiancé wished to be his widow. What was one more extra woman in that huge house already full of rickety relationships, an old concubine he treated as his mother, an oldish woman he treated as his wife. They wouldn't refuse her? She was too young to know her own mind and would ruin their good name by remarrying eventually. The usual reason. She would be forcibly escorted back to her own house where her father would kill her from shame.

He telephoned just before the Lunar New Year. "It's me. I'm back."

At the sound of his voice she seemed suddenly to lean back against solid wall although she had not moved from where she stood telephone in hand. The car was coming for her.

"Back?" Aunt Hung said.

"Yes."

The trouble Aunt Hung had had in getting a telephone of her own, the suspicions it aroused were justified now that a tryst had been arranged over it. She had a guilty pang at Aunt Hung's silence. As for the amah, the woman stole around nowadays as if pregnant by a ghost, expecting to give birth to some monster any day now.

He had won the battle of the South Pass after a long siege. He got dysentery at the front. Opium was recommended as a quick cure so he got the habit.

"I'll have a doctor end it as soon as I'm rested."

He would not let her see him lie down and smoke, wrapping his lips around the thick mouthpiece to make a slightly tilted snout. It was the vice of his father's generation like singsong girls. Both smelled of old men's spit.

"Did you miss me?" With an arm around her he strained to see her averted face. The question was sexual somehow. "Did you miss me?"

She finally gave a half-hearted stiff-necked nod.

"Do you smell it on my breath?"

"No." It was just a faint odor you associate with old people. She thought of opium as a handicap of the elderly. Still it was fortunate this was all he got from the war.

"The Third Chu is going to be married."

"Really? To whom?"

He muttered a name.

"What does he do?"

"Politician. She could have done better."

They spoke of other things. She suddenly smiled widely at him and burst out with, "I'm so glad."

"I knew you were dying to say that." He half laughed irritably and seemed to resent the comforting arms she put around him.

The next day he telephoned after eight in the evening. "It's me. I want to see you once more this year."

It immediately seemed to her also that it would be a year's separation otherwise. "Too late today."

"Tomorrow is New Year's Eve."

"No, that won't do."

"Say it's a show. The car comes right now."

"All right."

"I'm to go to the show with them," she mumbled to Aunt Hung.

"Tch! With the New Year upon us every family has business of its own. Nobody goes gallivanting around. Your father will speak," she whispered and it sounded frightening, his speaking at all.

After a silence Aunt Hung turned to the amah murmuring, talking fast, "Go up front and say the Marshal's House is taking Fourth Miss to a show."

The amah went.

"Well, hurry up and get ready, in case nothing is said. You can't go out like this."

They really went to see a movie. This started him taking her to shows and dinners where there was dancing. Either he was growing reckless or wanted to force the issue. His doctor always went along to give him injections for the opium cure. She had her hair done up to look as if it was cut, and wore new gowns and high heels kept at their secret house. Everybody was talking about them but she did not mind, not like with Aunt Hung. This was just the crowd's murmur, part of the lights and music. She did not get to hear what the Old Marshal said:

"Who can't he have for a concubine, it has to be my old friend's daughter. What kind of man does that make me? Marriage is out of the question even if he's free. We Chans don't have daughters-in-law that are laid first and married later."

Her father made his first move.

"I spoke to the principal of Peking University," he summoned her to say. "He will let you in as a listening student. You can try to catch up in a year or two."

No reason was given why she alone of the brothers and sisters was to go to school. The assumption was times were changing, college girls were sometimes preferred in marriage. In effect it set her free with the entire school day at her own disposal. If she went to the bad the blame was on modern education, the usual whipping boy. Better let her run wild than have it said that her father gave her away as concubine to the Chans. It eased the unspoken strain between the two houses. If the affair came to nothing she might still marry. Didn't the Third Chu?

Aunt Hung was oddly triumphant, the first time Fourth Miss had ever seen her excited. All these years of neglect and slights were avenged. The man was afraid. Her child had backing that had him cowed. Fourth Miss was her daughter as never before. She allowed herself to worry aloud:

"The times are unsettled. Better make your plans, don't put it off too long. Of course the Old Marshal is in a difficult position because of his feeling for the Tangs. But you don't want to fight over an empty name. Out of regards for your father he can't treat you wrong. The thing is for the Young Marshal to find the right person to speak to his father, someone who could get a word in. It's up to you to make up your mind. Men are never in a hurry," she whispered smiling, leery of calling attention to her knowledge of men as a singsong girl, careful not to hint that he might be as fickle as others. "I'm just reminding you as a bystander. I can see you don't lack decision. People will blame me for not speaking up earlier. For one thing it would be no use. It will just spoil things after being mother and daughter together."

Fourth Miss remained silent. By now it was rude and hurting never to have told her anything. But how was she to tell her that they never spoke of such things?

"So the Third Chu is married. Even got her husband a post. That's modern times for you."

Aunt Hung seemed particularly impressed by her keeping quiet about the Third Miss Chu's marriage. It made her slightly uneasy to have come to be loved for her supposed hardness.

Moon Festival was celebrated as usual in Peking despite the war with Canton, now split into Nanking and Hankow on their way north. He had been away for a long time on the Honan front. Still it was the happiest Moon Festival in her life. She had a schoolmate over, a girl alone in Peking, and walked her back to the dormitory. The family ricksha followed a few paces behind so they could ride any time they got tired. The low grey houses made the streets look still wider. Firecrackers pit-patted faraway with now and then a surprise banging away hollowly close by. All the shops were boarded up, everybody home by now for the reunion feast. The long street led straight up to the slate blue sky with the moon like a wheel of ice. The wind blew her veil into her mouth every time she spoke. She wore the dark red knitted shawl that no college girl was without and swung the box of moon cakes that her friend was to take home with her. They walked on the tram tracks until a tram bore down on them as big as a house clacking its bell that sounded like "I got the best man, the best, the best, the best." It was exactly what she had wanted when she stood right in front of the stage as a child with both hands on the boards and could never get up close enough. Now the cymbals were clapping down on top of her head.

He telephoned the next day. It turned out that he had come back the day before.

"Spent Moon Festival with his wife," Aunt Hung sniggered, indignant.

She just smiled. She herself had had to eat reunion feast with the family.

"Where's Dr. Liang?" she looked around the room when he made her sit down beside him.

"That turtle egg, I threw him out."

"What happened?" She had never seen him so angry.

"Those injections he gave me was a kind of morphine."

"Stop opium with morphine?"

"It's on purpose. To get me into the habit."

"Why, who is he?"

"He turns out to be Yang Yi-peng's man."

She searched her glossary of faceless names. Would that be the Old Marshal's most trusted aide?

"Why?"

"He hates me. It's all out in the open after the Koo Sing-ling incident."

The uprising in Manchuria. He didn't mean he was in it after all?

"That was to get him mainly."

Only partly against his father? The enormity of it instantly put her at sea. What happened to crown princes who rose against their father? Imprisonment, an imperial gift of poisoned wine for which you kowtowed in thanks toward the direction of the palace. Whatever he did it showed he was a man, not just So-and-so's son. Maybe she was also a little sad because he had done what he wouldn't do for her sake.

"But they say that you—" She stopped.

"That I lost my head gambling and whoring, didn't know what was going on in my own battalion?"

"Just that you were careless."

"I'm not such a fool. I played cards with Koo at the battalion club, yes. He's one of our better young officers. We both wanted change, but no chance of that as long as Yang was around. In the end there was no other way. It would have succeeded too but for the Japanese intervention."

"Why are they for the Old Marshal?"

"They don't want the Russians in Manchuria. Koo was allied with the Christian General and he's with the Russians."

She could not imagine him on the Christian General's side against his father. Since then he had defeated the General at South Pass. This year the two had been fighting again in Honan with the General on the side of the south.

Her silence made him add in his father's defence, "Some say the Old Marshal is pro-Japanese. Of course he has to get along with them because Manchuria is right next to Korea. But he always took this attitude: the small things could be talked over, the big things he would put off. Nowadays even the small things he will put off, the big things are definitely not negotiable. He never even carried out their terms for squashing Koo Sing-ling."

"What happened to Koo?"

"He was shot."

For a moment neither of them spoke. He had been spared because he was the son.

"Can't you tell the Old Marshal about being tricked? About the injections."

A slight shake of his head with a half blink dismissed the idea completely. But meanwhile other people would be telling the Old Marshal about his turning into an addict at his age.

"A funny thing the other day, shows the kind of people we

have around. Word came that the southern troops violated the first president's grave, so somebody suggested that we desecrate Sun Yatsun's body in return."

"Sun Yatsun is buried here?"

"In West Hill. Luckily Yieh Loh-fu was around that day, an old Nationalist. He persuaded the Old Marshal that these things were not done nowadays and anyway to check first. It turned out to be not the Nationalists but the Christian General's garrisons. Trees were chopped down, buildings robbed but the grave was untouched. So Yieh said to the Old Marshal, since Sun's remains happen to be in Peking we should protect it just to show we are big-hearted. So the Old Marshal ordered a detail of soldiers to the Temple of Green Clouds. Sure enough, in a couple of days several men went to the temple with picks and hoes. When they saw the sentries they loitered and left."

"Who were they?"

"Chi Yung-fu's men."

She gathered that they were from the first president's old troops.

"We're not so far behind. Why, the Nationalists themselves, two years ago when their rightists lost power to the left they came all the way here from Canton, into enemy territory as it was, just to hold a meeting in front of their leader's grave, and was known henceforth as the West Hill Conference Clique. Madame Sun herself—it was her idea to embalm him to last forever."

"He looks alive?" she cried.

"Yes, she got the idea from Lenin, she's pro-Communist. Of course she put it on her husband, said he had said it would be best if the body could be preserved. His followers were rather taken aback. For one thing the costs. In the end Russia gave them the glass coffin as a gift."

"Is she beautiful?"

"Big eyes."

"Which is more beautiful, she or her younger sister?"

"The younger is more lively. Madame Sun is lively too except that her husband took sick right away when they were here. I represented the Old Marshal to welcome him off the ship in Tientsin. It snowed the day we got to Peking. As we drove from the station there was a huge crowd besides the welcoming groups. People on top of all the roofs and trees with the big snow coming down." He confronted her almost indignantly. "The crowd was just as big in Tientsin, only the police chief drove them away to please Premier Tuan."

"Was Sun Yatsun really such a great man?"

"The thing is he represents the idea of a republic. At the revolution most people didn't know what happened. By the thirteenth year of the republic they really got to want it. Like women, when they are first married they don't know what it's all about but later they come to want it. Will you?"

"I don't know. I'm not married." She was sorry the minute it was out of her mouth, as if to remind him.

"So you're not. Getting independent, eh? Say whose man you are."

"Stop it."

"Whose man are you? Say it."

"Stop it. Was Madame Sun's sister with them that time?"

"No, just the two of them. He'd been invited down to form a government. There were high hopes among his followers that he'd be president. He called on the Old Marshal as soon as he arrived. I was with them. After the greetings the Old Marshal stood up right away saying, 'I Chan am a rough man, so I'd like to say frankly, it's my business to boost men. Today I may boost a man named Tuan. So can I boost a man named Sun. I only object to Communism. If we are to practise Communism I Chan would rather shed blood than go red.' This little speech when it got to Tuan's ears made him more suspicious than ever. Actually the talk only lasted half an hour. Sun of course denied he was pro-Communist. But there was Tuan, already installed. Sun went back to his hotel and conferred with his aides until after midnight. That same night he got ill."

"That's how he died!"

"A few months later. All this time Old Tuan wouldn't see him and never went to the funeral. The excuse was his legs were so swollen he could not get into his shoes. The head of a country and no shoes to wear!"

"At least he's gone away."

"He's having a good laugh on us. The government a vacuum after he stepped down. The regency cabinet with all our allies represented couldn't last of course. After the cabinet resigned nobody else would accept the posts. The Old Marshal was angry. 'Then just get anyone,' he said. Government employees have not been paid for six months. Ex-emperor Pu Yi still gets thirty thousand a month, from us personally. This respect for all higher-ups is all that's left of our king and country. Anyway all the people ever ask for is 'a Honan man to rule Honan' and 'a Shantung man to rule Shantung.' If they must be misruled they'd rather have one of themselves do it. As far as possible we let them have it. Any local person with enough armed men to overrun the area, gets from us a title or a post."

It did not sound good. "Is the war going to get here?"

"There's no telling about wars. As far as strength goes we have no fears. Last year Fung's troops did exceptionally good trench work at South Pass. But our cannons were so fierce, after several days of concentrated firing even the earth crust was turned over. Canton belonged to the school of revolutionaries with home-made bombs. Now that they have Russian arms and advisors naturally our allies are no match for them. Like Wu Pan-hu, when news came that his front was collapsing he sent the Big Sword Corps to chop down deserters. His soldiers had heard the Big Swords were coming and took shots at them through the train windows. The swordsmen never dared get off the train."

"What's the use of these allies?"

"Yes, everybody for himself. Fang of the southeast just sat still watching Wu get hit when he could have easily cut off the southern supply lines. When he was defeated in turn he bribed Long Legs to give him safe conduct to Mukden so he could come beg for help in person, traveling incognito in civilian clothes because he was a disgrace to the uniform. Seeing how he humbled himself the Old Marshal sent Long Legs to help him get back his five provinces." She had heard of their General Long Legs. "The Old Marshal is like that. As long as a man is your equal, even if he has been an enemy, always be generous and save him some face. The worst offence is to move against your superior. That's how Long Legs ganged with Fang managed to flatter the Old Marshal into heading the government himself. Subordinates don't count, but the support of your peers…"

"Has he become President?" she faltered.

"No, not President or Premier, just Grand Marshal. The Old Marshal is modest that way. All his life he has preferred to stay in the wings. This is already unlike him."

He stopped abruptly. She had also heard the saying, "Change and die." It was a bad sign when older people change their ways.

"The south is a mess too," she said.

"They have their kit of tools."

"They're Communists?"

"Not any more. Nanking has hitched a thread on England and America and thrown over Russia. Now Russia is looking to us to stop the south. The Old Marshal doesn't care, he had the Soviet Embassy searched anyway and published all the secret documents, proofs of their subversions. They're pushing hard here. It did look as though they had China going Communist."

"In the south?"

"Everywhere the southern troops went. Mass trials of land-lords. Dividing up the land. Cutting men's gowns short, the long gown is upper class. Also attacking churches and missions like the Boxers all over again. Foreigners do get themselves hated because the government kowtows to them and takes their part, then as now. A missionary is a power in the countryside. It's always popular to be against foreigners, and Communism sneaks in under cover. The people have their grievances and will have it out any way you let them. But the Communists are being purged, they lasted no longer than the Boxers."

"Is Madame Sun's sister married now?"

He smiled. "I don't know, haven't heard."

"How old is she?"

"About my age."

"She's not twenty-seven already?"

"I don't know, she herself didn't say. Foreignized women don't tell their age."

"She can't be not marrying ever?"

"There's no telling about those Christians."

"It's not because of you?"

"No, no."

"She must have liked you."

"She was looking for a ruler of China and I stood a chance of inheriting the position."

"You make her sound so hard."

"It's only natural that she should want to emulate her sister."

"Is she very beautiful?"

"No."

"No, tell the truth."

"There is a wonderful freshness that comes with going to school abroad. And she didn't come back all masculine and insufferable."

"Lucky the Old Marshal wouldn't let you get a divorce."

"It never came to that."

"Didn't you want to marry her?"

"If I did it had to do with the whole picture. A man may also want to marry into a certain house, like a lighted doorway everybody turns to—something you don't happen to have. After that crowd to see Sun Yatsun in the snow, any relations I can have with a man like that I won't mind having."

"But you have to like the girl."

"That of course. I used to get those ideas, not like now, no more stray thoughts."

"Did the Old Marshal know?"

"He took it as a joke. His son marrying the daughter of a fife-and-drummer! That's what they call her father. He used to play a harmonium doing missionary work near Shanghai."

The famous debutante was now a cozy figure in her own past. "I wonder why she never married."

"It may be difficult for her too. At her age, even a couple of years back all the men she met would be married."

He pulled the bell rope. The new doctor was fetched from another courtyard to give him the same injection as the other doctor had been giving him.

He was still pent up. "Let's go to West Hill."

"So late. The city gate will be closed."

"It will open for us."

It was growing dark as they got into the car with the doctor. They could hear from afar the gong at the city gate working itself up to a long frantic tzong-tzong-tzong-tzong-tzong-tzong, sounding an enemy attack or fire or flood, the end of the world. The car got round the mule carts that had just managed to squeeze in. One of the guards jumped off the running board and ran ahead shouting.

The gates swung open again and they drove through the tunnel in the iron-grey wall standing on black dust.

The long ride really seemed to get them away. But at West Hill Hotel they did not go into the dining room in case there was somebody they knew. They stood around the goldfish pond while Dr. Li went in to order soft drinks. She was wearing black glasses and a veil.

"You look like a war lord's concubine meeting a female impersonator in secret," he said.

It was not so romantic though. They ate dinner in their suite upstairs with the doctor. They spoke of places to see in the morning before going back, so it was settled that they would stay the night. She could say she was at a schoolmate's house but she wondered if she was going too far.

It was unnaturally silent in the country and the western-style hotel was dead quiet. Peking seemed a long way off with its vigilant drum and bell and city murmurs. Staying out all night, and in a hotel, she was so far out of bounds that she was no longer under the protection of the law. She felt ridiculously like a captive bride brought to a new village, finally under his power. Oddly enough he also looked embarrassed taking off his clothes not looking at her, smiling slightly, his eyes very bright. To escape the feeling of strangeness she quickly went to bed and under cover and slipped into his arms as soon as he got in. But he turned back the blanket and took his time sorting her out in the lamplight.

"What are you doing?"

An animal was feeding on her. She saw his bent head enlarged by perspective between her reared thighs and felt his hair brushing against her with a frenzy of terror. The flicks of his kisses furled petal-like in and around the bud of her inner self, intolerably. The resignation of the fallen prey alternated in her with some unformed yearning to get away somehow or devour in turn, be packed full of him. She tried to get up several times. At last it was him again smiling down at her, a little flushed. She took him almost gasping with relief, catching sips of a half glass of wine rocking on board ship. He filled her slowly with deep plunges and suddenly swung sideways like a fish swishing its tail, watching her face half laughing. He stopped to look and fondle.

"Bigger, aren't they? Haven't they grown?"

But they hardly talked all night, for a change.

7

Her father called her into his study and spoke in his deepest voice with an official ring.

"The political situation is tense. The Old Marshal is sending the family back to Mukden. Leaving tonight. He has sent for you. Perhaps it's best in times like these—saves worries on both sides.

Out of his friendship for me he is sure to treat you like a daughter. On your part however you have to learn to behave from now on. It's up to you yourself now. Tell your Aunt Hung to pack for you but there's no need to bring many things or people. Whatever you want can always be sent for later. Just dress warmly, it's cold outside the Pass. When the times are more settled you can come back and your Aunt Hung can also go and see you."

She had a wonderful trip. The Chans on their special train received her as a niece coming for a long visit. The Young Marshal's wife took her on as her special charge. She was to call her Big Sister from now on instead of Big Sister-in-law. Outside the Pass was China's Arctic. Sad princesses and palace beauties had been sent out there to marry the kings of the Huns. She was agreeably surprised by the heaving brown mountains and the grey sash of the Great Wall draped across them, buckled with twin square citadels. The scene never changed in the window, a picture screen being busily folded away, clackety-clack, clackety-clack, and still no end to it.

At the first stop next morning she looked out at a box car of soldiers halted on the next line. The soldiers were standing as if half out of the car. A peasant boy red-cheeked from the cold was eating his breakfast of fritter and bun. His thin face and neck came out of the padded uniform like the end of the fritter stick stuffed into the big sesame bun. They were talking and laughing a few feet away, yet soundless. She stared with a pleasant shiver around the heart, what she later thought was presentiment. The day after she got to Mukden the Old Marshal coming back the same way was assassinated by a mine. It was dangerous for the Young Marshal to come back but he managed it on troop trains dressed as a common soldier, with forced marches between rides.

When he turned up in the midst of the confusion and funeral preparations it was as if he had dropped down from heaven. He cried when he heard his father's last words were, "Has Little Six come back?" He was the sixth son of the clan.

He knew she was here. The aide stationed behind to take her out of the Pass in case of emergency had telegraphed him at the front.

"Father thought of us when he had so many things on his mind," he said to her.

"They say the Japanese did it," she said.

"Probably." His eyes shone curiously in the shadow of the army cap which he kept on even at night to hide the shaved head, part of the disguise.

To her it was a fitting end to their story, his coming back after such hardships. And they lived happily ever after. There was some truth in this ending to fairy tales which generally deal with young people and early success. What you get at that impressionable age stays with you. It was the only time when anyone can build things larger than life and in its own way lasting as long. At seventeen she had achieved the impossible, all that she had ever wanted. If there is a certain smugness in all young wives in addition to the reputed serenity of Oriental women, she was still more so, being younger and happier than any that she knew of. An unshakable placidity entered her soul like a second spine. Nothing that really mattered could happen to her any more.

"First we heard the Old Marshal had left for Mukden," he told her, "it looked as if we were retreating. We were fooling with a Ouija tray, it was a quiet night, so we thought to ask about the war. It wrote on the sand, 'The Grand Marshal is going home.' I was laughing, 'What wonderful fortune-tellers we are. Who doesn't know the Grand Marshal is going home?' That same night we got the telegram."

The train was wrecked on the railway bridge at the Fort of the Imperial Aunt.

He evidently found comfort in the story. If the supernatural exists in any way then maybe his father was still near. He was beset on all sides by the mourners sent by friends and foes alike. The Christian General, the Nationalists, the Japanese, the "king of Shansi" all had representatives at the funeral to pressure him into agreements, alliances, recognitions. He closed the Pass to General Long Legs and left him to be mopped up. He stopped the subsidies to Japanese personnel in Manchuria and sent for W. F. Ronald, known as the man to have with you in a pinch.

"They say they shot two people here," her old amah whispered to her.

"Where?"

"Over in the office building."

One was Yang, she heard later, the one who had got him into the morphine habit. In the evening he came in to change.

"Oh, get me the dollar in the trousers pocket."

He liked to play with the coin and had it gold-plated. He hefted it in his hand smiling.

"Last night I couldn't make up my mind about Yang and Ho so I tossed the dollar."

"No!" she said dismayed.

"People have been telling me they're unstable." The dread words "revolt" and "coup" were seldom said outright. "But you can't tell, people are jealous, and my differences with Yang are well-known. Now is not the time to remember grudges. So finally I said to myself, head for arrest, tails for execution. Three times to make sure."

"All tails?"

"All three times. I thought maybe this coin is lighter on one side. Try three more times, head for execution. And three times all head."

She shrank from the first president's round moustachioed face on the proffered coin. She did not believe in superstitions but she believed in him. He put it out of sight in his pocket quickly.

"I feel bad because of the Old Marshal."

"He'll understand now," she said.

"After a single interview with Yang, just back from studying from Japan, he had him start the munitions plant. That's how the Old Marshal hired people, whether relatives or strangers." His voice rose, thinned from distention so that she looked at him. His father could tell about people, yet had never relied on him so he must be no good. She did not figure that out at first, just thought confusedly of all the other men around his father that he disapproved of, like General Long Legs.

"That time we campaigned in the south I shared a room with Long Legs with just a curtain in between," he had said. "He called in three women and kept asking me, Have one? I just pulled the blanket over my head and pretended I was asleep."

Yet when they got to Shanghai he had played dominoes with Long Legs and the other officers in a hotel room for over a week, night and day, with singsong girls trooping in and out getting bonuses. He beat them at their own games and preferred women that were out of their reach.

"There was the furor about the virgin that Long Legs had booked from a Shanghai singsong house, before leaving for the front. A virgin for good luck, like sacrificing to the flag. It turned out that he did not 'see red', so he wanted the madam's blood instead. Actually who dares cheat him? The girl must have had a secret lover and didn't dare tell the madam."

Still Long Legs was a man of the times like the Old Marshal while he himself was just the son, still untried after many battles. It was always seen to that he did not lose, or at least not lose face.

"I asked Yang and Ho about the plant and the railway. They had to go and look up the answers. This time I summoned them here and they were still evasive. I walked out of the room. A minute later the door opened and several officers shot them down," he whispered with a scared smile. "Ronald just heard. He must be thinking he's got into a robbers' den."

"Did you tell him why?"

"I told him about the head and tails too."

"No. What would people think?"

"He must have had a shock already seeing me so changed from the Peking days." He looked at himself in the mirror.

"You're thin. You haven't got over the trip back."

She readily saw his addiction as the rest of the household did, as an ailment that was a nuisance, though sometimes whispered about behind his back as an Achilles' heel. All he needed was the time to take the cure once the crisis of his father's death was over. Now the pressure was too great.

"Like those Peking opera singers," he said, "all the better-known ones have to take opium to keep up the strenuous life."

"And to appease their women admirers," one of his friends said slyly.

He laughed. "They do have this problem."

There was this group of young men who used to ride with him, the sons of officers or big landowners. He invited them to hunting parties at the new villa he built at the North Graves where the Manchu emperors were buried. Fourth Miss loved the North Graves, massive architecture in the Samarkand style that the Manchus had toned down, here at its simplest in a forest of tall pines. The villa was just a group of little red brick houses. She heard there were girls at those parties. It was a rumor because of his bad reputation, he said. Another time it was some of the men's wives dropping in for the gambling after the hunt. So-and-so's wife "keeps a close watch." They both thought it was very funny.

She was still called Fourth Miss in the house but he was now known as having two wives. Big Sister was glad of her narrow escape. If Fourth Miss was not with them already he would want a divorce now that his father was dead. As it was there was no question of raising the issue in a time like this. The three years' mourning also ruled out any celebrations, a thorny point originally. A simple feast was too much like taking a concubine. "Wait and see what the Old Marshal says," the Fifth Old Concubine had said. Now the problem was solved on all sides. A few quiet kowtows within the family sufficed. Her status was equal but not legal.

The three of them lived in the same courtyard, for convenience's sake Big Sister said, so he could get his clothes and things at once instead of sending for them. It was the time-honored stipulation of wives who did not want to be left out of the picture. She generally got her way. The other two were too content to make an issue of anything. The house was a copy of the Peking palace on a small scale. Across a wall and rock garden stood the three-storeyed office building with wood curlicues and a calligraphic board in the Old Marshal's own handwriting, "Heaven's law is men's heart." Another motto over the garden gate: "Walk the straight and narrow." They were surrounded by a flock of houses for the staff and guards, the Side Arms Company and Automobile Corps.

"When the new house is ready we'll ask Ronald to stay with us," he said. "Now he's more comfortable in the hotel."

"Has he got a family?" she said.

"He was married once."

"In America?"

"No, he's never been back all these years. They met in China. She's from his home state. He must have been homesick. But she left him because he was too engrossed in China."

She laughed. "Only foreign women would mind a thing like that."

"At least that's the story. But he's known as a regular Confucius. Secretary Sung was comparing him to Confucius traveling through all the kingdoms looking for a ruler that would practise his teachings. To keep him from going south last year Old Chow specially created the Bureau of Statistics for him so he could collect figures to his heart's content. Americans believe in them. He got a thousand a month to run it. Old Chow said, 'That fool Ronald, the thousand was for him, I never expected him to hire a staff and pay out salaries.' What's more he paid them out of his own pocket after Peking fell. Nanking promised him to keep the bureau going but never paid him back in the end."

She loved to hear them talk. It gave her a feeling she had never had before, of sitting in a high pavilion open to the sun and wind looking clear across the plains to the Yellow River. It was all there before her even though muddied by all the unfamiliar proper names made still more confusing by Ronald's mispronunciations. He also said some incredible things, like he himself had paid for demonstrators against the Twenty-one Demands. In her year at college she had learned that the protest march was a milestone in the students' movement and national awakening. But she believed him, and at the same time felt a little dubious and affronted by the way everybody was made out to be such fools, Sun Yatsun for instance:

"A reporter asked, 'Are you a socialist, Dr. Sun?' He turned to me saying, 'Am I?' I said, 'You're everything a Nationalist has to be.'"

"So the good doctor is finally reburied in style, beside the Ming emperors," the Young Marshal said.

"In the most grandiose sugar cake. Over ten thousand people petitioned against having their houses torn down to build the highway across town just to get the casket to the mountain."

"How is it the body is not on display after all the trouble of preserving it?"

"They don't want to be copycat to Lenin now that they broke with the Communists."

"What do you think of the new brother-in-law and successor? He's got the ancestral tablet in both hands now."

She picked up her ears. That was the man who married his old love.

"I don't really know him, except through his brothers-in-law."

"Theirs is government by brothers-in-law."

"Was he really legally divorced?" The one time she spoke up she modestly addressed her question to the Young Marshal. They left her out of the conversation in the Oriental way with ladies.

"Yes," Ronald answered.

"Country wives are easy to handle," said the Young Marshal.

"In a case like this you can't just tuck a wife away in the country. And he'd gone as far as to turn Christian."

"What's this about his son denouncing him?"

"That's the son he sent to Russia in his Russian period. The

Russians always have sons denouncing their fathers. The boy is a Youth Pioneer. A Chinese Communist underground publication printed his open letter to his mother, accusing his father of betraying the revolution."

"And kicking his mother downstairs for asking him not to go to singsong houses," the Young Marshal chortled.

"That was when he was in business in Shanghai."

"Was that the wife he divorced?" she asked. She had seen the engagement photograph of Miss Soo-hoo and him, she round-shouldered in ruffled chiffon, with smiling eyes on a rather large soft face under marcelled waves, he standing behind her in uniform, tall, thin and clean-cut. Did she love him? She got what she was looking for, the ruler of China. And she was his own choice instead of the wife his family had foisted on him. There was a great difference there.

"Is it true he made a million on the stock exchange?"

"He lost it in the crash."

"Enough to make a man join the revolution."

"He'd joined early, in army school. But after the Nationalist defeat in Shanghai many went underground, some worked on the Exchange and met in singsong houses. He seemed to have merged into the scene rather well, stayed around for ten years."

"He's good at about-facing."

"He rode a dangerous current to the top. Trouble is nothing has changed. All the old forces gathering, more civil wars. Meanwhile Nanking doesn't do a thing that makes any difference. I stayed long enough to see they're time-wasters. Now I call them Nationa-lusts."

"Yes, same old China. If only we can kill off several million people. Then maybe we can get something done."

"That's the Bolshevik method."

"As long as it works."

"I don't know about that. The Great Experiment has been on for nearly ten years now and they're still famished. Militarily Russia is the one country nobody is afraid of."

"Here at least it got us back the foreign settlements in Hankow."

"They're the least of your worries. Get enough peace and order in the rest of the country and you'll attract as much investment. You don't even use the same money in all the provinces."

"If only we can hand over the country to some reliable foreign power for twenty-five years."

"Unfortunately that can't be arranged."

"Most of my countrymen will be angry at me for saying this, but they haven't tried to get things done, or never had a chance to try."

"I can see how you got known as a radical."

"Only because I'm my father's son and could speak more freely."

"I'm glad you're not of the prevailing view blaming everything on foreigners and unequal treaties. Actually China needs more foreign capital, more boards of control, not less. I say this although I fought the Consortium twice just as a newspaperman." He launched into the story of how he had tricked them out of the land tax marked down as security.

"Ronald talks a lot but he knows how to keep his mouth shut," he told her more than a year later. "He knew about Yang and Ho. They'd sent somebody to see him in Shanghai offering him two thousand pounds to go to London and negotiate a fifteen million pound loan to develop Manchuria. He said it couldn't be done. When he first came here he spoke to those two about it but they quickly changed the subject. He thought that was odd and suspected they wanted the money for a coup. It would have meant a lot to me if he'd told me this after they were executed. But he said nothing. That was real character. No matter who comes to him for advice it's confidential."

"Then how did you get to know?"

"He just mentioned it, now that we really know each other."

Ronald persuaded him to get rid of the drug habit and took charge of his diet, introducing some of his own favorite health foods. He could argue for hours about the relative merits of agar-agar and bran. He made him cut out the parties, played golf and swam and fished with him, took him on long hikes to tire him out completely. There were worries about assassination on country lanes. The Japanese Kwantung Army officers had been yelling around ever since he recognized Nanking as the central government, "Punish Chan Shu-tan, he betrayed us."

She was happy to see the two go off like boy scouts. But his health got so bad the doctor advised complete rest and seclusion for at least a month.

"The rumors will have me dead," he said at once. "There will be uprisings, an opening for the Japanese."

He went back to the drug. "I'll be the first to go for the cure when we have the hospital for it."

There were no funds for the hospital after building the university and a modern port. Settlers poured in from north and central China where there had been wars. The latest was the biggest yet, both sides had half a million men in the field. Three hundred thousand died. Both Nanking and the Christian General and his ally "the king of Shansi" pressed the Young Marshal to join them. He took the stand against civil wars but they kept at him.

She heard Ronald say at lunch, strangely upset, "So far nobody has touched it. The one thing that represents Chinese unity as a nation."

"The Chinese just see it as part of the unequal treaties," he said.

"If they seized the Customs on the pretext of customs autonomy, why install an Englishman as commissioner? Exchange one Englishman for another, that's what I don't understand."

"Old Yin has been too cooped up in Shansi. No experience in

foreign affairs."

"And to have Gravesend-Kemp of all people."

"He's unscrupulous enough. And a well-known writer."

"That makes it all right for him to do anything out here among the comic opera war lords. It's fun, and there may be a book in it."

They went to play golf. The next she heard was, "We're going in."

She thought it was agreed that he should stay out as long as possible.

"Only on condition that the Nationalists clean house and open up the government," Ronald had said. "And not just promises."

She did not want him to go to war and so was familiar with all the arguments against it—leaving Manchuria half empty, Japan would move in. Manchuria was more industrialized than any other part of China. The Nationalist representative had been all agog when he was taken over the munitions plant and it took three hours to drive him over the lot. The country was so big and potentially rich it would be more profitable to develop it than join in civil wars. In the final accounting the Old Marshal's wars had cost more than he got out of it.

"So you have your isolationists too," Ronald had said.

"Why does Ronald hate that Englishman so much?" she asked.

"Oh, Gravesend-Kemp. He's the kind of foreigner in China who's out for all he can get, and Ronald himself has always been scrupulous about money."

"They've known each other a long time?" Perhaps wives are prone to suspect their husband's best friend of using him. She felt uneasy and guilty.

"In Peking. Gravesend-Kemp wrote many books on China, said to be brilliant. Ronald also writes."

" 'Literary men are contemptuous of each other; it has been so since ancient times,' "she quoted laughing.

"And when was that said?"

"I don't know. About fifteen hundred years ago."

The coming test hung heavy over them. He was to enter what the newspapers called the Great War of the Central Plains and the Battle over the Nation. Japan was behind the other side. She never wanted to put him to any tests because they were unfair. The old saying was Do not judge a hero by success or defeat.

He went inside the Pass and sent for her as promised, along with Big Sister, as soon as he had found a house in Peking, avoiding the Marshal's House and any identification with the old regime. This time the Manchurians had come as the army of peace. The war was over the minute he appeared over the border.

His favorite story of the campaign was about Gravesend-Kemp.

"He wrote me at headquarters. Offered me two million in cash and a million a month if I would keep the Customs independent. I asked him to come and see me.

" 'Why did you do that?' Ronald said.

" 'I want to see an Englishman lose face.'

" 'Be careful. People will take it that you just didn't come to terms.'

" 'You'll be there as witness.'

" 'I don't know. He'd assume that you're interested. If you do work out something you'd have gained a friend and lost another. Because I'll have to leave you.' "

Ronald had threatened this before. He had happened to run into an old acquaintance in Mukden, an English baronet in the Indian civil service and then in the legation.

"What are you doing here?" Ronald asked.

"The Young Marshal asked me to be his advisor."

The Young Marshal announced at dinner at home, "Ronald threw down the gauze hat," the hat of office. "Jealous as a woman."

"Jealous as a woman indeed," Big Sister said. "Put out your hand and feel your own conscience."

"So Gravesend-Kemp came to headquarters. 'You simply must reappoint me,' he said.

"I said Why?

" 'Because of the money we can make together.'

" 'By robbing the Customs.'

" 'I wouldn't know what to do if you won't help me.'

" 'Ask Yin Shih-san.'

" 'He's run away.'

" 'Then you run away.'

" 'Will you give me a week?'

" 'Why?'

" 'I have to take care of my staff.'

" 'Give you a week to rob the Customs! I'll give you one day to hand it back to the proper authorities.'

"He hurried off. Two days later one of his employees shot him for the loot. Heaven knows it's difficult for a foreigner to get himself killed in China. Probably the first civilian since the Boxers. And for once England didn't send gunboats."

In those first hazy days of incredulous triumph the story was the one thing that made it real for her. Gravesend-Kemp was practically the only casualty of the war. The three hundred thousand anonymous dead was before he got in. Yin of Shansi still had the province to himself after temporary asylum in Dairen. The Christian General had retired with his wife and choice troops up a scenic mountain in Shantung. Nanking was satisfied to leave it at that. Keeping their names on the wanted list throughout the country was enough punishment. But for the death of the Englishman it was as baffling and dreamlike as a leaky pillow fight, punching into clouds of fluff. She got the impression that the interview at headquarters was the first high point of his life. He had finally proved himself and before Ronald who was the world.

"One odd thing," Ronald said, "in his first book you can see what impressed him most in the Boxers Rebellion was the looting. To think he'd die of it after thirty years."

" 'Peking Indiscreet'," she said.

"Yes. It's a good first-hand account. You can see him drooling."

"He also has a short story called 'Loot'."

"Oh? What's it about?"

"It's the same story."

"The British and Indians and Cossacks looting the palace?"

"Yes, he rewrote that into a short story eight years later."

"I'll be damned."

"I never knew you read him," the Young Marshal said happily.

"I got curious. You were talking about him."

He liked to show her off to Ronald but she generally kept quiet. Ronald was careful with her and was correct in paying her less attention than if she was an unmarried girl of the house. He loved to tease young girls, English-speaking ones perforce. But when a man had two wives it was safer to assume that they were old-fashioned, no matter how modern they seemed.

"He justified it all along," Ronald said. "They were Drake's pirates looting from the looters. The Manchu themselves had got it from the Ming emperors. As to the foreign-manned customs, theirs is the fruit of imperialist exploitation, although this may sound too Bolshie for him."

"So he was just doing what he had always believed in," the Young Marshal said.

"Writers are not supposed to. Barking dogs you know."

He was made Deputy Commander-in-chief of the Armed Forces of China and flew to Nanking with Ronald to attend the National Assembly. Rumors said he would never come back. Nanking would hold him or his father's old officers would take over Manchuria. He came back in two months. He had put an end to the war lords' era. The next time his wives went with him in their private plane. It was the twentieth century at last, thirty years late and he with two wives but he got in. China was in.

《少帥》
考證與評析

馮晞乾 ——文

《少帥》（The Young Marshal）是英文歷史小說，據張愛玲所言，創作念頭始於一九五六年，真正動筆在一九六三年左右。現存打字稿有八十一頁，共七章，約二萬三千英文字，是未完稿。本文分三部分討論《少帥》：一，創作歷程；二，史料考證；三，文學索隱。

一、創作歷程

> 　　我沒有寫歷史的志願，也沒有資格評論史家應持何種態度，可是私下裏總希望他們多說點不相干的話。現實這樣東西是沒有系統的，像七八個話匣子同時開唱，各唱各的，打成一片混沌。在那不可解的喧囂中偶然也有清澄的，使人心酸眼亮的一剎那，聽得出音樂的調子，但立刻又被重重黑暗擁上來，淹沒了那點了解。畫家、文人、作曲家將零星的、湊巧發現的和諧聯繫起來，造成藝術上的完整性。歷史如果過於注重藝術上的完整性，便成爲小說了。
>
> 　　　　　　　　　　　　　　　——張愛玲〈爐餘錄〉

　　一九六一年十月上旬，張愛玲暫別結婚五年的第二任丈夫賴雅，隻身從舊金山出發，先訪台灣，再赴香港。此行目的有二：其一是留港為國際電影懋業公司編劇，增加收入；其二是順道搜集寫作材料。赴港前，張愛玲寫了兩封信給鄺文美，提及她的寫作計畫。第一封寫於一九六一年九月十二日：

想在下月初一個人到香港來，一來因為長途編劇不方便，和Stephen〔宋淇〕當面講講比較省力，二來有兩支想寫的故事背景在東南亞，沒見過沒法寫，在香港住個一年光景，希望能有機會去看看。

另一封寫於同年十月二日：

USOA〔美國海外航空公司〕忽然改了時間表，兩星期一次飛港，（據說是因入秋生意清）十月三日一班機改十月十日。我為了省這一百多塊錢，還是買了十日的票。我寫信給Dick告訴他將去港[1]，他來信叫我在台灣逗留一天，住在他們家，什麼他都可以代辦。其實我那兩個非看不可的地方，台灣就是一個，我以前曾告訴你想寫張學良故事，而他最後是在台。（我想不告訴Dick為妥，你們覺得怎樣？）我本來打算幾個月後去台住幾個星期，但這班機也可以在台stopover〔中途停留〕，比下次去省錢。所以變計預備告訴Dick我想到台中或台南近土人的村鎮住兩星期，看看土人與小城生活。（我有個模糊的念頭土人與故事結局有關。）

張愛玲台灣之行，我們現在都知道，一個原因是為了蒐集關於「少帥」張學良的資料，以備日後寫小說時可以參考。第二封信可以印證此事。另外，上引書信還有兩點值得注意和玩味。

第一點：那兩支她想寫的東南亞故事指什麼呢？張愛玲所謂「東南亞」，定義大概比現在一般標準寬鬆，若照第二封信所言，「我那兩個非看不可的地方，台灣就是一個」，她很可能把台灣也包括在內[2]。然而《少帥》可以算作「背景在東南亞」的故事嗎？據現存打字稿，張愛玲還未寫到少帥幽居台灣的部分，已經把小說擱置了。至於另外一支故事，可能是那部沒有寫成的《鄭和》小說，因為場景涉及錫蘭[3]。然而這終究是不能確定的，我們只知道張愛玲對東南亞一直感興趣，即使在訪台十年後（即一九七一年）跟水晶見面時，她依然主動聊起「南洋的事」，詢及各種有趣的原始風俗——也許跟她來港時準備寫的東南亞故事有關也未可知[4]。

第二點：上引第二信說「我有個模糊的念頭土人與故事結局有關」，此句不但為未完的《少帥》添上一條耐人尋味的尾巴，更是窺探作者意圖的有趣線索。《少帥》體裁為歷史小說，以民國軍閥作背景，故事主線則是愛情，結局居然跟東南亞土人有關？這些貌似風馬牛不相及的元素該如何協調呢？雖然這是一個不存在的結局，但作者對故事的構想，某程度上也有助我們理解文本意義，正如海市蜃樓，本身即使虛幻，畢竟也是某個遙遠現實的折射。在本文第三部分，我會嘗試解釋一下這個想像中的結局到底如何跟小說相關。

言歸正傳，張愛玲抵台北後，時任美國駐台北領事館的文化專員理查德·麥卡錫先安排幾位年輕作家（包括白先勇、王禎和以及陳若曦）跟張愛玲見面，再讓王禎和帶她到花蓮觀光。然而賴雅中風的消息突然傳來，張愛玲只好結束台灣之旅，盡快赴港完成電影劇本，以賺取編劇費濟燃眉之急。

一九六二年三月十八日，張愛玲從香港回到美國，當時他們夫婦倆已從舊金山遷往華盛頓。這時期的張愛玲，一邊為生計替香港的電影公司撰寫劇本（如《南北喜相逢》和《一曲難忘》）[5]，一邊則為美國的文學事業而趕寫幾本英文小說。除了埋首於《雷峯塔》、《易經》外[6]，她又到國會圖書館查閱跟張學良有關的資料[7]，並正式動筆寫《少帥》。對張愛玲來說，一九六三年標誌著她人生的關鍵，這時期寫的小說也就別具意義，以下三信足以說明此點。第一封信是張愛玲寫給鄺文美的，日期為一九五五年十二月十八日：

> 有一天我翻到批的命書，上面說我要到一九六三（！）年才交運（以前我記錯了以為一九六○），你想豈不等死人？「文章憎命達」那種酸腐的話，應用到自己頭上就只覺得辛酸了。

第二封寫給賴雅，原信為英文，日期為一九六二年二月十日，我試譯如下[8]：

> 明年初只要一轉運，我們便一起遷居紐約。我很心急要交上六三年的大運——這是瘋話，也是我唯一的精神支柱——所以明年春左右就要完成《少帥》小說。這時機千載難逢，不容錯失，現在已經想奮發工作了。

第三封寫給鄺文美，日期為一九六三年一月廿四日：

> 今天是陰曆除夕，你知道我對明年抱著mystical〔神秘〕的希望，所以趁今天寫封信給你，別的以後再談。

由此看來，熱衷於命理和神秘學的張愛玲[9]，早已認定一九六三年就是她的事業轉捩點，而《少帥》正是其希望所在（給賴雅的信已一語道破）。但西諺說「書各有命」（Habent sua fata libelli），書的際遇根本不由得作者主宰，結果寫《少帥》的事一再蹉跎，不但趕不上六三年「大運」，多年後更以幻滅告終。有關《少帥》在一九六三年後的寫作進展，以及作者本人的心態轉變，現在只能參考她跟宋淇夫婦的通信了。以下順時序錄出相關書信，有需要時我會附上按語。

一九六三年六月二十三日張愛玲致鄺文美與宋淇書：

> 「少帥」的故事我想寫到三分之二才看得出結構，能告一段落，可以打出來交給Rodell兜售[10]，現在還差幾章。

按：現存的《少帥》打字稿共七章，據信上所言，即全書的三分之二，可見作者本來是計畫寫十章的。

一九六三年七月二十一日張愛玲致鄺文美與宋淇書：

> 這一向乘空在寫張、趙故事，本來可望一口氣寫到西安告一

段落，一看參考材料，北伐時期許多軍政事日期攪錯了，所以又有好幾處要改，這兩天正鑽在裏面有點昏頭昏腦。

一九六三年九月二十日張愛玲致鄺文美與宋淇書：

> 前天昨天又接連收到春秋和兩本書，裏面的材料好到極點，而且來得正是時候，替我打破了兩個疑團，我簡直興奮過度。

按：「兩本書」指何書不詳，單看信上這句話，大概不會聯想到《少帥》，而上下文也確實沒有提及《少帥》。我是在完成了本文第二部分的考證工作後，重看一遍張愛玲的信，才恍然大悟這句話的「深意」：重點是「春秋」二字。那是指一九五七年由姚立夫在香港創辦的半月刊《春秋》雜誌。迄今《春秋》已刊行逾五十年，除香港外，銷售遍及東南亞、歐美等地，內容以近代歷史和人物傳記為主，有很多珍貴的第一手史料。本文第二部分指出，《少帥》某些章節可能參考了刊於《春秋》的文章，這封信恰巧提供佐證，至少顯示張愛玲確實看過《春秋》。信中所謂「兩個疑團」，應該是指她寫《少帥》時碰到的歷史疑問，可見她非常重視資料的真確和完備，決不閉門造車。

一九六四年一月二十五日張愛玲致鄺文美與宋淇書：

> 小說還沒寫好，因為越寫下去，知道前面應當長，後面應縮短，所以老是只差一章就可以動手打了，也老是心不定。Dick去

年十月裏說，一得到關於賣「易經」的消息不論好壞就告訴我，這些時也沒信，我也沒問，因爲每次和他一談就使我恨不得馬上把張趙故事寫好，而又急不來。

按：假設《少帥》本來計畫寫十章，首七章的時代背景已知是一九二五年至一九三〇年，但第五章開始時還是一九二六年頭，可見前半部那幾個月寫得非常長；若小說以一九三六年西安事變作高潮，則餘下三章勢必一下子帶過六年。這個結構正符合張愛玲所謂「前面應當長，後面應縮短」。

一九六四年五月六日張愛玲致鄺文美與宋淇書：

> 少帥故事寫好的部分他〔指理查德・麥卡錫〕和Rodell看了都不喜歡，說歷史太confusing〔混亂〕，Rodell說許多人名完全記不清。我讀到新出的一本中國近代史的書評，說許多人名完全把他攪糊塗了，直到蔣出現才感興趣，所以我早有戒心，自以爲特別簡單化，結果仍舊一樣，難道民初歷史根本不能動？三年來我的一切行動都以這小說爲中心，現在得要全盤推翻，但目前也仍舊這樣過著，也仍舊往下寫著。

按：「三年來我的一切行動都以這小說為中心」，短短七章，居然費了三年功夫，可見即使《少帥》是未完稿，也確實貫注了作者數年的全副心力，不能以草稿目之。

一九六四年十一月十一日張愛玲致鄺文美與宋淇書：

同時Dick又找到一個人幫著賣它〔指英文小說稿The Rouge of the North（《北地胭脂》）〕，是從前做news commentator〔新聞評論員〕的，有個中國妻子在VOA〔美國之音〕做事。這人也喜歡「少帥」小說，並沒有被人名攪糊塗了，或者因為對中國近代史比較熟悉些。

一九六六年一月二十五日張愛玲致鄺文美與宋淇書：

昨天信上講申請grant〔獎助金〕，其實即使領到也是一年半後的事，所以我最後寫信去也只講《海上花》，不提少帥故事，希望到那時候已經寫完了。

按：所謂grant，是指向賴氏女子學院（Radcliffe College）申請資助翻譯《海上花》。一九六七年七月，張愛玲申請成功，遷居麻州劍橋。據此信所示，她在一九六六年頭仍未放棄《少帥》，更希望在一年半內寫好。

一九六六年九月九日宋淇致張愛玲書：

你的關於少帥的小說，是不是一看即知的thinly disguised〔略作掩飾〕的索隱體的小說？對蔣、宋二人有沒有牽涉到太明顯，或太unfavorable〔不討好〕的地方？盼在回信中告知。我有辦法可將中文version〔版本〕替你尋到地盤，不過如果政治性太濃，因而得罪了台灣的市場也犯不著。一共有多少字？是否故事性很濃？寫法比較傳統一點？自己如改成中文，須要多少時間？

一九六六年十一月十一日張愛玲致宋淇書：

少帥小說決無希望在台出版，因爲無論怎樣偏重愛情故事，大綱總是那樣，一望而知。我對英文本毫不樂觀，因爲民初背景裏人太多是個大問題。也還沒動手寫下去，可以不必擔憂英文本出版而使我自絕於台灣，至少現在愁不到那裏。要點是終身拘禁成全了趙四。

一九六六年十二月五日宋淇致張愛玲書：

少帥小說想想總是不妥。既然如此只好放棄了。

一九六六年十二月廿六日張愛玲致宋淇書：

「少帥」我不是沒顧慮到，也甚至於想著將來這裏碰來碰去沒人要，台灣倒已經知道了，只有他們感到興趣。但是實在愁不了這麼遠，在這裏有時候要對學生「講話」[11]，還要寫篇論文——本可拒絕，我也想試試看——自己的事總是揀有時限的先做，看來這部小說稿子還沒拿出來做下去，已經該收攤子了。同時因蔣年紀關係，將來的事也難說。

一九六七年三月二十四日張愛玲致宋淇書：

少帥故事我自從一九五六年起意，漸漸做到identification〔認同〕地步，跟你們別後也只有一九六三年左右在寫著的時候很快樂。寫完的部分有三個人看過，Marie Rodell說人多混亂，Dick McCarthy & Raymond Swing〔雷蒙德・斯溫〕（從前出名的commentator，他的中國太太在VOA做事，前些時到香港來，Mae也許見過）都喜歡，但是他們是中國通，Rodell較代表一般讀者。已經用gimmicks〔花招〕簡化一切，還搞不清，使我灰心得寫不下去。Dick認爲只要加點exposition〔說明〕。等有空我會再寫下去的，別的只好都「再說」了。Dick又對唯一的外國人端納（在這裏是美國人）表不滿──所以我早已對你們提出黃白戀愛的公式而不寫。

六〇年代有關《少帥》的通信到此為止。一九七一年，張愛玲與水晶會面，事後水晶在〈蟬〉一文中記下她的話，說「另外用中文寫的軍閥時代的長篇小說，寫了一半擱下來了，也想把它趕完」，顯然是指《少帥》[12]，至於「用中文寫」則似乎是水晶誤記。由此可知，即使到了七〇年代初，張愛玲還是打算把小說寫完的。

一九七六年，宋淇發表〈私語張愛玲〉，文中提到張愛玲有一本未出版的愛情小說，儘管沒有點明書題，但憑他的描述可推斷為《少帥》無疑：

她在美國的寫作生涯並不順利。長篇小說Pink Tears〔《粉淚》〕改了又改，始終找不到出版者。另一本愛情小說，因為人物太多，外國人攬不清中國人姓名的「三字經」，也沒有人要。如果改用中文寫，又怕其中人物有影射之嫌和近乎紅樓夢的「讔語」，不願輕率下筆。據我所知，這小說的主題很有吸引力，擱在那裏實在可惜。但願時來運到，慢慢有見天日的機會。

一九八一年十二月二十五日宋淇致張愛玲書：

你以前曾經用英文寫過一本以張學良為主角的小說，後來因外國人搞不清中國人的「三字經」，始終找不到出版商，中文版則你因為覺得有讔語，不敢拿出去。目前張已可公開活動，雙方因統戰關係，都在對他表示好感，倒是一個極好的出土機會。台灣方面比較起來對「老先生」最敏感，攻擊蔣經國沒有關係，對老先生如有何不敬則罪莫大焉。我現在正式建議你把《海上花》弄好後，立刻動手把它譯成中文。對老先生有不敬的地方可以沖淡一點，如果再有問題，最多在香港出版，金庸去了北京，訪問鄧小平，事後寫了篇長文，台灣拿他沒辦法，沒有把他的武俠小說禁止發行。〔……〕你這本「三字經」小說題材太好了，大時代背景，時代造成的英雄人物，然後有一段始終不渝的愛情故事。你無論如何要把它寫出來，如果夠得上水準，必是傳世之作。

一九八二年二月一日張愛玲致宋淇書：

「三字經」是Stephen〔宋淇〕記錯了，現在「三字經」指「丟那媽」等罵人的話，我不會用作題目。這故事雖好，在我不過是找個acceptable framework〔可接受的故事輪廓〕寫「小團圓」，能用得上的也不多。張作為一個愛國者──我因為傾向「聯合抗日就一定被吃掉」之說，（當時是有許多好人相信中共，所以有一股幾乎不可抗拒的吸力）總覺得他是被利用。當然，也有些英國人知道二次大戰一打，大英帝國就完了；難道因此就不抵抗希特勒？這些有先見之明的人至今受批評。不過太輕視男主角決寫不好。他禁閉的生活我找到些資料，也毫無心得，就有印象也是unflattering〔不討好〕。當時如果能寫下去，就也不去管台灣了，本來是個英文小說。

一九八二年二月二十二日宋淇致張愛玲書：

那本小說的「三字經」是你多年前信中提到的中國人的姓名，外國人看不懂，嫌煩，非常cute〔機智〕的pun〔雙關語〕，大概你忘了。你既然對男主角不同情，而且只有輪廓，不寫也罷。

按：關於「三字經」，張、宋兩方都說得有點纏夾。宋淇說那是張愛玲多年前用過的雙關語（她本人也忘記了），這是對的，但不是「信中提到」，而是在一九六八年發表的〈憶胡適之〉：「《海上花》許多人整天蕩來蕩去，面目模糊，名字譯成英文後，連性別都看不出。才摸熟了倒又換了一批人。我們『三字經』式的名字他們連看幾個立刻頭暈眼花起來，不比我們自己看著，文字本身在視覺上有色彩。」[13]

一九八二年三月十日張愛玲致宋淇書：

好故事難得，不然我也不會輕易放棄「三字經」（？還是不記得這書名），因為無論怎樣偏重私生活，難免涉及大局，而女主角是通過男主角眼中看出來的「王莽謙恭下士時」的中共，即使她有點懷疑也極有限。予人的印象曖昧。我甚至於想通過端納眼中——他離張就宋（美齡），給張的打擊很深。但是端納的工作（似乎大致是PR與寫演說稿）我更不懂了，雖有一本"Donald of China"，很壞，沒什麼用。

一九八二年四月二日宋淇致張愛玲書：

你那篇小說不寫也罷，給你一說，我才了解到牽涉如此之大。最近台灣傳記文學連載長文：西安事變回憶；中共據說也發表了他們手上的資料，拼命在他的身上做統戰文章。更犯不著捲進去，何況看你的口氣，對男主角並不同情，寫出來也不會討好。我起先以為故事有點像「傾城之戀」：一件驚天動地的大事成就了一段愛情，但從沒有想到這件大事影響到國運和億萬生靈。我想既然如此，可以告一段落，不必再花時去想了。

八〇年代有關《少帥》的通信到此為止。最後一回討論，則始於張學良在台灣獲釋。一九九一年三月十四日宋淇致張愛玲書：

少帥 —— 214

張學良於三月初獲得自由，想你已從聯合報航空版看到消息。〔……〕文美和我都記得你一度有意寫一冊以他的事蹟爲中心的小說，後因有「礙語」，所以只好擱置。當時我們都認爲設想很好。因爲中國的命運自東北起到西安事變，可以說都繫於他一身。這句話也許又有了三十年了，想你不一定再有精力來重拾舊山河，或許寫篇文章以誌其經過也可一解心中的結。

一九九一年四月十四日張愛玲致宋淇書：

對張學良我久已失去興趣，認爲他是個limousine liberal〔坐大轎車的自由主義者[14]〕，覺得irritating〔討厭〕——純粹我個人的偏見。

一九九一年五月二十七日張愛玲致宋淇書：

以前信上說過，我爲了寫「少帥」，對張知道得較多之後，覺得他像一般二世主一樣，沒眞正經過考驗，所以對自己沒信心，雖然外表看不出。東北易幟，固然是出於統一大義，而且獨力無望報父仇，也是他心深處寧願做他做慣的親信子任，甚至於傳人——蔣夫婦極力敷衍籠絡他，他也就當眞。當然蔣對他也確是有一種ambiguity〔模棱兩可〕。Dick McCarthy說蔣對張是眞視如子姪。（我也認爲因禁他是勢不能放。）同時張也是受端納影響。端利用他爲自己的政治資本，從coach〔訓練〕他（本想捧他爲國際舞台明星）升爲蔣夫人的coach。張終於對蔣政府感到幻滅，憧憬延安。蔣是個intuitive politician〔直覺敏銳的政治家〕，知道聯共抗日一定被吃掉。當時有些很能打仗的軍官都有恐共症。共軍是有一種mystique〔神秘可畏的氛圍〕。假定沒有西安事變，能拖到日本對美戰敗，中國固然沒面子，不能算戰勝國。但是即使內戰持續下去，得能免受大躍進與文革浩劫，總結賬的盈虧也很難說。我無法從趙四的觀點去看張，又not knowledgeable enough to write it from any other viewpoint〔沒有足夠知識從其他人的角度去寫〕，例如端納的。

一九九一年六月七日宋淇致張愛玲書：

　　張學良的事你分析得很對，目前不值得寫，也找不到適合的角度。

一九九一年八月十三日張愛玲致宋淇書：

　　還有關於張學良，兵諫在古代可能行得通，因爲世襲的君主地位穩固，不像現代的強人的image〔形象〕經不起重大打擊。蔣被脅迫抗日？造成張的民族英雄形象？稍有常識的人都知道絕對不行。當然張是自恃親同叔侄的特殊關係。使我想起天安門事件時NBC John Chancellor報道：「有些當權的高幹子弟打電話回家說：『今天我要出去。』指到天安門去。當天軍警就按兵不動。」最後還是出了事，同是錯估了自己的特權。（當然他們本人也仍舊能免禍。）

一九九一年八月三十一日宋淇致張愛玲書：

> 張學良已自由，去了美國，有人勸他寫回憶錄，據說他經考
> 慮後，不打算寫了。你信中講了不少關於他的話，我想我們應該
> write him off〔把他一筆勾消〕，做正事要緊。

以上所引，就是張愛玲與宋淇在信中論及《少帥》的所有重要
內容。這部小說的寫作經過與擱置因由，相信大家已掌握到一個梗概
了。總結一下：張愛玲最初對《少帥》期望甚高，覺得自己時來運
到，可以憑它在美國文壇打出名堂；寫了大約三分之二，她的出版代
理人卻大潑冷水，批評小說人名太多，歷史混亂，自此張愛玲便熱情
漸減，把它擱置多年，最後連對男主角的興趣也沒有了，這小說就不
得不放棄。

二、史料考證

> 這裏的故事，從某一個角度看來，可以說是傳奇，其實像這
> 一類的事也多得很。我希望讀者看這本書的時候，也說不定會聯
> 想到他自己認識的人，或是見到聽到的事情。不記得是不是《論
> 語》上有這樣兩句話：「如得其情，哀矜而勿喜。」這兩句話給我
> 的印象很深刻。我們明白了一件事的內情，與一個人內心的曲折，
> 我們也都「哀矜而勿喜」吧。
>
> ——張愛玲〈短篇小說集自序〉

現存的七章《少帥》，時代背景始於一九二五年，最後以少帥抵達南京作結（考諸史實，即一九三〇年十一月十二日）。正如作者自言，小說較「偏重愛情故事」（見前文所引一九六六年十一月十一日張愛玲致宋淇書），大致上以少帥陳叔覃（小說中張學良的化名）和周四小姐（小說中趙四小姐的化名）的相戀為主線，間或借飯局、閒聊的情節，穿插著當時的軼聞，讓歷史「像七八個話匣子同時開唱，各唱各的，打成一片混沌」[15]。這種寫法，不禁也令人想起張愛玲年少時讀過的歷史小說《孽海花》，其作者曾樸在序言〈修改後要說的幾句話〉中寫道：「想借用主人公做全書的線索，盡量容納近三十年來的歷史，避去正面，專把些有趣的瑣聞逸事，來烘托出大事的背景。」我認為這也是張愛玲寫《少帥》的一個指導原則，而這原則也在小說第二章通過角色的對話反映出來[16]：

「羅納先生一肚子軼聞，」教育部總長說完又用英文複述。
「不然還有什麼？」羅納說，「二十年來只有亂紛紛的登場人物，正是軼聞裏的那種腳色。」

現在先簡介一下張學良，為免冗長，這裏只側重與小說相關的時期和背景，餘皆從略[17]。張學良（一九〇一年至二〇〇一年），字漢卿，奉天海城人，奉系軍閥張作霖長子，綽號「少帥」。一九一一年四月，母親趙春桂（張作霖元配）病逝，自此交由張作霖繼室盧夫人撫養。武昌起義後，他隨父親到省城奉天。一九一五年參加反日本帝國主義二十一條運動。一九一六年春，他遵照父命，與自己不喜歡且年長三歲的于鳳至結婚。同年，師從奉天督軍署英文科科長徐啟東學習英語。一九一七年，經軍醫王少源介紹，參與奉天基督教青年會的活動，認識了一批外籍幹事，如普賴德（Joseph E. Platt）。自此，他漸受西方文化薰陶，愛穿洋服，喜打網球、高爾夫，思想、作風也遠比他父親一輩開明和摩登。一九一九年，張學良就讀東三省陸軍講武堂，與戰術教官郭松齡成為好友。一九二二年參與第一次直奉戰爭，任鎮威軍第二梯隊司令。奉系戰敗後，張作霖成立了東三省陸軍整理處，張學良任參謀長，頭銜雖不高，卻已實權在握。一九二四年第二次直奉戰爭爆發，張學良任第三軍軍長（郭松齡為副軍長），此時奉軍既經整頓，加上直系的馮玉祥倒戈，吳佩孚此役遂以大敗告終。

一九二五年就是《少帥》開始的時間。是年春，張學良被任命為京榆駐軍司令，進駐天津。六月，因「五卅慘案」而率奉軍抵上海，派兵入租界駐防。十一月，郭松齡反奉，一個月後兵敗被處死。一九二六年六月，率部進攻馮玉祥國民軍，七月進攻南口。一九二七年三月，率軍河南阻截北伐軍，兵敗。同年六月，張作霖在北京成立安國軍政府，自封「中華民國陸海軍大元帥」。一九二八年，蔣介石、馮玉祥、閻錫山、李宗仁聯合北伐，奉軍退回關外。是年六月四日，張作霖乘火車回奉天途中，在皇姑屯被日軍炸死。張學良被推為東三省保安總司令，年底宣布「東北易幟」，歸附南京國民黨政府。一九二九年一月，他處決了圖謀不軌的奉系元老楊宇霆和常蔭槐。一九三○年十一月，與政治顧問端納到南京，受到國民政府熱烈歡迎。一九三六年十二月十二日，與楊虎城一起發動「西安事變」，扣押蔣介石，逼他聯共抗日；十二月二十五日，張學良親自送蔣回南京，從此被軟禁。一九四六年底，被遷往台灣新竹，至一九九〇年才重獲自由。晚年與第二任妻子趙一荻定居美國夏威夷。如果要用一句話概括其為人、生平，最好就是借用史家唐德剛的說法——張學良是「花花公子和政治家、軍事家」的「三位一體」[18]。

張學良與趙一荻（原名趙綺霞，一荻只是洋名Edith的諧音）的愛情故事，多年來廣為流傳，但各個版本間的細節不盡相同，說法亦跡近小說，難以作準。張愛玲跟張學良沒什麼世交，談不上對他本人有深徹了解，關於他的街談巷語可能聽過不少，但這些粗糙的坊間傳說是遠不夠用來寫成小說的。五〇年代，她寫〈The Spyring〉（即〈色，戒〉英文版）時已說：「寫小說非要自己徹底了解全部情形不可（包括任務、背景的一切細節），否則寫出來像人造纖維，不像真的。」[19]因此要寫好《少帥》，除了參閱正史、傳記，她還要看大量野史、雜文，才能將故事說得肌理分明，瑣聞軼事穿插有致。這些資料來源是什麼呢？如果能看到她當年的參考材料，便可了解她剪裁拼湊的手法；了解到這種手法，便可更明白她的創作用心。由於我們沒有她的「參考書目」，所以也只能從現有文獻中找些蛛絲馬跡。她當時參考過的材料，比較能確定的有兩類：一是剪報、雜誌；二是美國國會圖書館的藏書，尤其是美國記者瑟勒（Earl Albert Selle）所著的《中國的端納》（Donald of China），此書在一九四八年由紐約Harper & Brothers 公司出版。

本來五十年前的剪報是不可能知道的，但《張愛玲私語錄》恰巧節選了一九六三年四月二日張愛玲寫給鄺文美的信[20]，當中說：

最近我又身體啾啾唧唧起來，病了幾天。寫小說看參考材料，找到今聖嘆講軍閥時代「陪斬」的一段[21]，不由得感謝Mae〔鄺文美〕歷年寄給我的新生晚報，從前實在美不勝收。

這一節書信何以見得跟《少帥》相關呢？原來在《少帥》第五章，有一段關於老媽子們講吳佩孚（小說中叫吳蟠湖）時代犯人斬首的情形，其中正提及「陪斬」。很明顯，張愛玲就是把那舊報專欄上的故事寫進小說裏去。但究竟小說化用這些史料的具體情況是怎樣呢？她引述軼聞時對原材料又有多倚重呢？以下將舉兩例，我們可直接看看小說與史料的異同。第一例是在《少帥》第二章，作者通過羅納的心聲插入一則張作霖的軼事：

> 當時老帥已經是統兵滿洲的軍官，北京特意任命了一個與他相得的總督。此人是呈遞秘密請願書，呼籲恢復帝制的十四省代表之一。論功行賞，他獲封一等公爵，老帥則是二等子爵，感到不滿。他召集一大群軍官同行去了總督的官邸，說道：「大人擁立皇上有功，想必要出席登基大典。特來請大人的示，定哪一天起程，我們準備相送。」
>
> 總督自知地位不保。「我明晚進京。」
>
> 老帥奉陪到底，召集軍官幕僚餞行。滿洲自此再無總督。新皇帝無暇他顧。

張愛玲從未提及這軼事的來源，但以我所考，她這段記事跟高拜石《古春風樓瑣記》的〈官場現形記——段芝貴浮沉錄〉其中一段很相似，雖經簡化，細節也略有改動，但行文遣詞還是見到亦步亦趨之跡。《古春風樓瑣記》於一九五八至一九六九年在台灣《新生報》副刊連載，這篇寫段芝貴的是早期作品，張愛玲很可能參考過[22]：

> 籌安會起，大典籌備已是密鑼緊鼓進行著，民國四年十二月二十一日，大封爵位，芝貴封一等公，不久作霖也破格得封二等子。
>
> 本來一個中將只能授為輕車都尉，張作霖以王占元封侯，憤請病假，段芝貴踵門視疾，也給擋駕不見，託人許以綏遠都統，又是不加理睬。實際這個身中面白美秀而文的張雨亭（作霖），早已偵知段芝貴挪用公帑，他密囑袁金鎧諸人，籌設「奉天保安會」，來個變相獨立形態，段芝貴大驚，電京請破格封給。
>
> 張作霖既如願以償，益發覺得北京的袁皇帝，正忙著黃袍加身，對關外是鞭長莫及，不趁這時候掃清臥榻，更待何時？
>
> 這一天的早上，張作霖、馮德麟等一班人率同高級軍官參謀，到督署見段，段見人多，詢他有何事故？張回道：「洪憲皇帝要登基了，大帥是開國元勳，特來請大帥的示，定哪一天起程，準備餞送。」
>
> 這傢伙也機警，觀色察言，已知來意，便答以「明晚回京」。果然第二天，張約同全體官佐僚屬，設筵歡送。

不難發現，所引《古春風樓瑣記》解釋了「作霖也破格得封二等子」的因由（引文第二段），到張愛玲筆下則完全省掉，相信是嫌它太長，但其餘情節則大致相同，尤其是老帥的話，顯然是從中文翻過來的。

再舉一例。小說第五章記徐樹錚（書中叫徐昭亭）被殺經過及他在白金漢宮園遊會的軼事，就跟薛觀瀾的〈馮玉祥為什麼要殺徐樹錚？〉一文所載非常相似，此文原刊一九五九年四月一日第四十二期《春秋》雜誌，張愛玲很可能參考過[23]。《少帥》如此寫：

> 「外國人叫他徐將軍。〔……〕他的高級秘書帶太太出席，那女人年過五十了，裹小腳，穿中國衣裳，但是她丈夫要她戴一頂很大的簪花草帽。有個年青的秘書不贊成，可是那高級秘書是前清的舉人，天下事無所不曉，說『哪有外國婦女白天出門不戴帽子的？』離御帳大約有六百碼的路，那女人小腳走不快，風還把她的帽子吹跑了。那年青秘書追趕帽子，可帽子在風裏忽左忽右，忽上忽下，好一會兒才抓住。喬治五世捧著肚子哈哈大笑。」
>
> 〔……〕
>
> 「過後徐昭亭跟那年青人說：『你大概沒有考慮吧，這對英皇是大不敬。』那秘書說：『那麼那美國首席大法官呢？他拍著英皇的背，一邊跺腳一邊大笑。』徐沒再說什麼。第二天倫敦泰晤士報講了追帽子的新聞，沒加評論，但是批評了休斯大法官，儘管他是英皇的老朋友。」

薛觀瀾在〈馮玉祥為什麼要殺徐樹錚？〉一文中則這樣寫：

一九二五年夏，白金漢宮有一盛大園遊會，此次有貴賓二人：第一個是美國大理院長前任國務卿休士；第二個便是中華民國特使徐樹錚。

〔……〕

是日隨徐樹錚入宮者，爲朱兆莘夫婦、陳維城及觀瀾等一行五人。朱夫人年逾不惑，小腳穿中裝，頭帶闊邊草帽，大而無當。觀瀾當時認爲不雅觀，不如不戴。但朱兆莘系前清舉人，甚守舊，他說：「外國婦女在白天出門那有不戴帽的。」

無何，朱夫人小腳走不快，朱恐誤時，頻加催促，她幾失聲而哭。從走廊步行至御帳，約長六百碼，走至中途，朱夫人的草帽突然被風吹落。我乃不假思索，拔步追拾之，惟帽隨風而轉，左右飛舞，良久始落我手。英皇佐治五世見此，捧腹大笑。有頃，徐樹錚對我說：「你大概沒有考慮罷，這對英皇是大不敬。」我答：「我絕未考慮及此，但美國大理院長休士狂拊英皇之背，且笑且躍，這你何以不說他是大不敬呢？」徐聞之，亦不再說了。次日倫敦泰晤士報載此，對觀瀾並未置評，但對休士之舉動，表示不滿。

另外，薛文又提出了一個較冷門的講法：「奉軍郭松齡因怨楊宇霆而倒戈，事前實獲張學良之諒解，張郭二人實皆受馮玉祥夫婦之慫恿。」《少帥》第六章，有一節也從趙四小姐（小說中叫周四小姐）的角度，想像少帥有份參與郭松齡（小說中叫顧興齡）的叛變，與馮玉祥（小說中叫馮以祥）勾結，目標也是要整掉楊宇霆（小說中叫楊一鵬）。但按一般說法或張學良晚年的口述歷史，他並沒有背叛自己父親[24]。在我看來，張愛玲對少帥叛變一事所採取的模棱兩可寫法，未嘗不是受到薛觀瀾的觀點影響；當然，她也可能只是寫出周四小姐的觀點——少帥是她幻想中的一個反父權人物——而未必有意坐實他是否真的叛變。

這類取材自剪報或雜誌的小說段落應該還有不少，但恐怕多無從稽考[25]。至於另一種材料來源，正如前文所言，就是華盛頓國會圖書館藏書。今天查國會圖書館的書目，也可找到一些張愛玲有機會讀到的書，例如魯泗《論張學良》（一九四八年由香港時代批評社出版）等等，但最重要的一部，無疑就是《中國的端納》。在《對照記》中，張愛玲回憶堂伯父張人駿時，就提起過《中國的端納》這部書[26]。端納（William Henry Donald）本來是駐中國記者，因緣際會下成為了孫中山、張學良和蔣介石的政治顧問，在中國近代史上發揮了一定的影響，他在小說中稱為羅納（W. F. Ronald）。

本文第一部分引了一九八二年三月十日張愛玲寫給宋淇的信，裏面說：「雖有一本"Donald of China"，很壞，沒什麼用。」儘管這樣說，但《少帥》中的若干小故事確實是直接從《中國的端納》（第二十章〈東三省與少帥〉尤為重要）移植過去的。姑舉七例說明：

1. 小說第二章寫羅納「幫助一個遭軟禁的反對派將軍藏身洗衣籃，潛逃出北京」，實際就是指端納偷運蔡鍔出城，事見《中國的端納》（下簡稱《中》）第一百七十六頁[27]。

2. 小說第四章寫羅納在第一次直奉戰爭時，因拉走了前線的電話線而扭轉戰局，事見《中》第二百二十九至二百三十頁。

3. 小說第七章寫少帥擲錢幣決定是否殺楊、何（即現實中的楊宇霆、常蔭槐）一事，見《中》第二百五十八至二百五十九頁。

4. 小說第七章寫楊、何付二千英鎊給羅納，要他到倫敦洽談，借款一千五百萬英鎊來開發東三省，羅納因此疑心他們叛變，事見《中》第二百五十六至二百五十七頁。

5. 小說第七章寫少帥拒絕貴甫森-甘（Gravesend-Kemp）的賄賂，不論情節或對白，都絕大部分跟《中》第二百六十四至二百六十六頁記張學良拒絕辛普森（Bertram Lenox Simpson）一事相同。

6. 小說第七章寫新聞記者問孫中山：「孫博士，您是社會主義者嗎？」羅納代答一句：「你是國民黨人所應是的一切。」其事其言皆載於《中》第一百二十六頁。

7. 小說第七章寫少帥說：「一樣的老中國。要是我們能殺掉幾百萬人就好了。也許那樣我們就可以有作為。〔……〕要是我們可以把國家交給某個可靠的強國，託管個二十五年多好。」這幾句也見於《中》第三百〇一頁，端納在一封信中轉述了張學良的話。

像這樣的例子其實還有更多，恕不逐一解釋。上面那麼不厭其煩地交代素材來歷，主要有兩個意義。其一，這證明了張愛玲確曾孜孜不倦搜集史料（尤其是軼事、野史一類），並甘心冒著剽襲的嫌疑，忠實地把這些素材逐一寫進小說。她為什麼要這樣做呢？因為沒有靈感寫不下去，只好順手牽羊聊以塞責？在我來看，這種寫法不過體現了作者素來服膺的美學觀——借用〈談看書〉裏引用法國女歷史學家佩奴德的話,就是「事實比虛構的故事有更深沉的戲劇性」。張愛玲在〈談看書〉裏又說自己喜歡「實事」,「並不是『尊重事實』,是偏嗜它特有的一種韻味,其實也就是人生味。」她因此很喜歡看比較可靠的歷史小說,「裏面偶而有點生活細節是歷史傳記裏沒有的,使人神往,觸摸到另一個時代的質地」[28]。體會到這種實事之美,就知道張愛玲決不是因為江郎才盡,挑得籃裏便是菜,隨隨便便把史料搬到小說裏去的。

在這套美學觀的基礎上,《少帥》以近乎記錄體的手法,勾勒出歷史人物某些真實而被忽略的側面,也小心翼翼移植了歷史事件中一些看似偶然、微末卻又往往意味深遠的細節──那是主流歷史教科書不會宣揚的「真實」(像〈燼餘錄〉寫香港淪陷),而這也正是她在〈自己的文章〉裏所謂的「較近事實」的、「參差的對照的寫法」。《少帥》第二章有一句話反映了作者的歷史觀:「現代史沒有變成史籍,一團亂麻,是個危險的題材,決不會在他們的時代筆之於書。真實有一千種面相。」張愛玲正是利用小說這種體裁,將真實的一千種面相兼收並蓄,通過種種富「人生味」的軼事來呈現「另一個時代的質地」。

我們考證小說的素材來歷,還有第二個意義,但那是在上述第一個意義的對照下才成立的:若張愛玲大部分情況都旨在「紀實」,力求拼湊一幅有實事韻味的歷史造像,那麼小說裏刻意偏離事實的每一處,即與上述第一意義不協之處,自然就別具深意了。好比在舞台上,不論如何鑼鼓喧天,演出者如何聲嘶力竭,只要布景露一點餡,就能立刻將觀眾拉回現實，所以小說世界中每一個「錯」，無論有意抑或無意，都必然暴露了作者存在處境的「真」。

上文舉出小說和素材相同之處，顯示張愛玲呈現歷史的手法正體現了她的美學觀；下文將辨析兩者之異，由虛入實，從其「露餡」處逐漸窺探作者的寫作策略，繼而剖析其「內心的曲折」，到本文第三部分，我們就以此為據，嘗試整合出《少帥》在張愛玲創作生涯中的獨特意義。《文心雕龍‧知音》：「夫綴文者情動而辭發，觀文者披文以入情。沿波討源，雖幽必顯。世遠莫見其面，覘文輒見其心。」評析的功用正在於此。

現在先講寫作策略。《少帥》既是小說，虛構是必然的，例如少帥與趙四的戀愛故事，具體情況就只有當事人知道，所以小說家也不得不借用自己的個人經驗（關於這點，將在本文第三部分詳論）。但前面已指出，張愛玲希望盡可能把真實的歷史寫進小說，那麼只要有足夠的資料作為參考，按道理她也不應該擅作改動。但現在小說卻有多處地方明顯不符史實——或準確點說，不符合張愛玲理應參考過的史料——那麼這些改動（也可視為謬誤）便大有可能反映了作者的寫作策略[29]。

改動第一個例子就是周四小姐的老父。首章說他跟老帥陳祖望（現實中的張作霖）「關係特殊」，第二章說他曾以「東北總督」身份提攜過老帥，而老帥亦曾助他解困，都完全跟歷史中的趙四小姐父親無關。真正的趙父叫趙慶華，在北洋軍閥政府時代曾任津浦、滬寧、滬杭甬、廣九等鐵路局長,又當過政府交通次長、東三省外交顧問,屬直系官員,談不上有恩於老帥。張學良認識趙四之前,以我所知,兩家人的關係僅限於:一,張是趙四兩位胞兄(趙燕生和天津大華飯店總經理趙道生)的朋友;二,趙慶華長女絳雪嫁了給張學良的法文秘書馮武越[30]。兩家並非世交。至於《少帥》中的周四父親,原型其實是趙爾巽[31],不是趙慶華。張愛玲為什麼要這樣改呢?若說她要掩飾小說人物的影射對象,那未免太可笑了。最簡單也最可能的解釋,就是張愛玲怕「民初背景裏人太多」(一九六六年十一月十一日張愛玲致宋淇書),所以要「用gimmicks簡化一切」(一九六七年三月廿四日張愛玲致宋淇書),令西方讀者不會看得一頭霧水。用趙爾巽取代趙慶華,一方面也許是張愛玲的幽默表現,純粹因同姓而戲改,另一方面則略過了對西方讀者沒有「戲味」的「直、奉」背景,而代之以較鮮明的「恩人」和「上、下級」關係,藉以加強劇情張力。

懂得張愛玲這種策略後,以下三處對史實的改動自也顯得順理成章。其一,在小說第二章,作者把羅納先含糊地寫成袁世凱復辟的始作俑者,繼而又寫他反復辟,充滿矛盾和戲劇性;然而現實中的端納則平淡得多,他一直只支持共和,真正挑起復辟論的外國人是Roy Scott Anderson,但張愛玲似乎為了塑造羅納成為「一個孤獨的冠軍」,「自己與自己對陣」,於是便把Anderson的賬,都統統算到端納的頭上去了[32]。其二,第二章說少帥幼年喪母,這是事實,但立即又杜撰一句「由五老姨太撫養成人」,而不是照史實說「由繼室二太太撫養成人」。西方讀者一看見「the Fifth Old Concubine」(五老姨太），加上小說第六章又說她「從前是小縣城的一個妓女」，大概會認定她地位不高，少帥的成長背景不會太好。張愛玲顯然不要少帥有太幸福的少年時代，而小說中多次提到他跟老帥關係緊張，也是要烘托出一個跟家庭疏離的、有少許反父權的英雄形象——但誰又想到張作霖的五房壽夫人在現實裏才是各房中最有影響力的一位呢[33]？這也許是張愛玲跟讀者開的一個玩笑，也許她根本就不知道五太太的威風。其三，第二章說周四小姐的親母早故，由失寵的側室洪姨娘撫養，而這位洪姨娘入門前也是堂子中人（singsong girl）；但現實中趙四之母為賢妻良母，沒有早死，也沒進過堂子，唯一值得一提的，是她因門第不高（本是盛宣懷家的丫頭），結果反被出身名門的二夫人（盛家小姐）爬過了頭，自己倒屈居第二[34]。張愛玲也許不清楚趙母故事，覺得沒有戲，但又不能不交代一兩句，於是便虛構出一個形象較鮮明的洪姨娘。通過這個角色，周四小姐與少帥的成長歷程便更接近，彼此也更有同病相憐的況味，於是感情發展也就更合情理了。

如此虛構、改寫之例當然還有更多，我不逐一列舉了。這手法也不限於《少帥》。張愛玲寫《雷峯塔》、《易經》兩本自傳性小說時，也為了增強戲劇張力或賦予象徵意義而改動事實。最明顯的例子是在《雷峯塔》結尾，琵琶（即現實中的張愛玲）的弟弟陵（即現實中的張子靜）懷疑被後母故意傳染肺結核，十七歲便英年早逝。張子靜實際上活到七十六歲。為什麼要這樣改寫呢？陵的死寫得很平淡，親人乍聞噩耗，表面上還若無其事，以戲劇張力來說簡直談不上是小說「高潮」。但張愛玲本來就要力避「三底門答爾」（sentimental），寫陵的死其實只是為了在小說收梢注入象徵意義，概括全書宗旨：藉著「抱著傳統的」弟弟的個體死亡，來象徵中國傳統文化的分崩離析——「雷峯塔倒下」[35]——所以她在敘述角色的個人命運時，其實已含蓄地隱寓著宏觀的歷史敘事和批判。《少帥》也是如此，本文第三部分將會補充。

張愛玲運用於《少帥》的寫作策略，這裏不妨總結一下：不管張愛玲多麼喜歡記實，她也要照顧市場，盡力令大眾接受，所以有時不得不簡化或改動史實；但即使基於市場考慮而需要改編部分歷史，正如上文所見，她也只是輕輕剪裁某些無關痛癢的枝葉，至於重要角色的生平、歷史大事的發展，以及能反映時代質地的軼聞，她都儘量忠於真實——因為實事自有其深沉的戲劇性，不必刻意加工也是上乘小說。

三、文學索隱

寫小說應當是個故事，讓故事自身去說明，比擬定了主題去編故事要好些。許多留到現在的偉大作品，原來的主題往往不再被讀者注意，因為事過境遷之後，原來的主題早已不使我們感覺興趣，倒是隨時從故事本身發見了新的啟示，使那作品成為永生的。就說《戰爭與和平》吧，托爾斯泰原來是想歸結到當時流行的一種宗教團體的人生態度的，結果卻是故事自身的展開戰勝了預定的主題。這作品修改七次之多，每次修改都使預定的主題受到了懲罰。終於剩下來的主題只佔插話的地位，而且是全書中安放得最不舒服的部分，但也沒有新的主題去代替它。因此寫成之後，托爾斯泰自己還覺得若有所失。和《復活》比較，《戰爭與和平》的主題果然是很模糊的，但後者仍然是更偉大的作品。至今我們讀它，依然一寸寸都是活的。現代文學作品和過去不同的地方，似乎也就在這一點上，不再那麼強調主題，卻是讓故事自身給它所能給的，而讓讀者取得他所能取得的。

——張愛玲〈自己的文章〉

上一部分比較小說與史實異同，能斬釘截鐵考證的，已說得差不多了。我本來就不打算為考證而考證，因為文學考證的功用，應該是協助讀者對文本獲得更深入的理解、更優雅的詮釋。你大可以嘗試詳考《少帥》裏每一件事的現實出處，但總有些地方無法客觀檢驗。我們只能在想像中沿著作者彎彎曲曲的意識長河流淌下去，希望跟她心內的桃花源不期而遇。但每人看事物的角度畢竟各有不同，這裏也只可以用我的角度來理解；而我自己也有很多不同的角度，如果真要滔滔不絕地解讀，便未免太喧賓奪主了，所以我只能選擇一兩個觀點討論。從那一兩個觀點出發，我儘量取我所能取的意義，至於那是否作者真要給予的，姑且存而不論。下文不算嚴格意義上的考證，大概只能按照王爾德的批評理論目之：評論是創作內的創作（creation within creation）。

讀者看張愛玲中、晚期的小說時，見她喋喋不休儘寫些日常瑣事，百思不得其解，很容易就不耐煩起來，其實她只是承繼了中國古典小說的含蓄傳統。看這時期的張愛玲，不是看她初出茅廬時為了趁早成名而堆砌的警句、比喻或意象，而是看她慘澹經營的伏筆和結構。含蓄，輕描淡寫，讀者初看不解，再看還是渾渾噩噩，但猛然省

少帥 —— 232

悟到什麼時，就會非常震動。這種作品要比《傳奇》的中、短篇難寫得多，也更難懂。《少帥》的特點，其實跟張愛玲眼中的《海上花》有共通處，「讀著像劇本，只有對白與少量動作」[36]，而為了重現對話的天然面目，甚至於刻意令人物的對白讀起來「散漫突兀」[37]——這時期她除了「參差對照」的寫法外，還強調中國古典小說「深入淺出」的優點，故事裏「人多，分散，只看見表面的言行，沒有內心的描寫」，「像密點印象派圖畫，整幅只用紅藍黃三原色密點，留給觀者的眼睛去拌和，特別鮮亮有光彩」，讀者讀小說時，「自己體會出來的書中情事格外生動，沒有古今中外的間隔」[38]。拌和的方式也許不是人人一致，但張愛玲肯定是期望觀者能自己體會的。我沒有辦法代表所有人，更不代表作者，我只能談談自己看到什麼。

要讀通《少帥》，我的方法就是設身處地去想：假如我是張愛玲，我又會寫什麼？明白了寫什麼，自然懂得她怎樣寫；反過來說，我也可以想想自己要怎樣寫，然後便可理解她決定寫什麼[39]。本部分將運用這個方法評析小說，首先探討《少帥》跟西方名著《愛麗絲夢遊仙境》的關係，再詳論周四小姐年齡的問題。

《少帥》和路易斯·卡洛爾（Lewis Carroll）的《愛麗絲夢遊仙境》（*Alice's Adventures in Wonderland*，以下簡稱《愛麗絲》）有什麼關係呢？首先要強調，張愛玲從未說過它們有關係，我只是在說我看到的關係。這問題牽涉兩部小說、兩位作者的比較，決不是三言兩語可以說得清的事。但略而不談也不妥當。了解兩書關係，不但有助闡釋《少帥》某些特殊文學意象，也讓我們看到張愛玲如何融會西方名著，令作品更廣泛地被接受。篇幅所限，我唯有盡量精簡，僅勾勒一些輪廓，留下的一大片空白，還有待高明之士填補。

張愛玲以英文寫《少帥》，目標市場在美國，寫作策略自然針對那裏的廣大讀者。能活用家傳戶曉的西方文學典故，觸發讀者想像，就可以讓他們有更深刻的共鳴，張愛玲是專業的英語作家，當然具備這種能力[40]，《少帥》內就有多個例證[41]。其中最重要的，是她對《愛麗絲》的暗中化用和指涉。例如在第四章，有一節從周四小姐角度寫她與少帥交歡時虛實交織的情境：

> 但是這張藍光勾畫的臉就在這裏，向她俯視微笑，嘴唇冷冰冰壓上來。他就在北京城這裏，鐘鼓延續著夜更，外頭聲音更大，黑夜的奇異與危機更覺迫切。古城後千迴百轉的時光兔窟和宮殿都在剎那間打通（For a moment it opened up the palaces and rabbit warrens of time behind the old city），重門一道一道訇然中開，連成一個洞穴或隧道。

"Rabbit warren" 本來是指相通的地下兔窟，又引申為巷陌縱橫交錯的地區或迷宮般的建築物，在《少帥》我認為是一語雙關，極難翻譯。留意 "...of time behind the old city"（直譯為「屬於古城背後的時間」）是 "the palaces and rabbit warrens"（直譯為「宮殿與兔窟」）的後置限定語，由於詞距相近的緣故，"rabbit warrens of time" 在讀者心中乍現的印象就是「時間的兔窟」。整段話在意象上慘澹經營，凝聚文字張力，務求在浪尖上的最後一句激起英語讀者的文學想像：現在跟古代的世界奇異地交疊著，彷彿是地下的時光兔窟在鐘鼓聲中被挖開了……

正是「時間的兔窟」一語，才令我聯想起《愛麗絲》的故事。《愛麗絲》那個通向奇境的「兔子洞」（rabbit-hole），當然有異於"rabbit warrens of time"，但我依然認為張愛玲是暗用了《愛麗絲》的典故，除了主觀感覺外，大致還有兩個理由。其一，兩部書中，兔子洞和時間的兔窟（或按其引申義理解）都通向某個奇境，加上字面和意思相近，自然容易觸發文學聯想。其二，兩部書還有其他共同元素，「兔子洞——時光兔窟」只是一例。至於其他共同元素，大致可以分三方面來說。

其一，《愛麗絲》和《少帥》的故事開端都是一個謎。《少帥》開場，府裏正在設宴，周四小姐混在一群女孩子當中，忽然街上有個男人把紙摺成同心方勝兒拋到樓上，紙上寫：「小姐，明日此時等我。」[42]男人是誰？小姐又是誰？第二天那男人也沒有來。這種開場不是很不可思議嗎？它在第一章結尾有一個變奏：朱五小姐叫周四小姐去找少帥，告訴他「有人在找他」，但大家都不知道是誰，也沒有時間地點。張愛玲在同一章先後兩次佈下疑陣，顯然希望讀者領略一點：《少帥》不單單是一部歷史小說，也不是普通的愛情故事，它要讀者抱著疑幻疑真的態度看待整個故事。《愛麗絲》開場，愛麗絲陪她姊姊坐在河邊百無聊賴，莫名其妙看見一頭有背心袋還會說話的兔子在趕路，兔子鑽進洞中，她又二話不說跟進去，整件事都不可理喻。這種莫名其妙的開場是《愛麗絲》的標記[43]，《少帥》似乎是模仿它的範式。

　　其二，《愛麗絲》和《少帥》都從女主角的觀點出發，她們被設定為旁觀者，自身和環境格格不入[44]，其他人的言行在她們都顯得有點荒誕、滑稽、難以理解。愛麗絲不懂得怎樣跟動物溝通，周四小姐記不住男人談話中的名字，內容也一知半解。例如在《愛麗絲》第三章，愛麗絲聽著老鼠、鴨子等動物的對話，覺得毫無趣味，後來見到牠們一本正經地賽跑、頒獎，又覺得非常可笑。《少帥》第二章，周四小姐覺得府裏男人的飯局很怪誕，圍坐著飲酒囂叫的人彷彿「圍成一圈的紅母牛被領進了某種比孔子還要古老的祭典之中」。跟愛麗絲的奇境一樣，周四眼中的男性世界很多時也是動物世界。

　　其三，《愛麗絲》和《少帥》最重要也最明顯的共同元素就是「魔法」。愛麗絲踏足奇境後，因喝下魔法藥水、吃了魔法餅乾而多次暴長暴縮，變成巨人或縮到極矮小。這些身材變化每一次都改變了她與周遭環境的力量對比。《少帥》的某些描寫也與這種魔幻情節暗合，例如第四章少帥與周四小姐定情之初：

　　　　在一個亂糟糟的世界，他們是僅有的兩個人，她要小心不踩到散落一地的棋子與小擺設。她感覺自己突然間長得很高，笨拙狼犺。

　　還是第四章，少帥跟周四親熱，兩人都彷彿拔高了成為神像：

彼此的臉咫尺天涯，都雙目低垂，是一座小廟的兩尊神像，巍巍然凸出半身在外，正凝望一個在黑暗中窺探肚臍上紅寶石洞眼的竊賊。

同一場，兩人交歡後平靜下來：

　　落地燈黃黯的光線下，這個陳設西洋家具的中式房間起了奇異的變化。熟悉的几案櫥櫃全都矮了遠了，貼牆而立，不加入戰鬥。

　　身材的放大縮小是相對於他人或外界而言的。家具變矮，便是自身變大了。還有一次縮放，出現在徐昭亭遇刺的第五章，也是交歡之後：

　　他們還是安全地身在半夜。他是一件她可以帶上床的玩具，枕邊把玩的一塊玉。

　　綜合這些例子，不難發現《少帥》的身材縮放與愛麗絲的體積變化有三個區別：其一，周四小姐只放大、不縮小，愛麗絲既放大又縮小；其二，周四小姐往往與少帥一同放大（除了在最後一例她憐愛地物化了男主角，讓他縮小），愛麗絲的縮放僅限於她自己；其三，以條件和效果而言，愛麗絲依賴外力（魔法飲品或食物）作出實質的縮放，但《少帥》那對情侶的體型變化只反映周四小姐的心理狀況，縮放的條件和效果僅存於周四的想像，並非客觀事實。

《少帥》裏的「魔法」究竟是什麼呢？第一章最後一段說周四小姐在帥府裏首次主動尋找自己暗戀多時的人，「她是棵樹，一直以來向著一個亮燈的窗戶長高，終於夠得到窺視窗內」——這是小說中周四小姐的第一次「變大」，但它主要隱喻漫長的成長和等待過程，還未算是「魔法」。到第三章，渴望再次見到少帥的周四小姐去了帥府：

　　　　今天變魔術的是個日本女人，才在上海表演過的，想必精彩。她們在少帥書房裏議論戲碼單，他好奇地瞥了她兩眼，然後幾乎再不看她。是頭髮的緣故。她頂著那個熱騰騰的雲海，沁出汗珠來。幾個月不見，她現在大了，他不再逗她了。朱家姊妹不在，其他女孩子也都沒什麼話說。他把別人從杭州捎給他的小玩意分贈她們。
　　　　「咱們走吧，魔術師該上場了，」一個女孩子說。
　　　　她正要跟著出去，他說：「這柄扇子是給你的。」
　　　　她展開那把檀香扇，端詳著。

　　這是小說的轉捩點，但交代得極含蓄——當然是作者故意的。周四小姐本來要去看魔法表演，這時少帥恰巧來了，戀愛也由此展開。這是一個戲劇性反諷（dramatic irony），劇中人尚且惘然，但敏感的觀眾已經心領神會：之後發生的愛情故事，其實就是周四小姐要去觀看的「魔法表演」。前面講的變形縮放，統統源於這種愛情魔法。然而誰是魔術師呢？以為是少帥的話，就是被作者誤導了（說到底寫作也是一場魔法表演）。只有魔術師自己才有資格承認根本沒有魔法。第五章少帥突然到周四小姐的家,她「見到他仗著權勢施展穿牆過壁的魔法」,禁不住興奮,隨即發現真實的少帥反不如她昔日的戀愛幻覺那麼動人:

在這房間裏她曾經對他百般思念,難道他看不出?常有時候她夜裏從帥府的壽宴回來,難得看到他一眼,然而感受卻那麼深刻,那麼跟她的舊房間格格不入,以致她只能怔怔望著窗子,彷彿在聽音樂。微弱的燈光映在黑漆塗金木框內空空的黑色窗格上,泛棕褐色。她不走到窗邊,只正對窗前站著,任一陣濕風像圍巾般拂拭她的臉,這時候現實的空氣吹著面頰,濃烈的感覺瀰漫全身,隨又鬆開,無數薄罳罳的圖案散去,歡樂的歌聲逐漸消散。相比那樣喧騰的感覺之河,他來到這裏的真身只像是鬼魂罷了。

〈第一爐香〉中,薇龍跟喬琪說:「我愛你,關你什麼事?千怪萬怪,也怪不到你身上去。」[45]這句名言也可以解釋周四小姐的想法。跟現實中很多人一樣,她只是愛上了愛情。她的幻想就是魔法之源,堂堂少帥不過是她的道具或助手,頂多是觀眾。愛情只有在幻想裏才是真實的,正如愛麗絲漫遊的奇境,也不過在她的夢中存在而已。

說《少帥》受路易斯・卡洛爾的《愛麗絲》影響,聽起來確實有點奇,但只要了解張愛玲的背景和比較她的其他作品,那影響其實一直都在。張愛玲八歲時同母親「搬到一所花園洋房裏,有狗,有花,有童話書」[46]——童話書她小時已看得極多,且印象甚深。她在一九三六年《鳳藻》校刊發表過一篇英文短故事，題作 "A Dream on the Journey"（〈書旅一夢〉），不但故事結構明顯襲自《愛麗絲》——場景更仿照《愛麗絲》第七章的「瘋茶會」——內文更明言「我步進一個奇境，那是連愛麗絲也未曾踏足過的奇境」（I walked into a mysterious wonderland, the wonderland that Alice had not gone in.）[47]。她寫《雷峯塔》時，已屢次用「魔法森林」、「魔法世界」來比喻琵琶母親的西式洋房[48]，可見《少帥》的「魔法」並非偶然、孤立的特例，而是構成作者內心世界的一大元素。又例如事物「縮放」的描述也不僅見於《少帥》，之前的《易經》和之後的《小團圓》也有[49]，只是沒有《少帥》那麼頻密。最後值得一提的是，《雷峯塔》有一節講琵琶懷疑自己的人生只是另一個人的夢，夢裏又疑心是另一場夢[50]，就不禁令人聯想起路易斯‧卡洛爾《走到鏡子裏》（*Through the Looking-Glass*）的情節：愛麗絲害怕自己只是紅國王的夢（參見第四、八兩章），結果發現是自己夢見了紅國王（第十二章）。兩部書都夢中有夢，夢覺難分，現實和幻想交錯成為地下迷陣，如同文本和文本也在互相指涉，每個細節都蔓生出一個宇宙，只要讀者稍一好奇，便會鑽進「連愛麗絲也未曾踏足過的奇境」，永遠找不到出路。

從兔子洞走出來後，現在讓我們討論一下周四小姐年齡的問題。為什麼要討論年齡這樣瑣屑的問題呢？普通讀者看小說，最關心情節、人物或文筆，鮮有留意小說背景年份、角色年紀之類等細節，更不會考究這些瑣碎數字的一致性。普通小說作者有見及此，自然也不會在讀者不關心的地方大做文章，否則就像莊子寓言所說，是向越人賣冠了。然而張愛玲是不一樣的小說讀者，舉兩個例：其一，讀

《紅樓夢》，她對年月了然於胸，作者偶有矛盾也瞞不過她，在〈紅樓夢未完〉便反駁周汝昌，指出書中年月並非絕對準確[51]；其二，讀《叛艦喋血記》，她仔細比較小說主角白顏跟他現實世界的原型海五德有什麼分別，更留意到作者故意把海五德年紀加大三歲，令角色「到了公認可以談戀愛的年齡，不至於辜負南海風光，使讀者失望。」[52]這裏可以見到張愛玲不是像某些自閉天才那樣下意識地記住所有數字，她之所以留意角色歲數，是因為她體會到小說作者的用心，知道「年紀設定」不過是寫作策略的一部分而已。看人家的小說也這麼不厭其煩講究歲數、年月，張愛玲自己寫小說就更不可能馬虎了[53]——何況她往往短、中篇也一寫經年，結果還要前後矛盾，這是無論如何也說不過去的事。

當年張愛玲寄《秧歌》給胡適品評，以考據見稱的胡當然不是普通讀者，立即發現角色歲數上的「矛盾」，於是回信給張說：「書中160頁『他爹今年八十了，我都八十一了』，與205頁的『六十八嘍』相差太遠，似是小誤。」但原來張是故意的，她回信解釋：「160頁譚大娘自稱八十一歲，205頁又說她六十八歲，那是因為她向兵士哀告的時候信口胡說，也就像叫化子總是說『家裏有八十歲老娘』一樣。我應當在書中解釋一下的。」[54]可見在張愛玲的小說裏，「矛盾」的、「不合理」的不一定就是疏忽，更可能是刻意為之。她期望讀者能反覆體會，在「破綻」中瞥見真相，借〈《紅樓夢魘》自序〉的話來說，「我不過是用最基本的邏輯，但是一層套一層，有時候也會把人繞糊塗了。〔……〕像迷宮，像拼圖遊戲，又像推理偵探小說。」

周四小姐的年齡，在小說中說得很清楚——簡直是太清楚，唯恐讀者錯過——但年齡背後的意義，卻需要讀者自己細心領略。為方便討論，我們不妨分兩個問題考察。第一個問題：小說為什麼要始於一九二五年？普通讀者看到這裏，大概已經禁不住疑惑：為什麼這個問題也會成為問題？要懂得問這問題，首先一定要知道張學良與趙一荻的相識經過——也許沒有多少讀者知道，但作者是不可能不知道的。我們只要知道「作者知道」，這就是一個非常有意義的問題了。

張學良與趙一荻的初遇年份、地點多年來眾說紛紜，我認為最貼近事實的，是採訪過張學良的郭冠英的說法：相識年份為一九二七，地點為蔡公館[55]。然而張愛玲只能依據道聽途說，《少帥》究竟參考了哪種講法呢？一直以來較流行的幾個說法是：張、趙相識年份為一九二六、二七或二八年，地點包括少帥的天津私邸、天津大華飯店和蔡公館[56]。張愛玲可能參考過《春秋》雜誌的一篇文章，當中說：「而她〔趙四〕與張學良相識的一歲，還正是二八盈盈十六之年。」[57]趙四小姐生於一九一二年，十六歲可以指一九二七或二八年。在《少帥》裏，周陳兩家關係特殊，周四在孩提時已認識少帥，所以不必等到二〇年代中期後才「初遇」，但作者也無妨安排他們在一九二六、二七或二八這三個較「熱門」或「真實」的年份開始相戀。結果很出人意表，張愛玲居然把這愛情故事推前到一九二五年——這是個非常「冷門」的年份，至少我在張愛玲可能參考過的史料中也找不到根據。這個改動似乎產生了一個恰巧跟《叛艦喋血記》相反的效果：令周四小姐在十三歲提早登場，推前「到了公認不宜談戀愛的年齡」。張愛玲為什麼要這樣做？

我有幾個想法。第一個很簡單，也是從寫作策略的角度考慮：以一九二五年開始，作者便有足夠空間把更多故事放進小說，令內容更豐富。例如第五章講徐樹錚（小說中叫徐昭亭）被馮玉祥（小說中叫馮以祥）刺殺，歷史上發生於一九二五年十二月三十日，若《少帥》一開始便晚於一九二五年，張愛玲便不太方便把薛觀瀾文章的小故事（參見本文第二部分）順時敘插進去了。但由現實中的十五六歲推前到小說的十三歲，大大影響了讀者對周四的觀感，女性那個成長階段的一年半載，可以有少女和女童的差別。作出如此重大的改動，張愛玲應該還有別的原因[58]。

一九六二年六月，史丹利‧庫柏力克（Stanley Kubrick）的電影《洛麗塔》（Lolita）在美國上映，戀童內容甚具爭議——原著小說的洛麗塔出場只十二歲，電影因題材太敏感，加大了兩年至十四歲——但美國票房報捷。張愛玲當然知道這部商業上成功的片子[59]。她是否基於某個市場考慮，有意將《少帥》寫成一個軍閥時代的洛麗塔故事呢？——當然周四小姐除了年紀，跟洛麗塔也沒有什麼可比之處。到了一九六三年，張愛玲正埋首寫作《少帥》，女權運動開始席捲美國[60]，女性角色被重新討論、定義。民國的十三歲女孩愛上比自己大十年的有婦之夫，義無反顧地談戀愛，不惜脫離家庭，體現了那些年的前衛的個人主義，而女孩年紀越小，對禁忌、權力的挑戰便越顯著，正好加強女權運動的主題。這當然是「gimmick」了。從這個角度看，在一九六三年的美國，寫一個十三歲中國女孩的愛情故事，還不乏性愛描寫，若能順著女性主義的潮流，這小說確實是前途無限的，說是「交運」也不為過。張愛玲也這樣想嗎？

我其實還有最後一個解釋。我因為覺得這個解釋更有啟發性，所以也寧願相信就是作者本意。小說以一九二五年開場，目的就是讓女主角能夠在十三歲登場——依作者標準，角色年齡應該符合史實——要她十三歲登場，其實是為了順理成章引用一首唐詩，帶出點題的「戲肉」[61]。這首詩見《少帥》第二章結尾：「娉娉嫋嫋十三餘，豆蔻梢頭二月初。春風十里揚州路，捲上珠簾總不如。」（是杜牧〈贈別〉詩，小說沒講出處。）作者緊接著寫：

> 從前揚州的一個妓女，壓倒群芳的美人與她竟然同齡，簡直不能想像。十三歲，照現代的算法不計生年那一歲的虛齡，其實只有十二。她覺得自己隔著一千年時間的深淵，遙望著彼端另一個十三歲的人。

這是第二章的收梢，也是一段點題的「戲肉」。可見周四小姐若非十三歲，那首唐詩便毫無用武之地。現在的問題是：何以非引此詩不可？它又如何幫助點題？首先要講講小說的其中兩個宗旨。其一，不管時代如何改變，女子始終承受著相同的命運，所以民國軍閥時代的周四小姐，即使跟唐朝揚州的妓女相隔超過一千年，也依然在共同命運的牽引下連成一線，一古一今互相對照。其二，現代女性既延續著古代女性的命運，那麼所謂「現代化」的意義便成為一個疑問了。這兩方面結合起來，張愛玲似有意借周四的個人命運，表達她對社會進步的懷疑，同時對「五四」的影響作出具有深刻意義的回應。

引用那首唐詩，無非為了合乎情理地舖排出第二章壓軸的周四小姐心聲，先藉此點破第一層宗旨，然後讓第二層在後文逐漸透露。

現在討論第一個宗旨，即周四小姐體現著古今女人的共同命運。張愛玲讀《紅樓夢》，留意到曹雪芹寫黛玉、晴雯的衣裙妝飾都含糊籠統，寫黛玉「就連面貌也幾乎純是神情〔……〕通身沒有一點細節，只是一種姿態，一個聲音。」曹雪芹這樣寫，是想借黛玉或晴雯描摹一個典型的女孩子，她沒有時間性，可以是任何時代的[62]。《少帥》的周四小姐也同樣面目模糊，沒有時間性。小說開場時，她混在一大群女孩子當中，作者從她的觀點寫其他女孩的衣著神態，對周四的描述就只有髮型──第三章開始時再一次寫髮型。第四章她往少帥一座房子幽會，下車時她「用頭巾掩面，像乘坐黃包車的女人要擋住塵沙」，然後「她帶著這張輕紗般的鴨綠色的臉走進去」；第六章周四小姐和少帥去西山飯店，「她戴著墨鏡，蒙著一層面紗」。張愛玲決不是單單為了劇情需要──幽會時要掩人耳目──才給她披上面紗的，作者還要藉此暗示女主角在男性世界喪失了主體性，因而面目模糊起來──這是小說家一石二鳥的高明手段，既服從情節需要，又暗寓了更高一層的意義。周四小姐這位相貌迷離的女子，不禁令人聯想起四○年代炎櫻設計的《傳奇》封面上有一個「非常好奇地孜孜往裏窺視」的現代女性人形[63]，沒有五官，彷彿也是一個典型。小說裏影射了很多歷史名人，張愛玲以紀實手法穿插他們的軼事，幾乎無一字無來歷，唯獨周四小姐則處處偏離史實，又面貌不清，可見作者本來就不是打算寫現實中的趙四。

周四小姐生於近代，千年來的中國傳統好像崩壞了，但過去所有女人的宿命還是如影隨形。什麼宿命呢？不外乎是婚姻、生育剝奪了個性和自由。第二章的收梢通過唐詩作出暗示，第四章結尾再來一個呼應，小說主題就更明顯了。當時少帥正要跟周四小姐一試雲雨：

> 他拉著她的手往沙發走去。彷彿是長程，兩人的胳臂拉成一直線，讓她落後了幾步。她發現自己走在一列裹著頭的女性隊伍裏。他妻子以及別的人？但是她們對於她沒有身分。她加入那行列裏，好像她們就是人類。

後來《小團圓》第八章寫之雍、九莉交歡也出現類似的隊伍，其中「五六個女人連頭裹在回教或是古希臘服裝裏」[64]，就不僅貫穿古今，且橫越中外，可見張愛玲要寫的不僅僅是中國女人，而是一切女人的典型，沒有時間性，也沒有地域性。這列女子對張愛玲顯然有特殊意義，否則也不會一而再地重寫了。另外值得一提的是，榮格（Carl Jung）主編的《人及其象徵》（*Man and His Symbols*）在一九六四年尾由Aldus Books出版，書裏收入韓德生（Joseph L. Henderson）的一篇文章，提到這個病例：某女子受過高等教育，婚後跟丈夫性生活不諧，有次做夢，看見自己置身一列像她那樣的年青女人隊伍當中，走在最前的那個被斷頭台砍下頭顱，後一個便挨次上前，如是者前仆後繼，她居然安心地繼續排隊，似乎願意承受同樣的命運[65]。《少帥》打字稿在一九六四年中已經完成，《人及其象徵》還未問世，也沒有證據顯示張愛玲看過這本書（儘管她肯定讀過榮格），但小說和病例中的「女性隊伍」毫無疑問有非常相近的寓意，似乎源於同一個集體潛意識的底層[66]。

通過周四小姐，張愛玲試圖總結所有女人的命運：不管什麼世代，女人只要能躋身那支由盤古初開以來一直為繁殖而捨身的行列，就會感到現世安穩；然而安全感的代價可能是要賠上個人靈魂，融入一個無名無姓的集體位格。這種女人普遍面對的異化過程，最容易體現於機械化的性交 （參見《少帥》第四章）；張愛玲為了凸顯這種女性處境，甚至不惜花上不合乎「歷史小說」應有比例的篇幅來寫周、陳的床戲，可知她真正偏重的是什麼。周四小姐在第二章末把自己跟揚州妓女混為一談，除了藉以點明小說宗旨外，本身也是一種修辭手法，所謂「預敘法」（prolepsis）——預兆了她和少帥的床戲。但作者要刻畫的決不是什麼魚水之歡，而是性愛過程中女人自我異化的荒謬感和悲哀。例如第四章寫周四小姐低頭看自己被吸吮過的一邊胸部時，從她角度所見的竟然是一個幾何圖形（「緩緩平伏的蒼白小三角形」），非常詭異。然而人類經驗中最極端、最普遍的異化畢竟是死亡，所以它往往被用作性交的隱喻。《少帥》裏的床戲根本是一幕幕有聲有色的恐怖片，說到底就是因為作者旨在寫的不僅僅是性交，而是作為異化隱喻的死亡。在張愛玲筆下，這種性愛中的死亡大概有兩個含義：其一是個人身分的死亡——體現於「女性隊伍」以及一些性交隱喻中，如第六章形容床上的少帥為「一隻獸在吃她」；其二是「生孩子生出死亡來」（見張愛玲〈談女人〉）的那種具有普遍性的死亡。

有必要解釋一下第二種死亡，它也許跟張愛玲小說內屢次出現的「神視性」情景有關[67]。我們知道大自然的質料是有限的，只能讓生命在不同個體上以此消彼長的形式流轉，一雞死方有一雞鳴，於是長久以來，死亡禁忌和性禁忌（跟生育相關）總是分不開的[68]。喜歡人類學的張愛玲自然知道這種聯繫，於是第四章寫少帥跟周四親熱，就憑空出現一群彷彿在監視她的「木雕鳥」[69]，第五章寫斬首時出現的凶神也是「一隻大鳥」——前者大概象徵生育，後者象徵死亡，兩者說穿了都不過是原始部族圖騰信仰的變奏。這樣先後兩處運用「鳥」這個古老圖騰的意象，只要讀者自己用眼睛稍為拌和一下，不難發現作者正是藉此暗示性與死亡的內在關係。換一個角度解釋這種關係，就是古今女人共同命運的一體兩面：正面是結婚、生育，彷彿充滿飛揚的生命力；反面是讓自己物化，淪為繁殖機器，只作為慾望對象而存在[70]，把一生都貢獻出來後，不過平白延續了物種，令世世代代的人可以生了又死，死了又生[71]。

　　女人的命運古今如一，是因為男人建立的世界其實並無二致。質疑歷史沿革、社會變遷的意義，拆穿「五四」後的所謂進步，我認為是《少帥》小說的第二層宗旨。這種略帶悲觀的懷疑態度（未至於是主義）其實是一種所羅門王式智慧。早在四〇年代，張愛玲已被舊約《傳道書》的厭世文辭所震動，而《少帥》的第二層宗旨，僅一句「太陽之下無新事」似乎已足夠概括[72]。正因為「太陽之下無新事」，所以一千年前的揚州妓女跟周四小姐才會承受共同的命運。在歷史的大舞台上，不同年代的人無意識地扮演著相同的角色，沒完沒了地搬演著同一齣戲，其實一切沒變[73]。不單是現代與古代的界線模糊了，文明和野蠻、進步和守舊也統統不再涇渭分明。於是《少帥》

第四章寫日暮的鐘鼓聲，周四小姐「聽上去像古時候」；第五章敘述「陪斬」那故事後，作者更直截了當寫道：

> 雖然這故事早於他的時代，她不知怎麼並不願意告訴他。那一定是吳蟠湖的時候。現在做法肯定不一樣了吧？可是一說起其實什麼都不會改變，他就難免惱火。

張愛玲在蘊釀《少帥》時曾跟鄺文美說：「我有個模糊的念頭土人與故事結局有關」[74]。軍閥時代的愛情故事結局居然跟土人有關？乍看來實在匪夷所思。但既然小說的一個旨趣是「太陽之下無新事」，人類社會不脫男女大欲的本能[75]，而那一列「女子隊伍」也自開天闢地以來便綿綿不絕，那麼即使張愛玲把女人的命運追溯到洪荒時代（第四章寫親熱場面時就提到返祖現象和穴居時代的新婚夜），其實也很符合小說的宗旨。至於土人將以什麼形式呈現呢？周四小姐會像一九六一年訪台的張愛玲般上花岡山觀看阿美族豐年祭？原始部族在她的「神視」或想像中顯現？抑或僅以畫外音交代？我們便不得而知了。

一九六五年，張愛玲為《世界作家簡介・一九五〇至一九七〇》寫過一篇英文自白。自白的寫作時間跟《少帥》很接近，其中對歷史和社會的看法顯然有助我們了解小說這方面的旨趣。下面節錄高全之的中譯本，我修訂了其中一句[76]：

> 然而，中國曾有腐敗與虛空，以及相信某種東西的需要。在

向內生長的近代儒學主義最後的崩潰之中，有些中國人在盛行的物質虛無主義裏尋求出路，相信了共產主義。就許多其他人而言，共產黨統治也比回轉到舊秩序要好得多〔按：原文爲"To many others Communist rule is also more palatable for being a reversion to the old order"，我認爲該譯作「對其他很多人來說，共產黨統治是向舊有秩序的一種回歸，因此也更容易被接受」〕，不過是以較大的血親──國家──來取代家庭，編納了我們這個時代無可爭議的宗教：國家主義。我最關切兩者之間那幾十年：荒廢、最終的狂鬧、混亂，以及焦灼不安的個人主義的那些年。在過去千年與未來或許幾百年之間，那幾十年短得可憐。然而中國未來任何變化，都可能萌芽於那淺嘗即止的自由，因爲在美國圍堵政策之外，還有其他更多因素孤立了中國。

張愛玲最關切的「荒廢、狂鬧、混亂」的幾十年，正是《少帥》時代背景，而陳叔覃和周四小姐兩位主角也確實體現了「焦灼不安的個人主義」。小說前七章不斷渲染歷史循環，女人的命運在同一主調上重覆，傳統的幽靈還在中國徘徊，但第七章結束時卻留下一條光明的結尾，彷彿變化還是可能的：

> 他已結束了軍閥時代。下一次南行，太太們也與他同坐一架私家飛機。終於是二十世紀了，遲到三十年而他還帶著兩個太太，但是他進來了。中國進來了。

儘管《少帥》沒有寫完，在這裏戛然而止，但這段話的作用是很明顯的，就是為往後中國的種種變化揭開序幕，暗中呼應著〈自白〉那句「中國未來任何變化，都可能萌芽於那淺嘗即止的自由」。然則《少帥》發展下去，也許會有更多筆墨寫中共的崛起以及各種意識形態之間的張力。但即使張愛玲要寫變化，大概也不會像拉奏凡啞林般讓人間的一切也向前流走，而是像胡琴般遠兜遠轉，「話又說回來了」，所以在第七章那個充滿光明的收梢中也不無反諷——不忘提醒讀者「過去」並沒有真的過去，「他還有兩個太太」。她筆下的「社會進步」很可能就如她在一九六三年發表的〈A Return to the Frontier〉（〈重訪邊城〉英文版本）最後一段所說：「進兩步，退一步——毛澤東說過這是他前進的方式。是跳舞也好，遊行也好，老百姓竭力地慢慢向前走著，希望比折磨自己的人活得更長。」[77]

可見歷史儘管一遍又一遍重覆，且進且退的前進還是可能的。然而人類社會在千迴百轉之後，到頭來又會否是「其實什麼都不會改變」呢？果真如此，張愛玲也不會徹底悲觀。人生的虛無終究和人間的色彩參差對照著，正如上文所論，只要加入那支在過去已存在千萬年的隊伍，還是會覺得現世安穩，也許就只有這樣跟古老的歷史一起「迴環往復」地活著，我們才能確保「比折磨自己的人活得更長」。這裏我不由得想起博爾赫斯的話：「在飛揚的年代，若設想人生只是一個不變的常數，是可以令人悲傷或憤怒的；而在下沉的年代（如現在），它卻帶來希望，因為任何恥辱、災禍或獨裁者都不能令我們枯竭。」[78]

拉雜地討論了小說的兩個宗旨，說得迂迴曲折，起點還是那個問題：小說為什麼要始於一九二五年？（另一個問法是：為什麼周四小姐要在十三歲登場？）答案在前文已經解釋了，再總結一句：不是一九二五年，周四小姐就不是十三歲；不是十三歲，唐詩中的揚州妓就不能喚起同齡的周四小姐共鳴，讓一古一今平行對照；沒有這古今對照，小說的主題便黯淡了。我這樣一層套一層地說下去，讀者也許忘了本來要考究的，始終還是周四小姐的年齡。我說過這件事要分兩個問題探索，現在輪到第二個了。上一個問題只要仔細分析文本，已經可以得到合情合理的解答；但現在這個問題非常隱秘，它不屬於《少帥》，而是指向作者本人，所以這問題不是用來闡釋故事，而是在說故事外的故事。我要問的是：為什麼在小說第七章少帥喬裝歸來時，周四小姐是十七歲而不是十六歲？

我們已知道周四小姐在一九二五年是十三歲，跟趙四小姐相同，張愛玲對歲數、年份向來是嚴謹的[79]；而我在第二部分也已說明，歷史大事的發展不牽涉「市場考慮」，不屬於作者改動的範疇。由此可以斷言：一，周四小姐年齡的增長，與趙四小姐必然是同步的；二，小說世界的歷史進程，與現實世界應該是一致的。依據小說這個內在邏輯，我們有如下推論：第五章以徐昭亭被殺開始，就是一九二六年頭，周四小姐那時也必然只有十三餘歲，即比第一章時僅大數月；第六章開始時，少帥「打贏了南口之戰」，在過陰曆年前回來了，可知是一九二七年頭；同一章過中秋節，是在少帥率兵河南、寧漢分裂、老帥陳祖望自封大元帥後，可知那依然是一九二七年。就在這個中秋節的第二天，周四和少帥見面，周問他孫夫人的妹妹（即現實中的宋美齡）多少歲，對話如下：

「她多大了？」

「跟我差不多大。」

「她不會已經二十七了吧？」

「我不知道，她自己沒講過。洋化的女人不提自己年齡的。」

　　簡言之，張愛玲（或小說裏的周四小姐）把一九二七年的少帥算作二十七歲。張學良生於一九〇一年六月，到一九二七年中秋，實歲二十六，小說這裏用的顯然是虛歲算法，準則跟第二章按實歲計算周四小姐的年齡不一致。但這種矛盾還是可以解釋的，甚至是故意的：在那個新舊交替的時代，實歲是所謂「現代的算法」（modern reckoning，見第二章尾），虛歲是舊式的算法，兩者可以並行不悖。在小說第七章，這種計算準則的不一致又再次出現：這時老帥被日軍炸死，少帥喬裝歸來，按史實必然是一九二八年；若第二章周四小姐在一九二五年是實歲十三，那麼到了第七章一九二八年，作者順理成章應該說她是十六歲。然而第七章卻這樣寫：

　　他歷劫歸來，這對於她是他們倆故事的一個恰當結局，從此兩人幸福快樂地生活在一起。童話往往是少年得志的故事，因此這種結局自有幾分道理。在那最敏感的年齡得到的，始終與你同在。只有這段時間，才可以讓任何人經營出超凡的事物，而它們也將以其獨有的方式跟生命一樣持久。十七歲她便實現了不可能的事，她曾經想要的全都有了。

張愛玲對角色年齡、事件年月向來錙銖必較，儘管十六歲（實歲）、十七歲（虛歲）都說得通，但按文理畢竟是十六歲較妥當，現在卻刻意把那人生「最敏感的年齡」（that impressionable age）強調為十七歲，這微妙的年齡調整我認為大有文章。從寫作策略的角度分析，十六歲或十七歲對一般讀者根本沒有分別，所以要解釋這個調整，我們要訴諸另一個角度——張愛玲似乎犯了一個佛洛伊德式筆誤，有意無意披露了自己內心深處的幻想，即改寫個人歷史的幻想。

作者早在第四章已埋下兩處伏筆（不熟悉張愛玲的西方讀者應該看不出弦外之音）。其一是周四小姐的內心自白：「她希望自己被囚禁，那麼他就會為了她而來」。其二是她和少帥對話：

> 「現在馬上說什麼是沒用的，你年紀太小。只會害你被囚禁。」
> 「你說過你會帶鎗來救我。」

這些話跟「十七歲」有關係嗎？在小說裏的確毫無關係。但對照一下張愛玲本人的成長經歷，那關係便非常明顯。一九三七年張愛玲十七歲，因為跟後母口角而被父親毒打並拘禁半年，其間得了沉重的痢疾，幾乎病死[80]。那大概是她一生中最黑暗、最接近死亡的日子了。對一般讀者「十七歲」可能沒有什麼意義，但在張愛玲而言卻是靈魂深處最不能磨滅的傷痕。在自傳性小說《小團圓》、《雷峯塔》裏，每提到「十七歲」時，總籠罩著陰森森的死亡黑影[81]。

懂得了這重內心曲折，我們讀到周四小姐幻想自己被囚禁而少帥來拯救她時，不期然便會覺得這是作者本人的心願。換言之，這是她對不諳其生平的異鄉讀者有意無意間吐露的「假面告白」。果真如此，我們便可以更深入地理解周四小姐的觀點，因為那根本是作者自己的投射。張愛玲不喜歡父親，代入了周四小姐的角色後也渴望少帥跟她同一陣線，於是小說第六章便寫周四想像陳叔覃背叛父親——說穿了也不過是作者的少女狂想曲變奏罷了——但張愛玲到底是清醒的，最後還是通過周四的心聲揭穿自己：

> 造反的皇太子是什麼下場？關押，賜死——面朝紫宮叩首謝恩，喝下毒酒自盡。無論他做了什麼，那也表明他是男子漢，不僅是某人的兒子。也許她還有點悲哀，因為他做了不會為她而做的事。

寫《少帥》時，張愛玲似乎幻想有這樣一位英雄，在她十七歲被囚禁時能夠千山萬水趕來，克服重重險阻拯救她，實現不可能的事，讓她得到她所希冀的一切。我這個猜想固然是無法證實的，但它至少有效解釋了小說與歷史的另一處分歧。小說裏周四小姐終於得到父親允許，可以跟少帥一起生活，「從此兩人幸福快樂」，是童話式大團圓結局；但事實是，趙慶華在趙四私奔後一連五天在報上刊登啟事，把她從祠堂中除名。也許可以替作者辯解，小說內兩家是世交，周父妥協是合理反應。但我的猜想也能自圓其說：張愛玲既代入了周四小姐，希望借她的美滿結局改寫個人歷史，那麼她最需要的自然不是人家的史實，而是自己的童話了。懂得她這個想法的人大概也會詫異，當時已四十多歲的張愛玲居然保留了一份屬於十三歲女孩的、充滿夢幻的童真[82]。也許只有在一部寫給洋人看的中國歷史小說裏，她才會如此肆無忌憚流露自己的少女夢，一個眾所周知在現實世界沒有實現，因此也格外苦澀的夢。《雷峯塔》裏，童年的琵琶總希望能無窮無盡的一次次投胎，「變成另一個人」，「她並沒有特為想當什麼樣的人——只想要過各種各樣的生活」[83]。成為別人，過不同的生活，享受無窮的可能性，這樣的人生就再也用不著抉擇，也不會有恨事了。中年的張愛玲儘管飽經世故，但童年時的幻想和渴望依然在她的小說裏時見端倪。

有人問過曾樸他的小說是不是事實的，他答道：「當然是事實。但情節有變換或顛倒，時間不盡同真事吻合，這是各小說家自序體的小說的常例，祇為所重的在情感，所以寫情感處全是真的，幾乎沒些子虛偽。」（參見曾樸《病夫日記》）完全可借來解釋張愛玲的寫法。如此說來，《少帥》雖是歷史小說，但它通過女主角所表達的情感，則很大程度是作者本人的。例如書中描寫陳、周床笫之事，任何看過《小團圓》或《今生今世》的人都會立即發現，張愛玲寫的只是自己和胡蘭成，甚至在語言、意象運用方面，《少帥》和《小團圓》也有不少相似或相同處[84]。事實上，張愛玲在八〇年代跟宋淇重提《少帥》時，已明確地說「這故事雖好，在我不過是找個accept-able framework寫『小團圓』，能用得上的也不多」[85]。宋以朗在《雷峯塔》、《易經》的引言中節錄了一九五七年九月五日張愛玲致宋淇書，談到自己寫《雷峯塔》、《易經》的計畫[86]：

新的小說第一章終於改寫過，好容易上了軌道，想趁此把

第二章一鼓作氣寫掉它，告一段落，因爲頭兩章是寫港戰爆發，第三章起轉入童年的回憶，直到第八章再回到港戰，接著自港回滬，約佔全書三分之一。此後寫胡蘭成的事，到一九四七年爲止，最後加上兩三章作爲結尾。

但結果《雷峯塔》和《易經》都沒有寫胡蘭成。我們知道《雷峯塔》、《易經》和《少帥》是她在一九五七至一九六四那幾年間先後創作的，因此大可推斷：在構思《雷峯塔》和《易經》的過程中，胡蘭成的事早已在腦海裏重溫過了，輪到寫《少帥》時，這些片段便「順著下意識」（張愛玲語，見水晶〈蟬〉）滑進陳、周的故事之內。當然這不可能是完全無意識的滑入，但也不是說她一開始便有預謀地、有計畫地把《少帥》寫成暗藏「張愛玲情史」的歷史小說。現實總不會那麼黑白分明。

想要了解真相，不妨回到創作的零點思考這個問題：張愛玲爲什麼要寫少帥與趙四這題材呢？必然是當中有些令她震動的地方了。不難發現，張學良有三方面跟胡蘭成很相似。其一，從事政治；其二，生性風流；其三，年紀都比女方大十年以上——少帥比趙四大十一年，而胡蘭成則比張愛玲年長十四歲。當然胡、張最明顯的矛盾是一個親日、一個抗日。但張愛玲對這類意識形態是淡漠的，所以還是讓胡蘭成投射到以張學良爲原型的角色身上。至於趙四小姐，我認爲是她在愛情上的奇遇觸動了張愛玲。趙四說過沒有西安事變，她跟少帥早就完了[87]，而張愛玲也自言小說的要點「是終身拘禁成全了趙四」[88]，彷彿趙四就是現實裏的白流蘇，且成全她的還不單單是一個城市的陷落，而是牽涉整個中國的興亡。通過這幾重想像中的關係，趙四和少帥的「童話故事」於張愛玲來說便有格外切身的意義。

張愛玲說：「在文字的溝通上，小說是兩點之間最短的距離。就連最親切的身邊散文，是對熟朋友的態度，也總還要保持一點距離。只有小說可以不尊重隱私權。但是並不是窺視別人，而是暫時或多或少的認同，像演員沉浸在一個角色裏，也成為自身的一次經驗。」[89]所謂「認同」、「沉浸」，就是張愛玲對宋淇說過的「iden-tification」[90]，似乎是她寫小說時的「方法演技」。考慮到這種創作方法，以及她在腦海裏跟角色建立的各樣關係，我們不難理解作者的少女夢何以會滑入「歷史」了。也許她在動筆寫《少帥》前，一心一意只想寫歷史小說，敘述人家的傳奇，只是越寫下去便越入戲，結果更不能自拔地要自己粉墨登場，躍身這充滿魔力的歷史舞台上[91]。那本來是「絕對不能夠走進去的，然而真的走進去了」（〈談音樂〉語），張愛玲就像王佳芝般臨陣變節，既出賣了趙四，也懲罰了主題。

正因為作者不自禁搶了角色的戲，自然也就「無法從趙四的觀點去看」張學良了[92]。能力所及的就只有「偏重愛情故事」，那是她的第一手經驗，最鮮活的素材。從這個角度看，不妨說《雷峯塔》、《易經》和《少帥》才是張愛玲六〇年代的「自傳」三部曲。七〇年代她寫《小團圓》，坦蕩蕩講她與胡蘭成的故事，已經豁出去了，於是那部未完的，「影射」自己的《少帥》便難免成為雞肋。按照本文第一部分所述，她最後一次表示有興趣完成《少帥》，是一九七一年跟水晶見面的時候，當時《小團圓》還未動筆[93]。到八〇、九〇年代跟宋淇重提此書，她已明言對張學良久已失去興趣了。當中的內心曲折，自然不必跟宋淇在信裏細說，但假如我這裏的解讀沒錯，結果也就只能如此了。《少帥》若能寫畢，那它應該是一部規模更大也更具雄心的〈傾城之戀〉，也許依然隱括著同一個啟示：現實是不可理喻的，沒有人知道哪個是因，哪個是果，全世界的歷史被改寫，就只為了讓一個女人守住風流的丈夫。

張愛玲說自己寫作時總是非常高興[94]，也許是因為她能夠在文字裏不斷輪迴，成為各式各樣的人，不論是歷史、小說或電影的世界也可任意穿越。在《少帥》的世界，張愛玲既是神遊於軍閥間的愛麗絲，也是迷倒大英雄的洛麗塔，更是被歷史成全了婚姻的趙一荻，灰撲撲的人生在剎那間幻化成紅的藍的童話故事。在這樣一部難產的小說裏，她至少開闢了一個平行宇宙，在那裏她過著不一樣的人生，異常快樂——這種快樂也特別叫人傷心。

註釋：

1.Dick是指理查德・麥卡錫（Richard McCarthy），上世紀五〇年代派港，任職美國駐港總領事館新聞處處長。張愛玲申請移居美國時，就由麥卡錫作保證人。

2.張愛玲一九六八年發表的〈憶胡適之〉，收錄了她一九五五年寫給胡適的信，兩處用到「東南亞」：「最初我也就是因為《秧歌》這故事太平淡，不合我國讀者的口味——尤其是東南亞的讀者——所以發奮要用英文寫它。〔……〕還有一本《赤地之戀》，是在《秧歌》以後寫的。因為要顧到東南亞一般讀者的興味，自己很不滿意。」所謂東南亞一般讀者，當然泛指星、馬、泰等地的華僑，但張愛玲當時的主要市場還有台灣，有理由相信她說東南亞時也把台灣包括在內。

3.關於《鄭和》小說，參見宋以朗〈張愛玲沒有寫的文章（上）〉，刊於二〇一三年七月二日《南方都市報》。

4.參見水晶〈蟬——夜訪張愛玲〉，收入《張愛玲的小說藝術》，台北大地，二〇〇〇年。

5.參見馮睎乾〈張愛玲的電影劇本〉，收入《張愛玲：電懋劇本集》，香港電影資料館，二〇一〇年。

6. 參見宋以朗〈《雷峯塔》/《易經》引言〉，張愛玲著，趙丕慧譯《雷峯塔》/《易經》，台北皇冠，二〇一〇年。

7.參見司馬新《張愛玲與賴雅》第八章，台北大地，一九九六年，第一五八頁。

8.英文原文："...we'll be going to N.Y. together early next year as soon as luck has turned. I'm in desperate haste to keep my date in desting[y] in '63—crazy talk but, my only mental prop—by finishing the Young Marshall novel around next spring. It's now or never & I'm in a working mood." 參見高全之〈倦鳥思還——張愛玲寫給賴雅的六封信〉，《張愛玲學》，台北麥田出版，二〇〇八年，第三九六至三九八頁。

9. 參見〈張愛玲語錄〉：「從前胡ＸＸ就說我寫的東西『有鬼氣』。我的確有一種才能，近乎巫，能夠預感事情將如何發展。我覺得成功的一定會成功。」收入宋以朗主編《張愛玲私語錄》，台北皇冠，二〇一〇年，第五〇至五一頁。 關於張愛玲的「預感」，詳見這條語錄的附注，《張愛玲私語錄》第五六至五七頁。

10. Rodell即Marie Rodell（瑪莉‧羅德爾），是張愛玲在美國的出版代理人。

11. 一九六六年九月，張愛玲往俄亥俄州牛津（Oxford, Ohio）的邁阿密大學（Miami University）作駐校作家，為期七個半月。所謂「對學生『講話』」，參見一九六六年十月十二日張愛玲致劉紹銘書：「今晚我到Badgley〔巴傑利，邁阿密大學教授〕家吃飯，別人並沒來找我。有兩處學生找我演講，我先拖宕著，因為Badgley說我不如少講個一兩次，人多點，節省時間。」此信見劉紹銘〈落難才女張愛玲〉，收入《張愛玲的文字世界》，台北九歌，二〇〇七年。

12. 司馬新《張愛玲與賴雅》第九章說，一九七一年張愛玲與水晶
會面時，「她已寫完《少帥》」，此處有誤。見《張愛玲與賴
雅》，台北大地，一九九六年，第一八一至一八二頁。

13. 張愛玲在「多年前信中」提及她正在寫的一部長篇英文小說（指
《雷峯塔》與《易經》），的確也說過內容相近的話，但沒有用
「三字經」一語。一九五七年九月五日張愛玲寫信給鄺文美與宋
淇說：「這小說場面較大，人頭雜，所以人名還是採用『金根』
『金花』式的意譯，否則統統是Chu Chi Chung式的名字，外國
人看了頭昏。」

14. 「坐大轎車的自由主義者」含貶義，尤指那些一邊大談自由平等
博愛，一邊卻享受著特權的人（例如他們會坐豪華大轎車四出招
搖，不理會耗油量大、佔的空間又多）。

15. 據張愛玲那本具自傳性質的小說《雷峯塔》所記，她小時候已聽
見父親（小說中叫沈榆溪）跟客人大講軍閥的事：「榆溪只和客
人清談，在室內繞圈子，大放厥詞，說軍閥的笑話，叫他們老
張、小張、老馮、老蔣。琵琶想聽，政治卻無聊乏味。」參見張
愛玲著，趙丕慧譯《雷峯塔》，台北皇冠，二〇一〇年，第二〇
九至二一〇頁。

16. 本文所引《少帥》文字，皆依據鄭遠濤的中譯本。

17.本文簡介的主要參考資料為：一，張友坤、錢進、李學群編《張學良年譜》，社會科學文獻出版社，二〇〇九年；二，唐德剛《張學良口述歷史》，台北遠流，二〇〇九年；三，張學良《雜憶隨感漫錄——張學良自傳體遺著》，台北歷史智庫，二〇〇二年。

18.參見唐德剛〈論三位一體的張學良將軍〉，收入唐德剛《張學良口述歷史》，台北遠流，二〇〇九年。

19.參見宋以朗主編《張愛玲私語錄》，台北皇冠，二〇一〇年，第五四頁。

20.參見宋以朗主編《張愛玲私語錄》，台北皇冠，二〇一〇年，第一八四頁。

21.「今聖歎」是程綏楚（一九一六至一九九七，字靖宇）的一個筆名。他是湖南衡陽人，一九五〇年移居香港。六〇年代初，在《新生晚報》副刊上以「丁世五」為筆名，開設了一個專欄〈儒林清話〉，張愛玲看到的很可能是這專欄。現在繁、簡版的《張愛玲私語錄》皆把「今聖歎」誤印作「金聖嘆」。

22.高拜石《新編古春風樓瑣記（壹）》，北京作家出版社，二〇〇三年，第一四〇至一四一頁。

23. 本文第一部分引一九六三年九月二十日張愛玲致鄺文美與宋淇書，說：「前天昨天又接連收到春秋和兩本書，裏面的材料好到極點，而且來得正是時候，替我打破了兩個疑團，我簡直興奮過度。」可證張愛玲確實看過《春秋》雜誌。薛觀瀾的〈馮玉祥為什麼要殺徐樹錚？〉分四期在《春秋》連載，白金漢宮園遊會一事載第三期。此外，《少帥》至少還有兩處顯然參考過《春秋》：其一是《少帥》第二章講革命黨人召集會議，欲推周四小姐之父為都督，老帥到場護周，以鎗拍案，說自己「不同情革命」，這是參考了射陵外史〈張作霖——張學良父子（二）〉，載一九五九年一月十六日第三十七期《春秋》雜誌；其二是《少帥》第六章講有人要損毀碧雲寺孫中山遺體，則參考了慕意〈葉恭綽與國民黨的關係〉，載一九五九年一月十六日第三十七期《春秋》雜誌。

24. 參見唐德剛《張學良口述歷史》第四章，台北遠流，二○○九年，第一六四至一六八頁。

25. 如第二章寫袁世凱（小說只稱之為「首任大總統」）變身大蛤蟆一事，乃坊間習聞的傳說，難以推斷張愛玲從哪裏讀到或聽到。丁中江有《北洋軍閥史話》一書，一九六二年起在台北《大華晚報》逐日連載，第一章「北洋時代」就提到袁世凱這則怪事，張愛玲也許看過，姑且引錄於下：

　　民國六年馮國璋曾說過一段掌故：據說真正促成袁世凱要做

洪憲皇帝的，是袁身邊端茶捶腿的小廝。原來袁世凱每日習慣午睡兩小時，睡醒後必先喝茶，使用一隻最心愛的玉製茶杯。有一天小廝端茶時突見袁所睡的床上躺著一隻大癩蛤蟆，這一驚，失手便把玉杯跌落地上，當然四分五裂。幸好沒有驚醒袁世凱，小廝嚇得哭了起來，慌忙把地上掃淨，便去找袁世凱的一位老家人請教。老家人見小廝嚇得哭哭啼啼，便動了惻隱之心，乃教他如此這般。待袁世凱午覺睡醒，小廝換了一個茶杯奉茶，袁接過來大為疑惑，便問道：「玉杯呢？」小廝戰戰兢兢地回答：「求大人開恩，小的打碎了。」袁大怒：「打碎了，這還了得。」小廝眼淚已流了出來，細聲地說：「小的端茶進來時，看見床上睡的不是大人。」袁厲聲問：「是什麼？」小廝說：「是一條五爪金龍橫躺在床上，小的嚇了一大跳，一不小心便把玉杯跌碎了。」袁的面色突然好轉，聲調也緩和下來說：「胡說，不許在外邊講，讓我聽見打斷你的狗腿。」袁說完便在抽屜裏拿出十塊洋錢給小廝說：「這個賞給你。」小廝接了賞錢，歡天喜地而去，一場天大的禍事便如此這般化為烏有。

26. 張愛玲《對照記》圖四：「多年後我才恍惚聽見說他是最後一個兩江總督張人駿。一九六〇初，我在一個美國新聞記者寫的端納傳（《中國的端納》，*Donald of China*）上看到總督坐籮筐縋出南京圍城的記載，也還不十分確定是他，也許因為過去太熟悉了，不大能接受。書中寫國民政府的端納顧問初到中國，到廣州去見他，那時候他是兩廣總督。端納貢獻意見大發議論，他一味笑著直點頭，帽子上的花翎亂顫。那也是清末官場敷衍洋人的常態。」參見張愛玲《對照記》，台北皇冠，二〇一〇年，第一四頁。

27.引用的頁碼以這版本為準：Selle, Earl Albert, *Donald of China*
（New York: Harper & Brothers, 1948）.

28.參見〈談看書〉，張愛玲《惘然記》，台北皇冠，二〇一〇年，
第六五至六六頁。

29.對於寫作策略，張愛玲向來是非常自覺的。她在一九四四年發表
的〈論寫作〉已經說：「將自己歸入讀者群中去，自然知道他
們所要的是什麼。要什麼，就給他們什麼，此外再多給他們一
點別的〔……〕作者可以儘量給他所能給的，讀者儘量拿他所能
拿的。」參見張愛玲《華麗緣》，台北皇冠，二〇一〇年，第一
〇三頁。在〈關於〈傾城之戀〉的老實話〉又說：「寫〈傾城之
戀〉，當時的心理我還記得很清楚。除了我所要表現的那蒼涼的
人生的情義，此外我要人家要什麼有什麼，華美的羅曼斯，對
白，顏色，詩意，連『意識』都給預備下了」。參見張愛玲《華
麗緣》，台北皇冠，二〇一〇年，第二二七頁。事實上，張愛玲
自己也曾經像我現在分析《少帥》般分析人家的小說，如三〇年
代的美國暢銷書《叛艦喋血記》，她便在〈談看書後記〉中「鍥
而不捨的細評起來」，她解釋：「原因是大家都熟悉這題材，把
史實搞清楚之後，可以看出這部小說是怎樣改，為什麼改，可見
它的成功不是偶然的。同時可以看出原有的故事本身有一種活
力，為了要普遍的被接受，而削足適履。它這一點非常典型性，

不僅代表通俗小說，也不限西方。」參見〈談看書後記〉，張愛玲《惘然記》，台北皇冠，二〇一〇年，第一〇九頁。小說怎樣改（史實）以及為什麼改，也是本文的討論焦點，儘管我比較關注改動與詮釋文本意義的關係，多於小說在市場上成敗的因由。

30.王益知《張學良外紀》，香港南粵出版社，一九八九年，第六頁。

31.趙爾巽與張作霖的故事，參見唐德剛《張學良口述歷史》第一章，台北遠流，二〇〇九年，第八一至八三頁。從另一角度想，張愛玲有沒有可能真的搞錯了趙四小姐父親的身份呢？一九六三年，徐鑄成《金陵舊夢》由香港致誠出版社出版，書中收有〈不抵抗的「銑電」〉一文，初刊香港《大公報》副刊，此文正是張冠李戴，誤把趙四小姐當作趙爾巽第四女。在時間上，的確不能排除張愛玲看過徐鑄成文章的可能，但我認為機會不大，理由有二：一是《金陵舊夢》專講民國政壇舊聞，但除了將趙爾巽記作趙四之父這一處外，《少帥》別的地方再沒有參考過《金陵舊夢》的痕跡；二是張愛玲肯定參考過的《春秋》雜誌，有一篇署名東北舊侶所撰的〈俱往矣！少帥聲威、風流趙四〉，已清楚記述了趙慶華乃趙四之父，文章載於一九五九年八月一日第五十期《春秋》雜誌。因此，張愛玲不大可能搞錯，應該是她刻意改動史實的。

32.關於挑起復辟論一事，詳見《中國的端納》第一七〇至一七六頁。

33. 參見〔民國〕陳灝一《睇向齋談往》，上海書店出版社，一九九八年。《睇向齋談往》有「五太太」一則，記張作霖五太太事：「就東北言，最貴之太太，莫逾于所謂五太太者。〔……〕作霖性褊急，易怒，怒時無人敢攖其鋒，獨五太太可以一言止之。」張學良晚年自述，也說父親張作霖很聽「五母親」的話，見唐德剛《張學良口述歷史》第二章，台北遠流，二〇〇九年，第一〇一頁。

34. 趙夫人故事，可參考：一，郭冠英〈趙四的故事〉，《聯合報》，二〇〇〇年七月三日；二，陸靜嫣、李蘭雲、吳靖：〈草長鶯飛春暮懷人風雨江南——懷念在台灣的趙一荻四妹〉，一九八三年十一月十九日至十二月二十四日《團結報》，見范克明、周亞蘭：《張學良傳》，武漢長江文藝，二〇〇二年，第一五一頁。

35. 《雷峯塔》裏，作者已經頗明白地提示了讀者陵的結局寓意何在：「我們都突破了，琵琶心裏想，各人以各人的做法。陵是抱著傳統的唯一的一個人，因為他沒有別的選擇，而他遇害了。」參見張愛玲著，趙丕慧譯《雷峯塔》，台北皇冠，二〇一〇年，第三三八頁。

36. 參見張愛玲〈憶胡適之〉，《惘然記》，台北皇冠，二〇一〇年，第二四頁。

37.一般人交談時，說話總是散漫突兀，張愛玲在〈紅樓夢未完〉已經明確點出：「乾隆百廿回抄本，前八十回是脂本，有些對白與他本稍有出入，有幾處更生動，較散漫突兀，說話本來是那樣的。是時人評約翰‧俄哈拉（John O'Hara）的『錄音機耳朵』。百廿回抄本是拼湊的百衲本，先後不一，筆跡相同都不一定是一個本子，所以這幾段對白與他本孰先孰後還待考。如果是後改的，那是加工。如果是較早的稿子，後來改得比較平順，那就太可惜了，但是我們要記得曹雪芹在他那時代多麼孤立，除了他自己本能的判斷外，實在毫無標準。走的路子是他漸漸暗中摸索出來的。」參見張愛玲〈紅樓夢未完〉，《紅樓夢魘》，台北皇冠，二〇一〇年，第一六頁。

38.參見張愛玲〈談看書〉，《惘然記》，台北皇冠，二〇一〇年，第七二至七四頁。她早年有一段話談古中國衣服的圖案，跟她在〈談看書〉所表達的文學觀頗為一致，同樣強調觀者要在無數的點與點間看出各式各樣的圖案：「這裏聚集了無數小小的有趣之點，這樣不停地另生枝節，放恣，不講理，在不相干的事物上浪費了精力，正是中國有閒階級一貫的態度。惟有世上最清閒的國家裏最閒的人，方才能夠領略到這些細節的妙處。製造一百種相仿而不犯重的圖案，固然需要藝術與時間：欣賞它，也同樣地煩難。」參見張愛玲〈更衣記〉，《華麗緣》，台北皇冠，二〇一〇年，第二三頁。

39.這種解讀方法不是我的原創，三百多年前的大文評家張竹坡在

〈金瓶梅讀法〉早已說過：「看《金瓶》，把他當事實看，便被他瞞過，必須把他當文章看，方不被他瞞過也。（四十）看《金瓶》，將來當他的文章看，猶須被他瞞過，必把他當自己的文章讀，方不被他瞞過。（四一）將他當自己的文章讀，是矣。然又不如將他當自己才去經營的文章。我先將心與之曲折算出，夫而後謂之不能瞞我，方是不能瞞我也。（四二）」

40. 張愛玲的英文有時遭論者詬病，尤其是批評她筆下角色的英語對白不夠道地，參見劉紹銘〈輪迴轉生：張愛玲的中英互譯〉，陳子善編《重讀張愛玲》，上海：上海書店，二〇〇八年，第二二六至二三〇頁。對白不夠道地，我不敢斷言到底是她力不從心抑或刻意為之，但張愛玲大概也意識到這個問題的原因。她在一九七三年九月二十日致信宋淇，提到寫 "Stale Mates"（後譯成中文為〈五四遺事〉）的情況：「用中文還是英文思想，與你一樣，不過對白總是中文，抽象思想大都英文，與一向看的書有關。」別的英文小說應該也是如此。她的英語對白確實時有硬譯之嫌，但那似乎是為了營造疏離感或保留一種中國氣氛而甘心付出的代價。至於她的英文敘述文字，儘管未能說是自成一家，但起碼道地，流暢，詞彙豐富，是專業作家的英文。理查德·麥卡錫對張愛玲的英文文筆有以下評語：「初讀《秧歌》頭兩章，我大為驚異佩服。我自己寫不出那麼好的英文。我既羨慕也忌妒她的文采。」參見高全之〈張愛玲與香港美新處——訪問麥卡錫先生〉，《張愛玲學》，台北麥田出版，二〇〇八年，第二五三頁。

41. 例如《少帥》第二章暗用了舊約聖經的「紅母牛」（red cow）典故，恰到好處地隱喻周四小姐眼中的怪誕場面：「幽會地點就是他們倆談話的院子，裏頭一屋子圍在大紅桌布前的豬肝色的臉，有些人面無笑容，站著狂吼，或勸酒或推辭，或邀人劃拳，這種屬於男性的儀式於她一向既怪誕，又完全無法理解，圍成一圈的紅母牛被領進了某種比孔子還要古老的祭典之中。那些外國人極力保持微笑，高高的白衣領托出灰暗的深棕色頭部，像照片一樣。難怪他與外國人為伍，不和她父親那樣的人應酬往來。」所謂紅母牛祭典，是指《民數記》第十九章的潔淨儀式。張愛玲以它作為隱喻，形象化了周四小姐的困惑，西方熟悉聖經的讀者一看定必心領神會。這紅母牛祭典有什麼「無法理解」呢？有必要略為解釋一下。《傳道書》第七章二十三節說：「我曾用智慧試驗這一切事。我說，要得智慧，智慧卻離我遠。」猶太人釋經文獻《米德拉什》（Midrash）對此節的詮釋，就是說所羅門王在慨嘆自己無法理解關於紅母牛的上帝誡命──由此可見，以「紅母牛」隱喻怪誕、不可理解的情景確實恰到好處。當然古中國也有紅牛祭祀，如《檀弓》所記：「夏后氏尚黑……牲用玄；殷人尚白……牲用白；周人尚赤……牲用騂。」《洛誥》：「王在新邑，烝祭歲，文王騂牛一，武王騂牛一。」（騂是赤類，這裏俱指紅牛。）但考慮到張愛玲的寫作對象是西方讀者，且周禮也沒有任何「怪誕，又完全無法理解」的地方，對小說這隱喻的唯一合理詮釋，相信就只有訴諸舊約了。

42. 張愛玲這樣寫，也許是受到某個傳聞啟發。《春秋》一篇文章說：「張學良與趙四之間，只經過了一段很短的時間，據說，在遊宴中小張寫了一張紙條，只有『我愛你』三字，趙四尚在雛年，而立即委身相事。」參見東北舊侶〈俱往矣！少帥聲威、風流趙四〉，收入一九五九年八月一日第五十期《春秋》雜誌。

43.例如利維特（Jacques Rivette）的片子《塞琳和朱麗上船去》（*Céline et Julie vont en bateau*，法語片名其實一語雙關，較隱晦的含意是「塞琳和朱麗被捲入一個荒唐的故事」）就是《愛麗絲》的變奏，開場是朱麗坐在公園看魔法書，塞琳像《愛麗絲》的兔子般匆匆路過，丟三拉四的模樣，然後朱麗跟著她。為什麼會這樣呢？完全沒有解釋。

44.張愛玲在散文〈華麗緣〉、小說《小團圓》第九章都用了「點和立體」來比喻女主角跟周圍的人群格格不入。例如《小團圓》說：「這些人都是數學上的一個點，只有地位，沒有長度闊度。只有穿著臃腫的藍布面大棉袍的九莉，她只有長度闊度厚度，沒有地位。在這密點構成的虛線畫面上，只有她這翠藍的一大塊，全是體積，狼狽的在一排排座位中間擠出去。」參見《小團圓》，台北皇冠，二〇〇九年，第二六五頁。這個比喻也許來自《愛麗絲》第八、十二章：愛麗絲是立體的人，紙牌國王、王后等人則是平面。

45.參見張愛玲〈第一爐香〉，《傾城之戀》，台北皇冠，二〇一〇年，第五九頁。

46.參見張愛玲〈私語〉，《華麗緣》，台北皇冠，二〇一〇年，第
　一四八頁。

47.參見祝淳翔〈新發現的張愛玲早期英文習作〉，刊於二〇一四年
　四月六日《東方早報》。

48.《雷峯塔》：「聖誕節露為孩子們弄了很大一棵樹，樹梢頂著天
　花板。〔……〕她和珊瑚掛起了漂亮的小飾品，老媽子們幫著
　把蠟燭從樹頂點到樹根。〔……〕蠟燭的燭光向上，粉紅的綠
　色的尖筍。蠟燭的氣味與常青樹的味道混和，像是魔法森林裏的
　家。」「姐弟倆帶著小狗躺在地毯上看英文童書上的插畫，英文
　還看不懂。書上的樹寶塔似的綠裙展開來，吊著鳳梨和銀薊。西
　方特為孩子們創造的魔法世界歡喜得她不知如何是好。」參見
　張愛玲著，趙丕慧譯《雷峯塔》，台北皇冠，二〇一〇年，第
　一六二至一六三頁。這裏的「魔法森林」原文為 "an enchanted
　forest"，「魔法世界」是 "the magic world"，參見Eileen Chang,
　The Fall of the Pagoda（Hong Kong: Hong Kong University Press,
　2010），pp.128-129。《雷峯塔》另一段說：「她們拿沙發墊子給
　她在地板上打了個舒服的地舖。躺在那裏，她凝望著七巧桌的多
　隻椅腿。核桃木上淡淡的紋路渦卷，像核果巧克力。剝下一塊就
　可以吃。她終於找到了路，進了魔法森林。」參見《雷峯塔》，
　第三一四頁。這裏的「魔法森林」原文為 "the magic forest"，參
　見The Fall of the Pagoda, p.263。

49.《小團圓》:「不過那麼幾秒鐘的工夫。修女開了門,裏面穿堂黃黯黯的,像看了迴腸蕩氣的好電影回來,彷彿回到童年的家一樣感到異樣,一切都縮小了,矮了,舊了。她快樂到極點。」參見張愛玲《小團圓》,台北皇冠,二〇〇九年,第四四頁。類似情景也見《易經》,參見張愛玲著,趙丕慧譯《易經》,台北皇冠,二〇一〇年,第一二五頁。值得一提的是,自《易經》、《少帥》開始到後來的《小團圓》,有濃厚自傳色彩的女主角都是只放大,不縮小;但四〇年代張愛玲初識胡蘭成時,曾送他一張刊於《天地》雜誌上的照片,後面題了幾句話:「見了他,她變得很低很低,低到塵埃裏,但她心裏是歡喜的,從塵埃裏開出花來。」參見胡蘭成〈民國女子〉,《今生今世》,台北遠景出版,二〇〇四年,第二七六頁。

50.《雷峯塔》:「碰到這種時候她總納罕能不能不是她自己,而是別人,像她在公園看見的黃頭髮小女孩,只是做了個夢,夢見自己是天津的一個中國女孩。〔……〕靠著浴缸單薄內捲的邊緣,她用力捏自己,也只是悶悶的痛。或許也只是誤以為痛,在夢裏。要是醒過來發現自己是別的女孩呢?躺在陌生的床上,就跟每天早上清醒過來的感覺一樣,而且是在一幢大又暗的屋子裏。〔……〕怎麼知道這是真實的,你四周圍的房間?她做過這樣的夢,夢裏她疑心是一場夢,可是往下夢去又像是真實的。說不定醒著的真實生活裏她是男孩子。她卻不曾想到過醒來會發現自己是個老頭子或老太太,一輩子已經過完了。」參見張愛玲著,趙丕慧譯《雷峯塔》,台北皇冠,二〇一〇年,第六三至六四頁。

《小團圓》有一段相應的話：「有時候她想，會不會這都是個夢，會忽然醒過來，發現自己是另一個人，也許是公園裏池邊放小帆船的外國小孩。當然這日子已經過了很久了，但是有時候夢中的時間也好像很長。」參見張愛玲《小團圓》，台北皇冠，二〇〇九年，第二一九頁。

51. 〈紅樓夢未完〉：「第六十四、六十七兩回，一般認為不一定可靠，但是第六十四回上半回有兩條作者自批，證明確是作者手筆。矛盾很多，不止這一處。〔……〕周汝昌排出年表，證明書中年月準確異常。但是第六十四回七月黛玉祭父母，『七月因為是瓜菓之節，家家都上秋季的墳』，是七月十五，再不然就是七月七。接著賈璉議娶尤二姐，初三過門，當是八月初三。下一回，婚後『已是兩個月的光景』是十月初。賈珍與尤三姐發生關係，被她鬧得受不了。然後賈璉赴平安州，上路三日遇柳湘蓮，代三姐定親。『誰知八月內湘蓮方進京來』。那麼定親至遲是七月。怎麼三個月前已經是七月？周汝昌根據第六十九回，臘月尤二姐說嫁過來半年，推出婚期似是六月初三，認為第六十四回先寫七月，又退到六月，是『逆敘』。書中一直是按時序的。」參見張愛玲〈紅樓夢未完〉，《紅樓夢魘》，台北皇冠，二〇一〇年，第一五頁。

52. 參見張愛玲〈談看書後記〉，《惘然記》，台北皇冠，二〇一〇年，第一〇八至一〇九頁。

53.張愛玲會仔細考慮讀者反應，小說角色的年齡從來都不是隨意設定的。她說過：「〈傾城之戀〉裏的白流蘇，在我原來的想像中決不止三十歲，因為恐怕這一點不能為讀者大眾所接受，所以把她改成二十八歲。」參見張愛玲〈我看蘇青〉，《華麗緣》，台北皇冠，二〇一〇年，第二八三頁。

54.參見張愛玲〈憶胡適之〉，《惘然記》，台北皇冠，二〇一〇年，第一三至一五頁。

55.參見郭冠英〈趙四的故事〉，《聯合報》，二〇〇〇年七月三日：「張趙是一九二七年在天津認識的，男的二十七歲，女的只有十五歲，故早年張皆稱趙為小妹。〔……〕一九二七年，京津地區的權貴子弟常在『蔡公館』跳舞，張、趙在舞會中認識。當時是奉軍鼎盛的時代，張學良是風流成性，張、趙是否即相好，尚不可知。」一九二七年這說法跟張學良晚年的其他口述紀錄是吻合的，他說：「我跟太太（指趙一荻）認識的時候，她才十六歲。」語見唐德剛訪錄，王書君著述《張學良世紀傳奇（口述實錄）》上卷，山東友誼出版社，二〇〇二年，第一六〇頁。趙四小姐生於一九一二年，一九二七年就是虛歲十六。（順帶一提，王書君這本書雖記錄了張學良的說法，卻把張趙認識時間定於一九二六年四月，不知何據。又王書君在少帥的口述後附記故事，大多採自坊間舊聞，未經核實，是一部體例混亂的書。）另外，據趙四小姐的胞兄趙燕生晚年回憶，他是在一九二六年認識張學良的，之後張每次到天津，趙燕生和他家姊妹都會跟少帥到交際場所遊玩。參見文思編《我所知道的張學良》，北京中國文史出版社，二〇〇三年，第二七至二八頁。綜合上述資料，趙四認識少帥，不會早於一九二六，而以一九二七年最有可能。《少帥》影射他們自一九二五年開始相戀，是不符史實的。

56. 張學良和趙四相識的時、地，我嘗試綜合多年來較流行的四個說法：其一，是一九二六年前後，地點在少帥位於天津舊法租界三十二號路五十四號的私邸，參見王益知《張學良外紀》、趙雲聲〈趙四小姐與張學良將軍〉；其二，是一九二八年，在天津大華飯店舞廳，參見孫玉清〈張學良在台灣〉、張德榮〈紅粉知己——張學良和趙綺霞的愛情〉；其三，是一九二六年前後，在張學曾（張學良三弟）岳父的蔡公館，參見曹振中〈將軍手撥乾坤轉，淑女心期玉雪清——朱洛筠談張學良夫人趙一荻〉。以上三說皆引自范克明、周亞蘭：《張學良傳》第六章，武漢長江文藝，二〇〇二年。其四，是一九二七年在大華飯店，參見張永濱，《百年少帥張學良傳》，北京團結出版，二〇〇〇年，第六八頁。

57. 參見東北舊侶〈俱往矣！少帥聲威、風流趙四〉，收入一九五九年八月一日第五十期《春秋》雜誌。

58. 中譯者鄭遠濤對這問題的看法，我認為也值得參考，以下是他的批注：〈國語本《海上花》譯後記〉指出在傳統中國「戀愛只能是早熟的表兄妹，一成年，就只有妓院這髒亂的角落裏還許有機會。再就只有聊齋中狐鬼的狂想曲了。」《少帥》有一場戲中陳叔覃覺得周四小姐看上去「像是一個鬼」，正是指向聊齋一類故事。另一方面陳周的戀愛模式又有點類似「早熟的表兄妹」，兩家有世交，而且女方確實早熟。唯因早熟，家裏人才會放鬆警惕讓兩人私下來往。《紅樓夢魘》考證寶玉、黛玉諸人的年齡，可見張愛玲對愛情故事中的年齡問題非常注意。據她的看法，曹雪芹在改寫歷程中將寶黛年齡一次次減低，使故事寫實。「中國人的伊甸園是兒童樂園」（參看該書〈三詳紅樓夢〉）。

59.張愛玲在〈國語本《海上花》譯後記〉說：「浣芳雖然天真爛漫，對玉甫不是完全沒有洛麗塔心理。納博柯夫名著小說《洛麗塔》──拍成影片由詹姆斯梅遜主演──寫一個中年男子與一個十二歲的女孩互相引誘成姦。」參見《海上花落》，台北皇冠，二○一○年，第三五三頁。

60.張愛玲在〈談看書〉和〈對現代中文的一點小意見〉也談過六○年代美國的婦運。參見《惘然記》，台北皇冠，二○一○年，第四五至四六頁及第一五九頁。

61.張愛玲寫作有一個傾向，就是不惜花大量篇幅來襯托即使只有一兩句的「戲肉」。一九七九年七月十五日張愛玲致宋淇書：「上次講歷史小說，其實我並沒有故事可寫。〔……〕目前想寫的小說，都是為了故事裏的一點『戲肉』。」所謂「戲肉」，我認為是指作者揭示小說意義的一刻，形式可以是一句話或一個情景，它可以用來解釋，甚或顛覆之前發生的一切。試舉一例，張愛玲在一九七六年四月二十六日寫信給宋淇說：「我也曾經顧慮到頭兩章〔指《小團圓》〕人太多，港戰又是我從前寫過的，連載沒吸引力。這兩章全為了『停考就行了，不用連老師都殺掉』這句話，Ferd〔賴雅〕從前看了也說就是這一句好。」這句話就是「戲肉」，點出了一種人生的諷刺——寄生在日常生活中的咬嚙性小煩惱，往往要付上致命的代價才能除掉，終究得不償失。

62. 參見張愛玲〈紅樓夢未完〉，《紅樓夢魘》，台北皇冠，二〇一〇年，第一七至一八頁。

63. 參見張愛玲〈有幾句話同讀者說〉，《華麗緣》，台北皇冠，二〇一〇年，第二九五頁。

64. 《小團圓》：「他坐了一會站起來，微笑著拉著她一隻手往床前走去，兩人的手臂拉成一條直線。在黯淡的燈光裏，她忽然看見有五六個女人連頭裹在回教或是古希臘服裝裏，只是個昏黑的剪影，一個跟著一個，走在他們前面。她知道是他從前的女人，但是恐怖中也有點什麼地方使她比較安心，彷彿加入了人群的行列。」參見張愛玲《小團圓》，台北皇冠，二〇〇九年，第二五六頁。

65. 原文如下："She dreamed she was in a line of young women like her-self, and as she looked ahead to where they were going she saw that as

each came to the head of the line she was decapitated by a guillotine. Without any fear the dreamer remained in the line, presumably quite willing to submit to the same treatment when her turn came."參見 Joseph L. Henderson, "Ancient Myths and Modern Man," in Carl G. Jung, ed., *Man and His Symbols*（New York: Dell Publishing, 1968）, p.129。

66. 《少帥》和《小團圓》裏那一隊排成直線的女人，也令我們想起〈談跳舞〉散文中的東寶歌舞團：「提起東寶歌舞團，大家必定想起廣告上的短袴子舞女，歪戴著雞心形的小帽子。可是她們的西式跳舞實在很有限，永遠是一排人聯臂立正，向右看齊，屈起一膝，一踢一踢；嗆地一聲鑼響，把頭換一個方向，重新來過；進去換一套衣服，又重新來過。西式節目常常表演，聽說是因為中國觀眾特別愛看的緣故。我只喜歡她們跳自己的舞，有一場全體登台，穿著明麗的和服，排起隊來，手搭在前面人的背上，趔趄著腳，碎步行走，一律把頭左右搖晃，活絡的頸子彷彿是裝上去的，整個地像小玩具，『絹製的人兒』。把女人比作玩具，是侮辱性的，可是她們這裏自己也覺得自己是好玩的東西，一顆頭可以這樣搖那樣搖——像小孩玩弄自己的腳趾頭，非常高興而且詫異。日本之於日本人，如同玩具盒的紙托子，挖空了地位，把小壺小兵嵌進去，該是小壺的是小壺，該是小兵的是小兵。從個人主義者的立場來看這種環境，我是不贊成的，但是事實上，把大多數人放進去都很合適，因為人到底很少例外，許多被認為例外或是自命為例外的，其實都在例內。」這段話用來闡釋小說中

「女子隊伍」的意象似乎不錯，兩者同樣有女人被集體物化的傾向。參見張愛玲〈談跳舞〉，《華麗緣》，台北皇冠，二〇一〇年，第二一九頁。

67. 《少帥》第四章寫一群女子（包括她自己）化為木雕鳥，而《小團圓》第五章也有兩處提及此鳥：其一，九莉與之雍親熱時，「門框上站著一隻木雕的鳥〔……〕雕刻得非常原始，也沒加油漆，是遠祖祀奉的偶像？」其二，九莉打胎後，「夜間她在浴室燈下看見抽水馬桶裏的男胎，在她驚恐的眼睛裏足有十吋長，畢直的欹立在白磁壁上與水中，肌肉上抹上一層淡淡的血水，成為新刨的木頭的淡橙色。凹處凝聚的鮮血勾劃出它的輪廓來，線條分明，一雙環眼大得不合比例，雙睛突出，抿著翅膀，是從前站在門頭上的木雕的鳥。」這隻神秘的鳥，先後在張愛玲筆下出現三次，每次也跟性或死亡有關，它究竟象徵什麼？作者自己沒有解釋，但最相關的說明見於她在一九七六年四月二十六日寫給宋淇的信：「《小團圓》是主觀的小說，有些visionary〔神視性〕的地方都是紀實，不是編造出來的 imagery〔文學意象〕。就連不動感情的時候我也有些突如其來的ESP〔超感官能力〕似的印象，也告訴過Mae。」她告訴鄺文美（Mae）的ESP經驗，參見《張愛玲私語錄》，台北皇冠，二〇一〇年，第八四頁，注五四。

68. 參見巴塔耶（Georges Bataille）《情色論》（*L'Erotisme*）第一部分第四章「繁殖與死亡的相類」，當中又說屍體臭腐與性交穢物同樣中人欲嘔。究其通章要旨，不外乎：「長期或短期而言，要繁殖，則生育者必需死亡，而生育從來就只是在拓展滅亡（正如一代死了，必有新一代來臨）。」（longue ou brève échéance, la reproduction exige la mort de ceux qui engendrent, qui n'engendrent jamais que pour étendre l'anéantissement（de même que la mort d'une génération exige une génération nouvelle）.）巴塔耶提供了一個理論基礎，讓我們理解為什麼張愛玲筆下的性愛，總是跟死亡、嘔吐扯上關係，例如《少帥》第四章寫性交：「還在機械地錘著打著，像先前一樣難受，現在是把她綁在刑具上要硬扯成兩半。突然一口氣衝上她的胸口。就在她左一下右一下地晃著頭時，只見他對她的臉看得出神。『我覺得要吐出來了。』」《小團圓》第八章寫之雍與九莉親熱：「泥譚子機械性的一下一下撞上來，沒完。綁在刑具上把她往兩邊拉，兩邊有人很耐心的死命拖拉著，想硬把一個人活活扯成兩半。還在撞，還在拉，沒完。突然一口氣往上堵著，她差點嘔吐出來。他注意的看了看她的臉，彷彿看她斷了氣沒有。」參見張愛玲《小團圓》，台北皇冠，二〇〇九年，第二五七頁。《赤地之戀》第七章寫戈珊的獨白：「她需要的是一種能夠毀滅她的蝕骨的歡情，趕在死亡前面毀滅她。而他不斷地使她記起死亡。有時候他使她已經死了，他是個痴心的嬰孩伏在母親的屍身上吮吸著她的胸乳。」參見張愛玲《赤地之戀》，台北皇冠，二〇一〇年，第一五四頁。

69.我認為張愛玲這種「神視」（vision）或幻覺源自她讀過的原始部族信仰，如木鳥化為嬰兒，也許跟阿藍塔人（Arunta）的轉生觀有關：一個女人在某處感到受孕，正是在那處等待轉世的亡魂進入她的身體所致，而屬於那地方的圖騰就成為嬰兒的圖騰。可參考Sigmund Freud, "Die Infantile Wiederkehr des Totemismus", in *Totem und Tabu*。《少帥》第四章中的女子化鳥，類似一些馬拉尼西亞人（Melanesians）或西非的部落信仰，即人有「另一個我」或「外在靈魂」附於動物；而在澳大利亞東南部某些部族中，更會按性別區分這些圖騰動物，如Wotjobaluk族相信他們的男族人與蝙蝠命運相連，女性則與夜鷹禍福與共。可參考James G. Frazer, *The Golden Bough:A Study in Magic and Religion: A New Abridgement from the Second and Third Editions,* ed. Robert Fraser（Oxford: Oxford University Press, 1994），774-784。張愛玲喜歡人類學，也許讀過《金枝》，她小說中描寫的神視，我認為就是這些部族信仰的大雜燴，其中也攙和著一些個人幻想。作為文學意象，那群監視周四小姐的木鳥既是第四章末「女子隊伍」的預兆，也是她們的隱喻。

70.近年已有科學研究證明，人（不論男女）觀看女性的方式確實是局部的，往往只把她們等同於性徵所在的身體部位——把女人「物化」——但觀看男性時則從整體去看，而非視作身體部位的總和，參見Sarah J. Gervais, Theresa K. Vescio, Jens Förster, Anne Maass, Caterina Suitner, "Seeing women as objects: The sexual body part recognition bias", *European Journal of Social Psychology,* 2012。

71.關於女人的命運，可比較張愛玲〈傾城之戀〉這一段話：「白公館有這麼一點像神仙的洞府：這裏悠悠忽忽過了一天，世上已經過了一千年。可是這裏過了一千年，也同一天差不多，因為每天都是一樣的單調與無聊。流蘇交叉著胳膊，抱住她自己的頸項。七八年一霎眼就過去了。你年輕麼？不要緊，過兩年就老了，這裏，青春是不希罕的。他們有的是青春——孩子一個個的被生出來，新的明亮的眼睛，新的紅嫩的嘴，新的智慧。一年又一年的磨下來，眼睛鈍了，人鈍了，下一代又生出來了。這一代便被吸收到硃紅灑金的輝煌的背景裏去，一點一點的淡金便是從前的人的怯怯的眼睛。」參見張愛玲《傾城之戀》，台北皇冠，二〇一〇年，第一八四頁。

72. 胡蘭成說：「愛玲看到《傳道書》，非常驚動，說是從來厭世最徹底的文辭。她唸給我聽，『金練折斷，銀罐破裂，日色淡薄，磨坊的聲音稀少，人畏高處，路上有驚慌』，又道，『太陽之下無新事』。」參見胡蘭成〈鵲橋相會〉，《今生今世》，台北遠景出版，二〇〇四年，第四二六頁。

73. 張愛玲說：「中國人的天堂其實是多餘的。於大多數人，地獄是夠好的了。只要他們品行不太壞，他們可以預期一連串無限的、大致相同的人生，在這裏頭他們實踐前緣，無心中又種下未來的緣分、結冤、解冤——因與果密密編織起來如同簟席，看著頭暈。中國人特別愛悅人生的這一面——喜歡就不放手，他們的脾氣向來如此。電影《萬世流芳》編成了京戲；《秋海棠》小說編成話劇、紹興戲、滑稽戲、彈詞、申曲，同一批觀眾忠心地去看了又看。中國樂曲，題目不論是《平沙落雁》還是《漢宮秋》，永遠把一個調子重複又重複，平心靜氣咀嚼回味，沒有高潮，沒有完——完了之後又開始，這次用另一個曲牌名。」參見張愛玲〈中國人的宗教〉，《華麗緣》，台北皇冠，二〇一〇年，第一九〇頁。

74. 參見本文第一部分一九六一年十月二日張愛玲致鄺文美書。

75. 人類的世界之所以「太陽之下無新事」，可以從張愛玲的文章中歸納出兩個原因。其一，人不論男女，總害怕隨著時代而沉沒，「為要證實自己的存在，抓住一點真實的，最基本的東西，不能不求助於古老的記憶」，所以人跟傳統很難徹底割裂，參見張愛玲〈自己的文章〉，《華麗緣》，台北皇冠，二〇一〇年，第一一六頁。其二，社會現象的變或不變，取決於人心這個更根源的範式變或不變，「去掉了一切的浮文，剩下的彷彿只有飲食男女這兩項」，參見張愛玲〈燼餘錄〉，《華麗緣》，台北皇冠，二〇一〇年，第七五頁。果真如此，那麼只要飲食男女的大欲尚存，任何時代的生活也終究離不開古老的本能。在《少帥》第七章，就連中國最高的權力機構也被戲稱為「連襟政制」，可見在張愛玲沒有什麼是不能用「男女大欲」的角度來理解的。

76. 高全之《張愛玲學》，台北麥田出版，二〇〇三年，第四〇九至四一〇頁。張愛玲這段自白，一個重點是說人必需抓緊或依附一些東西：以前是家庭為中心的儒家倫理體系，現在就是吸納了國家主義的共產政權。這種觀點我懷疑是赫胥黎啟發的，他在一篇文章寫道：「Men cannot live in a chronic state of negation; the voids of thought and feeling must be filled, and if we reject the divine, its place will inevitably be taken by some idolatrous ersatz. 〔…〕 With the decline of Christianity, such God-worship as had existed went out; the idolatrous worship of the Church was exchanged for the equally idolatrous worship of the State and the Nation」。大意是說，人的思想感覺不能長期懸空，總得被某些東西填滿，以前是基督教，如今就是國家民族。參見Aldous Huxley, "Variations on a Philosopher," in *Themes and Variations*（New York: Harper & Bros, 1950）。我們只要把赫胥黎所說的基督教用儒家代替，就是張愛玲〈自白〉的其中一個要點了。

77. 原語為：“Advance two steps, retreat a step—Mao Tse-tung has said this is his way of making progress. Whether dance or march, the people drag on, hoping to outlive their tormentors.”參見張愛玲〈A Return to the Frontier〉，《重訪邊城》，台北皇冠，二〇〇八年，第八〇頁。文中所引為我的翻譯。

78. 原語為：“En tiempos de auge la conjetura de que la existencia del hombre es una cantidad constante, invariable, puede entristecer o irritar: en tiempos que declinan（como éstos），es la promesa de que ningún oprobio, ninguna calamidad, ningún dictador podrá empobrecernos.”見Jorge Luis Borges, "El Tiempo Circular", *Obras Completas*

1923-1972（Buenos Aires: Emecé Editores, 1974），p.396.

79.參見本文第一部分一九六三年七月二十一日張愛玲致鄺文美與宋淇書：「這一向乘空在寫張、趙故事，本來可望一口氣寫到西安告一段落，一看參考材料，北伐時期許多軍政事日期攪錯了，所以又有好幾處要改，這兩天正鑽在裏面有點昏頭昏腦。」足證作者極力追求小說裏歷史事件日期的準確無誤。

80.參見張愛玲〈私語〉，《華麗緣》，台北皇冠，二〇一〇年，第一五二至一五五頁；張愛玲《對照記》圖二十六，台北皇冠，二〇一〇年，第四八頁；張子靜《我的姊姊張愛玲》第三章，台北時報文化，一九九六年，第八九至九一頁。

81.《小團圓》第三章寫九莉患傷寒住院：「單人病房，隔壁有個女人微弱的聲音呻吟了一夜，天亮才安靜了下來。早晨看護進來，低聲道：『隔壁也是傷寒症，死了。才十七歲，』說著臉上慘然。她不知道九莉也是十七歲。本來九莉不像十七歲。她自己覺得她有時候像十三歲，有時候像三十歲。以前說『等你十八歲給你做點衣服，』總覺得異常渺茫。怪不得這兩年連生兩場大病，差點活不到十八歲。」參見張愛玲《小團圓》，台北皇冠，二〇〇九年，第一四九至一五〇頁。試比較《雷峯塔》：「珊瑚道：『等你十八歲，給你做新衣服。』珊瑚一向言出必行，但是琵琶不信十八歲就能從醜小鴨變天鵝。十八歲是在護城河的另一岸，不知道有什麼辦法才能過去。」參見張愛玲著，趙丕慧譯

《雷峯塔》，台北皇冠，二〇一〇年，第二四一頁。我更發現《雷峯塔》有一個特點，就是作者似乎刻意避開了琵琶的十七歲，不是不寫當時的事，而是不直接說她是十七歲。《雷峯塔》有兩處寫珊瑚提醒琵琶她十六歲了（見《雷峯塔》第二三六、二九六頁），我在上文也引了「等你十八歲」云云一段，偏偏就不說她十七歲如何。唯一提到「十七歲」的一處，就是陵在十七歲病死（見《雷峯塔》第三四一頁），卻是作者無中生有的，彷彿在暗示弟弟代替了她，成為那個舊式家庭的犧牲品。綜合以上例子，「十七歲」對張愛玲來說就是死亡、苦難、大劫的象徵。

82.宋淇在〈私語張愛玲〉也說：「從這些小地方，可以看出愛玲是多麼的天真和單純。」見《張愛玲私語錄》，台北皇冠，二〇一〇年，第二八頁。《小團圓》最後的那個夢也充滿童真。

83.參見張愛玲著，趙丕慧譯《雷峰塔》，台北皇冠，二〇一〇年，第一二〇頁。

84.聊舉數例相較，恕不盡錄：《少帥》第一章結尾：「她是棵樹，一直向著一個亮燈的窗戶長高，終於夠得到窺視窗內。」《小團圓》第六章結尾：「她像棵樹，往之雍窗前長著，在樓窗的燈光裏也影影綽綽開著小花，但是只能在窗外窺視。」參見張愛玲《小團圓》，台北皇冠，二〇〇九年，第二二〇頁。《少帥》第四章描述少帥：「他低著頭，臉上一絲微笑，像捧著一杯水，小心不潑出來。」《小團圓》第四章寫邵之雍：「沉默了下來的時候，用手去捻沙發椅扶手上的一根毛呢線頭，帶著一絲微笑，目光下視，像捧著一滿杯的水，小心不潑出來。」參見《小團圓》，第一六四頁。《少帥》第四章記少帥說：「我小時候有一回出去打獵，捉到一隻鹿，想帶回家養，抱著它在地上滾來滾去，就是不鬆手。最後我睏得睡著了，醒過來它已經跑了。」《小團圓》第五章記邵之雍說：「鄉下有一種麂，是一種很大的鹿，頭小。有一天被我捉到一隻，力氣很大，差點給牠跑了。累極了，抱著牠睡著了，醒了牠已經跑了。」參見《小團圓》，第一八七頁。《少帥》第四章：「他探身揮了揮煙灰，別過頭來吻她，一隻鹿在潭邊漫不經心啜了口水。」《小團圓》第五章記邵之雍吻九莉：「他講幾句話又心不在焉的別過頭來吻她一下，像隻小獸在溪邊顧盼著，時而低下頭去啜口水。」參見《小團圓》，第一八七頁。胡蘭成在《今生今世》說：「又問我們兩人在一淘時呢？她〔張愛玲〕道，『你像一隻小鹿在溪裏喫水』。」胡蘭成〈民國女子〉，《今生今世》，台北遠景出版，二〇〇四年，第二九五頁。

85.參見本文第一部分一九八二年二月一日張愛玲致宋淇書。

86.參見宋以朗〈《雷峯塔》/《易經》引言〉，張愛玲著，趙丕慧譯《雷峯塔》/《易經》，台北皇冠，二〇一〇年，第三頁。

87.趙一荻曾對張學良說：「不是西安事變啊，咱倆也早完了，我早也不跟你在一塊堆玩了，你這個胡三仔，我也受不了。」參見唐德剛《張學良口述歷史》第三章，台北遠流，二〇〇九年，第一一二頁。

88.參見本文第一部分一九六六年十一月十一日張愛玲致宋淇書。

89.參見張愛玲〈憫然記〉，《憫然記》，台北皇冠，二〇一〇年，第二〇五頁。

90.參見本文第一部分一九六七年三月二十四日張愛玲致宋淇書。

91.張愛玲這心態令我們想起《少帥》第一章周四小姐看戲的一幕：「她感到戲正演到精彩處而她卻不甚明白，忍不住走到台前，努力要看真切些，設法突出自己，任由震耳的鑼鈸劈頭劈腦打下來。〔……〕在戲園裏，她見過中途有些人離開包廂，被引到台上坐在為他們而設的一排椅子上。他們是攜家眷姨太太看戲的顯貴。大家批評這是粗俗的擺闊，她倒羨慕這些人能夠上台入戲；儘管從演員背後並不見得能看到更多。」

92.參見本文第一部分一九九一年五月二十七日張愛玲致宋淇書。

93.《小團圓》醞釀了很多年，但要到一九七五年才正式開始寫。參見宋以朗〈《小團圓》前言〉，《小團圓》，台北皇冠，二〇〇九年，第四頁。

94.水晶〈蟬──夜訪張愛玲〉記張愛玲說「她寫作的時候，非常高興，寫完以後，簡直是『狂喜』！」〈張愛玲語錄〉：「寫完一章就開心，恨不得立刻打電話告訴你們，但那時天還沒有亮，不便擾人清夢。」參見《張愛玲私語錄》，台北皇冠，二○一○年，第五二頁。一九七六年四月四日張愛玲致宋淇書，也提到寫《小團圓》時有「euphoria」（狂喜）感覺，參見宋以朗〈《小團圓》前言〉。一九六七年三月二十四日張愛玲致宋淇書：「少帥故事我自從一九五六年起意，漸漸做到identification地步，跟你們別後也只有一九六三年左右在寫著的時候很快樂。」

小團圓

這是一個熱情故事，我想表達出愛情的萬轉千迴，
完全幻滅了之後也還有點什麼東西在。——張愛玲

從幼年傳統家族在新舊世代衝擊中的爭鬥、觀念對立的父母籠罩的陰影，到讀書時修道院女中千面百樣的同學、戰時人與人劍拔弩張的緊繃感……點點滴滴的細碎片段，無一不在九莉生命刻下印記，並開出繁盛的文字。而就是這種特殊的文采，吸引了邵之雍天天來拜訪九莉。他眼中的光采像捧著一滿杯的水，他說就算這文章是男人寫的，也要去找他，所有能發生的關係都要發生。二十二歲還沒談過戀愛的九莉，覺得這一段時間與生命裏無論什麼別的事都不一樣，恍如沉浸在金色的永生中，讓她不顧一切，即使之雍被說是漢奸、即使他是有婦之夫……

讀中國近代文學，不能不知道張愛玲；讀張愛玲，不能錯過《小團圓》。《小團圓》是張愛玲濃縮畢生心血的顛峰之作，以一貫嘲諷的細膩工筆，刻畫出她最深知的人生素材，餘韻不盡的情感鋪陳已臻爐火純青之境，讀來時有被針扎人心的滋味，因為故事中男男女女的矛盾掙扎和顛倒迷亂，正映現了我們心底深處諸般複雜的情結。墜入張愛玲的文字世界，就像她所寫的如「渾身火燒火辣燙傷了一樣」，難以自拔！

易經

張愛玲自傳小說三部曲
《小團圓》、《雷峯塔》、《易經》終於完整問世！

雖然家族秘史謎雲滿佈讓琵琶很迷惘，但童年畢竟是悠長而美好的。十八歲那年，她因爲惹怒了父親與後母，驚險地逃出那個囚禁她的豪宅，去投奔母親與姑姑。原本母親打算讓琵琶去英國留學，卻遇上了戰爭爆發，只好安排她去香港大學唸書。烽火很快地威脅到香港，學生們也開始過著戰戰兢兢的日子。隨著香港被日軍佔領，琵琶不得不中斷學業，她和比比商量要一起回上海，她相信只有故鄉能與自己的希望混融！爲了拿到船票，琵琶必須發揮從小累積的世故與智慧，即使那要冒上生命的危險……

接續《雷峯塔》的故事，《易經》描寫女主角十八歲到二十二歲的遭遇，同樣是以張愛玲自身的成長經歷爲背景。張愛玲曾在寫給好友宋淇的信中提及：「《雷峯塔》因爲是原書的前半部，裏面的母親和姑母是兒童的觀點看來，太理想化，欠眞實。」相形之下，《易經》則全以成人的角度來觀察體會，也因此能將浩大的場面、繁雜的人物以及幽微的情緒，描寫得更加揮灑自如，句句對白優雅中帶著狠辣，把一個少女的滄桑與青春的生命力刻劃得餘韻無窮！

華麗緣 散文集一·一九四〇年代

哪怕她沒有寫過一篇小說,她的散文也足以使她躋身二十世紀最優秀的中國作家之列。

——【中國現代文學史研究家】陳子善

張愛玲的散文創作時間橫跨五十年,本書收錄一九四〇年代的作品。這是她引領風華、意氣風發的盛產期,這個時期的題材多半取自她的生命紀錄、豐沛情緒與獨特見解。篇篇奇思妙想,洋溢著對俗世的細膩觀察,表面上恍如絮絮叨叨的私密話語,卻又色彩濃厚、音韻鏗鏘、意象繁複、餘韻無窮,完全呈現出張愛玲獨具一格的美感!

惘然記 散文集二·一九五〇~八〇年代

張愛玲散文創作的成就在神韻與風格的完整呈現上已經超過了小說!

——【東海大學中文系教授】周芬伶

比較起四〇年代的那種華麗風格,這時期的題材多為回顧過往,筆法也顯得越來越清淡,自我的喜怒哀樂較為隱藏,更符合她追求的簡樸蒼涼美學。隨著生命進入另一階段,張愛玲對世事人情的體會更加透徹,文字描繪的功力也轉變得更成熟,並時時透現出她對創作的無比熱忱!

對照記 散文集三·一九九〇年代

除了「驚豔」,似乎沒有適當的形容詞可以概括她的散文風格。 ——【逢甲大學中文系教授】張瑞芬

這段時期她的作品較少,以〈對照記〉為代表。〈對照記〉是張愛玲挑選出自己與親友的照片,最末並加收一張拿報紙的近照表示自己還活著,讓我們感受到這位幾乎被讀者「神化」的才女幽默親近的一面。而這些性格也顯露在她其餘的小品中,俏皮語隨手拈來,但絲毫不減其獨特的韻味,反覆閱讀,每每有新的感動與想像,也難怪張愛玲的文字永遠能讓我們沉吟低迴、留連忘返!

傾城之戀
短篇小說集一．一九四三年

凡是中國人都應當閱讀張愛玲的作品！
——【中央研究院院士】夏志清

一九四〇年代，抗戰淪陷期的上海文壇出現了一位奇才——張愛玲，她發表了一系列描繪平凡男女的殘缺愛情故事，立刻掀起一陣狂熱！每一篇看似真實的浮世情事，卻又帶著大時代驚心動魄的傳奇色彩，並拓展了女性批判的視野，也難怪會讓評論家們反覆鑽研、萬千讀者迷戀傳頌，果然是「傾城」的不朽經典！

紅玫瑰與白玫瑰
短篇小說集二．一九四四年～四五年

張愛玲的時代感是敏銳的，
敏銳得甚至覺得時代會比個人的生命更短促。
——【名作家．評論家】楊照

談論到張愛玲的小說特色，幾乎不免要提到文字華麗、比喻創新、體裁大膽、意象繁複、色彩濃郁……這些外在的技巧，但讓追隨者最難以企及的，應該是她累積的智慧與世故的體悟。張愛玲的小說不只描敘出一段精采的來龍去脈，還囊括她對人性、對生命的思索，並充滿文學藝術的渲染力，值得一而再、再而三地細細品味！

色，戒
短篇小說集三．一九四七年以後

許多人是時間愈久，愈被遺忘，
張愛玲則是愈來愈被記得。
——【名作家．評論家】南方朔

隨著環境、時代、心境的變遷，張愛玲的小說進入轉變期，雖然她的靈感仍以上海和香港雙城為主，並保有一貫冷眼看世情的敏銳，但手法卻更加圓融成熟，最明顯的是從早期濃烈外放的風格，逐漸凝鍊昇華為自然素樸，更接近她所追求的創作理念。

國家圖書館出版品預行編目資料

少帥／張愛玲 著．宋以朗◎主編
-- 初版．-- 臺北市：皇冠，2014.9
面；公分．--（皇冠叢書；第4417種）
（張看・看張；2）
譯自：The Young Marshal
ISBN 978-957-33-3104-9（平裝）

857.7   103016664

皇冠叢書第4417種

張看・看張 2

少帥
The Young Marshal

作　　者—張愛玲
主　　編—宋以朗
譯　　者—鄭遠濤
發 行 人—平雲
出版發行—皇冠文化出版有限公司
　　　　　台北市敦化北路120巷50號
　　　　　電話◎02-27168888
　　　　　郵撥帳號◎15261516號
　　　　　皇冠出版社(香港)有限公司
　　　　　香港銅鑼灣道180號百樂商業中心
　　　　　19字樓1903室
　　　　　電話◎2529-1778　傳真◎2527-0904
美術設計—王瓊瑤
初版一刷日期—2014年9月
初版十刷日期—2022年11月
法律顧問—王惠光律師
有著作權・翻印必究
如有破損或裝訂錯誤，請寄回本社更換
讀者服務傳真專線◎02-27150507
電腦編號◎531002
ISBN◎978-957-33-3104-9
Printed in Taiwan
本書定價◎新台幣 300 元／港幣 100 元

• 張愛玲官方網站：www.crown.com.tw/book/eileen
• 皇冠讀樂網：www.crown.com.tw
• 皇冠Facebook：www.facebook.com/crownbook
• 皇冠Instagram：www.instagram.com/crownbook1954
• 皇冠蝦皮商城：shopee.tw/crown_tw